*The Dangerfield
Diaries*

By the same author

The Lorimer Line
The Lorimer Legacy
Lorimers at War
Lorimers in Love
The Last of the Lorimers
Lorimer Loyalties
The House of Hardie
Grace Hardie

The Dangerfield Diaries

Anne Melville

GRAFTON BOOKS

A Division of the Collins Publishing Group

LONDON GLASGOW
TORONTO SYDNEY AUCKLAND

Grafton Books
A Division of the Collins Publishing Group
8 Grafton Street, London W1X 3LA

Published by Grafton Books 1989

A CIP catalogue record for this book is available
from the British Library

ISBN 0-246-13517-4

Photoset by Rowland Phototypesetting Limited
Bury St Edmunds, Suffolk
Printed and bound in Great Britain by
William Collins Sons & Co. Limited, Glasgow

Prologue

Kingsgelding is a secret village; a village avoided by the march of history. Roman conquerors, plague carriers, the armies of Yorkists and Lancastrians, Royalists and Parliamentarians, the builders of canals, railways and trunk roads: none of them has passed this way. Wherever they have begun their journey, wherever they are going, there has always been an easier route somewhere else.

The white horse which has given Kingsgelding its name is older than Domesday. When its shape was first etched on the chalky slope of the down, it was without any shadow of doubt a stallion. Probably it was while the Norman church was being built that the priest set his parishioners to hack holes in the side of the hill and to plant a coppice which still obscures the exaggerated outline of the stallion's anatomy. Not, presumably, because a Norman was any more prudish than his earthy congregation, but because the Church in Norman times was determined to stamp out the English cult of the green men of the hills, with which the horse was associated.

More than eight hundred years later, at the beginning of the twentieth century, the green men still held sway on the hills. No amount of thundering from the pulpit was able to convert the midsummer ceremony of cleaning the white horse into anything but a pagan festival. Giggling and whispering, the younger members of the community would abandon the weeding as the sun set, and put the coppice to a wholly appropriate use. Almost all the village weddings at the turn of the century took place in October and each couple's first child, healthy

1

and full-term, was born in March and christened in June.

The christening scheduled for three o'clock on Sunday, 18 June 1904 had, however, nothing to do with the green men of the hills. It could be assumed with confidence that the Honourable Ainslie Anne Dangerfield had been conceived in the Jacobean tester bed at Kingsgelding Hall, between sheets embroidered with the family crest. There was a pattern of life ordained for the daughters of the Dangerfields and this one had not yet had time to rebel against it.

She had been born in the usual manner and the usual place – for Kingsgelding Hall was large enough to have a birthing room reserved for such occasions. Very soon, dressed according to tradition in a christening robe of Honiton lace and wrapped in a three-hundred-year-old shawl of gossamer lightness, she would be carried into a church almost filled by the alabaster effigies of her ancestors. Already it was fragrant with the scent of roses and lilies and sweet peas, cut from the gardens of the Hall before breakfast.

With still an hour to go before the party from the Hall were expected to appear, the rector had already dressed for action. The flowers so carefully arranged by Lord Dangerfield's head gardener and one of his journeymen were to do double duty, gracing the earlier assembly of a humbler family. Researchers who come in modern times to check dates in the Kingsgelding parish register are astonished to discover that Ainslie Dangerfield's name immediately follows that of Gilbert Stanley Blakey. How extraordinary, they exclaim, that such implacable enemies, opposing figures in one of the famous trials of the nineteen-thirties, should have been born in the same place and at the same time!

Well, not quite at the same time. The register of christenings is misleading. The daughter of a baron was brought to church as soon as her mother had recovered her strength and figure. But May Blakey, the swineherd's wife, produced babies with an annual regularity in her mud-floored cottage – and, to economize on cake-making, brought them to the christening font in batches. Gil Blakey was already four years old when his name was inscribed in careful copperplate.

Wearing a jacket that was too tight for him and handed-down

trousers that came below his grazed but unusually clean knees, he viewed the proceedings with doubt and alarm. His father wisely kept a tight grip on his collar while the three younger children were dealt with, in case he should make a bolt for the door. Only once did Gil give evidence of a natural unwillingness to accept the voice of authority as gospel truth. The moment came when his two-year-old brother was christened Augustus George.

'No he i'n't!' exclaimed the four-year-old in disbelief. ''E's called Stinker!'

This was a minor distraction. The ceremony was concluded speedily so that the four little Blakeys, heathens no longer, might be ushered away well before the party from the Hall arrived. The two groups did not meet even in the churchyard, for Lord Dangerfield had a private gate and path to the church which was built by his own ancestor on his own land.

In years to come, the children christened on this occasion could be expected to encounter each other from time to time, for Lady Dangerfield was charitably inclined and her husband did his paternalist best to find employment for the sons of his servants. Little Ainslie, as she grew older, would help her mother to carry bowls of broth or bundles of baby clothes to villagers in need of them, and May Blakey was likely to lay claim to more than most.

As for Gil Blakey, the swineherd's son, he could hope to be summoned to the steward's office at Kingsgelding Hall after leaving school at the age of twelve. If his talents proved suitable, he might find himself holding a horse for his young mistress to mount. But that was as far as any relationship could be expected to go.

The two christenings, after all, took place in 1904. Ainslie Anne Dangerfield and Gilbert Stanley Blakey had been born into a society in which differences of class were clear-cut and everyone knew his place. Those were the golden years, at least for those at the top; and nothing, it seemed, was going to change.

3

One

Like all untidy people, Lady Ainslie is accustomed to boast that she can put her hand straight on to anything she wants. More often than she deserves this proves to be the case; but on the evening before her admission to hospital, as she contemplates the miscellany of diaries on the highest of her bookshelves, she is forced to admit defeat.

Those incidents which are to be separated from the rest, so that they shall remain private for ever, present themselves clearly to her mind. She can visualize the page on which each has been recorded, remembering the colour of the ink, the jagged shape formed by the handwritten lines and a selection of marks particular to individual places and times – a smear of candlewax from her bedroom in Kingsgelding Hall; a splash of red wine from her days as a medical student; the charring of a page rescued after the bombing of her home in 1941; brown coffee circles from a House of Commons mug set aside when a telephone rang. What she cannot always identify are the covers which enclose the items she is looking for. She stares up at the jumble of notebooks and sighs.

'No good,' she says aloud. She has lived alone for forty years and always speaks clearly to herself. Mumbling is a sign of old age. 'They'll all have to come down.'

The task is exhausting. Her first-floor flat is converted from a spacious house built sufficiently early in Victorian times to have its entertaining rooms above ground level. The old drawing room serves her as both sitting room and study, and one wall of it is lined with bookshelves from floor to ceiling. The room is fifteen feet high and Lady Ainslie is only five foot two – and eighty-three years old. After she has backed down the library steps nine or ten times, clutching half a dozen notebooks in one hand and the mahogany pole with the other, she is forced to sit down for a few moments.

While resting she studies the diaries now spread around the floor. There is little uniformity about their appearance. These are journals of record, not mere lists of future engagements. She remembers just once, in 1921, trying to squeeze her daily thoughts into the meagre half inch allowed by a bird-watcher's diary; ever since then she has rejected any book which by dates and printed lines tries to suggest that all days hold the same interest as each other.

She has never attempted to confine a year neatly within a single notebook, so that to track down any particular date she must now first collect together four or five instalments of the year in question.

'Chronological order, then,' she says, beginning the sorting process. A few of the diaries date themselves at a glance. It was at the respective ages of nine and seven that Caro and Martin discovered a new notebook to be the perfect Christmas present for their grandmother, and for several years the covers they chose reflected their own taste for bright cartoon characters. But Snow White and Donald Duck guard no great secrets. So many politicians since those days have poured their memories on to tape recorders that her own cautious indiscretions would arouse no interest now even if she wished to release them. They can all go back on the shelf.

More recently, Lady Ainslie has found for herself the perfect size of volume and bought a dozen at once. They are still on the high shelf, and can stay there, for the uniformity of their mock-leather bindings rightly indicates a lack of variety in the events they chronicle. Within their covers, no doubt, is an accurate picture of an old lady living alone; a life peer who conscientiously attends debates and committees in the House of Lords but who is no longer privy to Cabinet secrets or the gossip of the Commons. There is nothing controversial there; nothing that she needs to hide.

The very first of her diaries, equally innocuous, also remains in its place at the other end of the shelf. As Lady Ainslie stares up at it now, waiting for her breathing to steady itself, she summons to her mind the memory of how her addiction began.

That diary, the handsomest of them all, was given to her when she was thirteen by her brother Edward. The instructions with which he accompanied the gift are a direct cause of her exertions on this evening more than seventy years later. The volume was his leaving present as he went off to war in 1917. No mock leather then, but two hundred white pages bound in green calf, with her initials tooled in gold and a clasp with a tiny padlock to close the book against prying eyes.

'This is a selfish present,' Edward admitted as he watched her unwrap it. 'I want you to write down everything that happens at home while I'm away. What people say, how the horses do, when the trees come into leaf, when the swallows fly off – anything that changes: everything. Then I can read it when I come home on leave and feel that I'm still part of what's going on. But you mustn't let anyone else read it – or even know that you're writing it. It's to be a secret between you and me.'

'Why?'

'It's the only way to be straight – to set down what you notice without thinking about it. If you suspect there's the slightest chance that someone else might see, then you'll leave out things which might offend them or make you feel ashamed. Or else you'll put things in that you want them to believe. People who leave day-books around are really expecting them to be read, even though they may pretend to be indignant when it happens. Tell yourself that you and I are the only ones who'll read it ever, and you can put everything down – even the bad-tempered bits – exactly as it is. Promise?'

'Promise.'

She kept her promise, beginning the task by candlelight that very night – and even after so many years she can remember the first entry word for word.

Edward left for France today. He looked immensely smart in his new uniform. Tara moped all morning and then began to howl so loudly that she had to be shut in the stables, because none of us could comfort her. How did she know that Edward wasn't just going back to school?

She wrote the diary exactly as her brother asked until the day when she copied out on a tear-spattered page the War Office telegram which announced his death. From that time on she has recorded the events of her life for her own eyes only.

Edward was right. Because her resolve never to show anyone what she writes has always been uncompromising, she has been able to risk setting down not only her own secrets, however shameful, but other people's. And it is for the most part other people's secrets, rather than her own, which must be protected, even though many of those concerned will by now be dead.

For a period of eight years in her Harley Street surgery and her Bethnal Green clinic she helped many women desperate to have children to get their wish. But other women had different wishes – wishes which in those days were punishable by law – and not all of these did she turn away. As they pleaded with her, many scandals and disloyalties in high places were necessarily revealed. It was not safe to leave their full case notes where an inquisitive nurse might see them. The problem was solved by incorporating the background details into her private diaries. She used initials and a home-made code, but it will not present much difficulty to anyone determined to crack it. That is something she has already had reason to know.

So the time has come to take precautions. To throw the record of her working years into a fire or a shredder would be easy, but somehow unnerving. Although believing that she has come to terms with the shortness of the time left to her, she is not yet ready to act on that belief. She accepts the risk of death under anaesthetic as a possibility, but does not really expect it to happen. To shed the past is to turn her back on the future.

Gathering her strength again, she makes three more journeys up the steps and then lowers herself stiffly to kneel on the rug. The task of sorting the notebooks is not after all too difficult. The feel of each accomplishes what a view of its spine could not. As she touches it, she knows at once what period of her life it records. Quickly she arranges the diaries in chronological order and then goes through them again, stacking them into two piles.

The diaries from the larger pile she returns, taking it slowly, to the top shelf. Then she packs almost all the others into a cardboard carton which she has carried home from the supermarket. Three remain unsorted. Her hands hover over them, undecided. Are they especially precious or especially dangerous?

'Stop waffling!' she commands herself, shaking her head in frustration at the difficulty of making a choice; but is unable to obey her own order. The three notebooks, their fate still uncertain, are put to one side. Returning her attention to the cardboard box, she throws in at the top a few magazines which contain articles written by herself. They are her file copies, but she will never want to read any of them again.

A buzzing startles her. It is two years now since Martin, her grandson, installed an Entryphone system for her as a Christmas present. She is not at all the kind of elderly person who refuses to use new inventions just because of their newness, and is glad to be spared unnecessary journeys down the stairs to be confronted only with an unwelcome double-glazing salesman or Jehovah's witness; but it still takes her a few seconds on each occasion to remember what to do.

Today it proves to be the giver who is making use of his own gift.

'Martin darling!' She presses the buzzer and waits at her private front door while he climbs the stairs and presents to her a smiling face decorated by a black eye. 'Gracious, you've been in the wars! Is this football match duty again?' For Martin is a policeman and, although a graduate, is condemned by the rules of the service to do two years in uniform on the beat, with compulsory weekend overtime whenever the local soccer team has a home match. But he shakes his head with a laugh.

'No. A rugger match; playing, not guarding. Self-inflicted wound, you might say. There's nobody roughs up a police fifteen as much as another police fifteen. Good game, though.' He has a rugby player's build: broad-shouldered and with long, muscular legs which power a devastating speed whenever he has a ball under his arm or a runaway mugger in his sights.

'Come into the kitchen. I was just going to make myself a hot drink. But perhaps you'd rather have a beer.'

'Good guess!' Knowing his way around, he opens the refrigerator and takes out a bottle of the Ruddles County which is always waiting for him there. 'I only called to wish you all the best tomorrow. And to ask what your visiting times are?'

'Any time between two and eight. But you're not to worry about that, Martin. I know you're not likely to be free then. And I shan't be pining for visitors. I'm always happy in my own company – and prefer to enjoy yours when I'm feeling at my best.'

'I'm afraid you're right: it won't be easy for me to get in. But I'll be thinking of you. You've told Dad, I take it.' His father, Lady Ainslie's only son, although loosely attached to an English university, spends most of his working life in the South Seas. When asked by her friends what Leonard is doing these days, she takes refuge in a vague suggestion that he is compiling tribal dictionaries; his own description of his subject is linguistic geography.

At the moment he is in a remote area of Papua New Guinea, testing how long it takes for a word newly introduced into the local pidgin language by the arrival of video films in the urban areas to spread to the villages. It is because he and Madge have spent so much of their married life far from civilization and schools that their two children, educated in England, are closer to their grandmother than to their mother.

'No, not yet. I'll mention it in my next letter, in a few days' time.'

'But –'

'What's the point, Martin dear? Suppose I write today. He gets the letter in a week or a month, and then what can he do but feel worried until he hears again? Whereas if I wait until next week I can tell him that I've had an operation and that all is well and there's nothing to worry about.'

'Yes, I suppose you're right.' Martin's first reaction may have been conventional, but he is an unsentimental young man. 'Well, I'll keep in touch through Caro. And before I go, is there anything I can do for you?' It is understood between them that she will always reserve any heavy tasks for him to tackle.

'No thank you, darling.' If he catches sight of the box in the drawing room he will certainly offer to move it somewhere, so she shows him straight out from the kitchen.

Returning to the box herself, she seals it with a wide parcel tape. Then she telephones the Jaffreys in the flat below. She has already discussed with them what they should do if she does not return from hospital, and they will be expecting her summons now. It would have been easy for her to knock on the floor, as they frequently suggest. But although Lady Ainslie accepts the fact that she is old, she is determined to avoid the stereotypes of old age. It is not yet time for her to become an elderly tyrant banging a stick for attention. She invites them up for a late-night drink; they take the box with them when they leave.

Now for a last look at the high shelf. Although the diaries are more generously spaced than before, Caro and Martin are unlikely to notice the difference. But the three which she has set aside remain on the floor. What is she going to do with these?

Two of the three diaries have an identical appearance: they are ruled notebooks of the kind used by schoolchildren in the nineteen-thirties. The backs of their dark green covers are printed with useful information about chains and furlongs, rods, poles and perches.

The third is prettier, its cover designed like the embroidery sampler of a Victorian child, with a space for the owner's name to be inscribed in the centre. All three notebooks were bought and filled in 1938. Has the time come for her to destroy them?

'Girls can't keep secrets.' It was nine-year-old Gil Blakey who said that to her, almost eighty years ago. 'They always tell in the end.' These are the diaries which can reveal not just her patients' secrets, but her own. Why has she not added them to those which the Jaffreys will burn if she dies? Why is she not tearing them to pieces at this moment? Does she secretly want the truth to be known? She stands still and finds herself thinking about that nine-year-old boy tickling trout in a stream.

'Girls always tell in the end.'

Two

There was something in the air on that autumn afternoon in 1909: a secret known only to the grown-ups. Constance was just a baby and Edward was away at school, but Ainslie was five years old; old enough to be told what was going on. She could feel excitement rushing through the house and gardens like a forest fire leaping from the crown of one tree to another, far above her head. But no one would explain. All her questions were given the same answer. 'Wait and see. You might be getting a surprise come teatime.'

Usually such an atmosphere grew only when her brother was expected home for the holidays. At such times horses were exercised and groomed with special care, guns were cleaned, fishing tackle inspected and windows thrown open to air rooms not in daily use. But Edward had only just left and would not be back until December. Tara, his bitch, who could always tell when her master was expected, was not padding impatiently up and down. Instead she stretched herself lazily in the sun, only occasionally raising one of her floppy ears in curiosity at all the coming and going.

Little Constance had a temperature that day.

'She'd best stay in the warm,' said Nanny Frensham, who more usually claimed that fresh air would blow any headaches or illnesses away. 'Peggy will take you for your walk.'

Ainslie was pleased about that, knowing that the walk would be more fun with only the nursery maid to look after her. Peggy was a village girl who knew the answers to questions. She could say where to look for rabbits and water rats and dragonflies and meadow larks. Best of all, she wouldn't keep reminding Ainslie to behave like a young lady. There would be no cross reprimands if her young charge were to stuff her gloves in her pocket or stamp in puddles.

Even Peggy seemed to have been infected by the general excitement on this particular day. She and Ainslie skipped along the lane hand in hand. It was the wrong lane, though.

'You said we could go to the stream,' said Ainslie accusingly.

'And so we shall, me love.'

'This isn't the way.'

'It's one way.' They were walking towards the village. Peggy began to slow up as they approached the smithy. A young man broke off from a conversation with the farrier and turned to smile at them.

'Afternoon, Peg.'

'Afternoon, Ken.'

'Let you out of prison, then, have they?'

'Just taking Miss Ainslie down to walk by the stream. No time for chattering now.'

'Be seeing you, then.'

Peggy did not slacken her pace during this encounter, nor did she release Ainslie's hand. Turning to stare, Ainslie found herself dragged along, almost losing her balance.

'Why's Ken dressed like that?' She knew the farrier's son, who often helped his father by holding the horses steady while they were being shod.

'He's joined the army, that's why. Smart, his uniform, isn't it?'

'Will he have to kill people?'

'Not many, I don't suppose. And only fuzzy-wuzzies if he does.'

'Will he eat them?'

'Lord, what an idea! What put that into your head?'

Ainslie was remembering the time when her father showed her the pens in which his pheasant chicks were reared. She found it hard to understand why so much care was taken of baby birds just so that they could be shot, and was not entirely convinced by the argument that it was wrong to kill for the sake of sport

13

but not to shoot what God had provided for food. She would have liked to continue the conversation with Peggy, but they were both startled when a nine-year-old boy jumped down from a tree just ahead of them.

'Gil Blakey! Why aren't you in school?'

Gil was one of Peggy's six brothers. He was shabbily dressed and none too clean. His hair, recently shaved off in the battle against head lice, had begun to grow again, as stiff and golden as barley stubble. According to Peggy he was a little terror both at home and at school; but he always behaved politely to his sister's young charges and now looked at Ainslie, neatly dressed in her blue coat and frock and black stockings, in a friendly manner.

'Friday, i'n't it?' he reminded his sister. 'Got two detentions this week, ha'n't I, for not learning my Scripture verses. But if I don't go to school at all, they can't keep me in, can they?' He gave an impudent, gap-toothed grin, pleased with the cleverness of his solution. Peggy, who had never found much use for reading and writing herself, wasted no time in criticism but put her brother's truancy to good use.

'Then you can look after Miss Ainslie for me for half an hour,' she said. 'She likes to play at damming the stream, and I don't fancy getting my skirts wet. Take her as far as the pool. No further, mind. You're to stay with her. If she comes to any harm, it's on your head.'

'Can I take my boots off?' asked Ainslie.

'You know right enough what Nanny would say to that.'

'But *can* I?'

Peggy beckoned her close to whisper. 'We'll have a secret, you and me,' she said. 'When we gets back, and Nanny asks, we've been walking along the meadow path and through the spinney, choosing leaves for you to press in that contraption of yours. Not a word from the one or t'other of us about boots or streams or Gil or anything else. How about that?' She held out her little finger, crooked for Ainslie to hook her own small finger through it. A tingle of the day's excitement passed from Peggy into Ainslie. It had to do with more than secrets. Something was about to happen.

14

What happened, after they had splashed their way along the stream, was that Gil sat her down on a rock near the edge of the deep pool and commanded her to keep still. Obeying orders, Ainslie watched as his grubby fingers became suddenly gentle. He stroked and tickled a slender speckled trout to the surface of the water before cupping his hands and lifting it out.

'Come and look.' He held the fish in front of her for a few seconds and then tossed it back into the pool.

'Why did you do that?' asked Ainslie. 'You could have eaten it for tea.'

'I'd get whipped out of my pants if your father found I was helping myself to his fish.'

'You do it all the time,' Ainslie said as confidently as though she knew it for a fact instead of only guessing. Then an explanation for his action occurred to her. 'I wouldn't have told on you.'

'Yes you would.'

'No I wouldn't. It would have been a secret.'

'Girls can't keep secrets. Not for ever. They always tell in the end.'

'I don't tell. You can't say I do.'

'Don't suppose you've ever had a secret worth telling.' Gil picked her a handful of almost-ripe blackberries to show that he did not mean to quarrel. But Ainslie was staring up into the sky with wide-eyed amazement.

'Look at that!'

Gil followed her look and, sharing her astonishment, dropped the blackberries. A huge yellow balloon, as large as a house, had appeared over White Horse Hill and was drifting towards them. A basket hung below the balloon, carrying three people. One of them was tugging at ropes and the other two were pointing and waving.

'Come on,' said Gil.

'Where?'

'To see where it's going, of course.'

'Peggy said –'

'Peg won't mind as long as you're with me. This way.' He took

15

her hand to tug her along. By now the balloon was hidden from them by trees, but Gil looked at the clouds to see which way the wind was blowing, and made for Kingsgelding Hall. 'How about that, then!' he exclaimed as they emerged from the wood.

The balloon was coming down to earth, silently, gently, just beyond the ha-ha which kept the pleasure grounds of the Hall safe from grazing sheep. Ainslie saw her father and mother standing on the terrace, waving in welcome, while the servants formed an avenue behind them. For a moment she was cross, because she ought to have been there too. Being sent out for a walk had made her late for the surprise. She put her resentment to use by resuming an earlier argument.

'You said I couldn't keep secrets. But I kept the secret about the balloon going to my house, didn't I?'

'You didn't know.'

'I did so.' Ainslie told the lie with such conviction that Gil was almost convinced. Then he gave a short laugh to show that he didn't believe her. Ainslie would have liked to sulk, but was too interested in what was going on. 'How do they make it come down?' she asked, unable even to understand what made it stay up in the first place.

Gil, equally puzzled, shook his head. The children watched as two of the gardeners hurried to catch the ropes which dangled towards the earth and to make them fast. Two people, a man and a woman, were helped out of the basket by their mechanic, who handed their luggage down after them.

'D'you think they'd let me have a ride?' Ainslie was about to run straight home across the park, but Gil held her back.

'You'll get Peg into trouble if you go home without her.'

Ainslie hesitated. But she could see that the balloon was being pegged down, to stay where it was for a little while. She allowed Gil to take her back to the stream where Peggy, flushed and untidy, was calling her name anxiously.

The two children gabbled out their story, but Peggy did not share their excitement. Knowing that her brother was bound to boast of what he had seen, she ordered him not to mention that he had company at the time. Ainslie for her part was instructed in what she might or might not tell Nanny Frensham about the events of the walk. The details did not bear much relationship to what had really happened.

The seeds of change, so casually scattered on that autumn day, were to germinate and grow at very different rates, as though a sower had mingled acorns with rape seed.

Peggy was dismissed without a character as soon as it became obvious how she and the farrier's son had spent their hour of privacy. When she learned that Ken Bainton had died of dysentery on the troopship without ever learning of his impending fatherhood, she did her unsuccessful best to end the pregnancy. Not until many years later did it occur to Ainslie Dangerfield that there was an indirect connection between her own life and that of the shambling, jerking, dribbling child who was to be seen hanging about the Blakeys' cottage. But when the realization did at last dawn, it perhaps influenced her choice of specialization after she became a doctor.

Gil's life was changed by the events of that morning as dramatically as Peggy's. The postman who gave him a lift home on his bicycle crossbar sent him to repeat his excited chatter to the village postmistress, who supplied local news to the county newspaper. The next day – beneath a photograph of a society beauty who had chosen an adventurous way to begin her honeymoon with the son of a duke – the words 'observed by nine-year-old Gilbert Blakey' swept away his previous contempt for reading and writing and the disciplines of school.

An ambition to provide more stories for the newspaper – and to read them when they were printed – carried him within two years from the bottom to the top of the village school merit list. Ainslie's father, surprised to find intelligence and ambition developing in his swineherd's cottage, paid for the boy to go on to grammar school – though Gil, thinking that he had been awarded a scholarship, was unaware of this. The hot air balloon had lifted him out of the mud.

As for Ainslie herself, she had learned in the course of that day that girls are expected to behave differently from boys and that the difference is not always to their credit.

'Girls always tell in the end!' She resented the taunt and was

17

determined never to deserve it. Peggy, instructing her to say that she had been in her nursemaid's sight all afternoon, provided her first secret – but it was the wrong kind of secret. To tell lies was naughty. Keeping a secret was different. It meant not talking about something which was true. She was quite willing to conceal from Nanny Frensham the fact that she had been left alone to play with Gil, but only by silence. So as she walked home that afternoon she sorted out in her mind what it would be safe to say and what must be left out if Peggy were not to get into trouble.

Ainslie's instinct to conceal other people's secrets would one day come into conflict with Gil Blakey's determination to reveal them. Without either of them realizing it at the time, the seed of their later quarrel was sown on the bank of a stream in 1909, as a hot air balloon drifted overhead.

Three

On the morning when she is to enter hospital Lady Ainslie awakens early, as usual. Even as a young woman she has never needed much sleep, and her years in government have accustomed her to working an eighteen-hour day. She has just finished her breakfast when the telephone rings.

'It is I,' says Caro. 'Your favourite granddaughter. Of necessity, since you have no other. Have you listened to the news? The ambulancemen have rejected the arbitration award and declared a Day of Action.'

'Yes, I heard.'

'Which being translated means a Day of Inaction. So that helpless little old ladies waiting patiently to be transported to hospital will wait in vain.'

'I may be old,' says Lady Ainslie briskly. 'I will even admit that I'm little. But I am most certainly not helpless. Not until the surgeon gets at me, at least. I wasn't expecting to be collected by ambulance. Dame Freda's Foundation is approximately ten minutes' walk from the Palace of Westminster, to which I have successfully transported myself every working day for the past forty years.'

'You're not going to walk into hospital alone and carrying a suitcase,' says Caro. 'I shall be round to pick you up in twenty minutes.'

'Quite unnecessary, dear. Since this is a special occasion, I'd already decided to treat myself to a taxi instead of going by Tube. There's no problem.'

'Twenty minutes,' repeats Caro, and rings off.

19

Lady Ainslie smiles to herself. Caroline is her favourite person in any category and a visit from her always adds a sparkle to the day. This fact does not, however, prevent her from performing an exaggerated act of disapproving shock as she opens the door a quarter of an hour later.

'My dear child, what *have* you done to your hair!'

Caro's style of dressing has always been idiosyncratic. She makes most of her own clothes, copying any fashion which takes her fancy, whether it is a pair of baggy trousers from a Persian miniature, a shapeless shift from a silent film of the Twenties, a nipped-waist costume from Dior's New Look of the late Forties or a modern man's evening suit. In the past, even the most bizarre outfit has been given a link with normal appearances by her beautiful long blonde hair. Today, however, her head is crowned with upward-pointing short spikes of dark crimson.

'Had it restyled,' says Caro, stooping to kiss her. 'Boring, boring, looking the same for ever. "Posh punk, please," I said to the snipper. I've always regretted missing out on this sort of thing first time round. Think yourself lucky that I didn't get myself shaved for a Mohican. Don't look so sniffy, Nanna. If you gave your hair a purple rinse I wouldn't say a word.'

'But I don't, do I?' Lady Ainslie's hair, cut short at the nape of the neck but saved from severity by a natural wave, has been silver for years. 'Will it wash out?'

'There's a pretty compliment!' Caro steps inside and closes the door. 'Rest assured, dear Nanna; nothing is for ever. My hair will grow again and if the colour doesn't fade or rinse away I can always dye myself back blonde and become once again the sweet English rosebud you have known and loved.'

'How do you achieve the hedgehog effect?' Lady Ainslie leads the way into the kitchen, where the coffee percolator is bubbling.

'With something called gunge.' But now it is Caro's turn to be taken aback. 'What have *you* been doing to your kitchen?'

'A little spring cleaning, that's all. Will you carry the tray for me, dear?'

Caro leads the way into the sitting room. As she sets the tray down on a coffee table she looks suspiciously around.

'What's been going on here?' she demands. 'In all the twenty-five years of my life I've never known this flat to look other than cosily lived-in. In other words, chaotic. What's happened to half a century of Hansard? The embroidery you started when you broke your ankle eight years ago? The dusty dried flowers that Martin gave you for your seventieth birthday? And – my God! – the Lowry! Nanna, you haven't been burgled, have you?'

'No.' Lady Ainslie sits down and pours out two cups of coffee. 'But burglary has been on my mind. Suppose some newspaper gets hold of the information that I'm in hospital, and prints it. It would be as good as announcing that this flat will be unoccupied for the next few weeks. It seemed only sensible to take precautions. And the Lowry must be very valuable by now, although it didn't cost me much.'

Her purchase of the picture – a townscape of mean streets and terraced houses – came in the first excitement of her conversion to Socialism; the idea that the artist might one day become famous did not at the time enter her mind. Instead, she used the picture to attack her father, asking him as she held it up whether he realized the cramped conditions in which ordinary people lived while he enjoyed the spaciousness of Kingsgelding Hall. It is ironic that although her own party, by its wealth tax and death duties, has been responsible for Kingsgelding Hall crumbling into disuse, it is the Tories who have helped the matchstick figures in the Lowry painting to become householders.

'Anyway,' she adds now, 'it seemed only sensible to take precautions. Especially as it isn't insured.'

'Nanna!'

'Do I detect middle-class capitalist shock beneath those crimson spikes? It's not simply that the premiums are horrendous. I wouldn't even be allowed to start paying them until I'd installed a burglar alarm – and in this part of the world it's the people with alarms who get burgled. The box seems to act as a proclamation that there's something inside the property worth having. Besides, I've always felt it would spoil my pleasure in looking at the picture if I knew how much a week it was costing me to have it on the wall. So. It will be hanging in the Jaffreys' flat downstairs while I'm away.'

She pauses for a moment to visualize it there and then

21

continues more briskly. 'I haven't much else of more than sentimental interest,' she says. The Dangerfield family pictures and silver were correctly bequeathed to Constance, whose marriage brought her a Scottish castle and a Bayswater mansion in which to house them. As someone disapproving of inherited wealth, it did not even occur to Lord Dangerfield's elder daughter at the time of her father's death that he was using his will to punish her for choosing to earn her own living. 'After losing so much in the Blitz, I vowed never to let myself become attached to objects again. What there is, I've hidden. Let me show you.' She stands up and moves towards the fireplace.

'No need,' says Caro. 'I'll help you get it out again when you come home. You can tell me then where to look. Unless you're afraid that you might forget where you put it.'

'Certainly not.' Lady Ainslie, who is proud of her memory, reacts with indignation, but nevertheless insists on easing the electric fire away from the fireplace in order to point out a black plastic sack stuffed up the never-used chimney.

Caro stares at her for a moment, frowning slightly, and then crosses the room to the large desk in the bay window. Without asking permission she begins to open the drawers, noting the unusual neatness and near-emptiness of each. Turning, she points an accusing finger.

'You have assured me,' she says, 'that you will be paying a brief visit to hospital in order that a tumour of the transverse colon, or something of the sort, may be removed. The operation is described as a major one only because of the area it affects. The growth to be removed, you have stated categorically, is causing you discomfort because of its size, but is non-malignant.'

'Correct,' says Lady Ainslie, sitting down to enjoy her coffee.

'Do you mean that I'm reporting you correctly or that you were reporting the actual state of affairs correctly?'

'Both. Now come and sit down, dear. We need to be off in ten minutes.'

'Then why all this?' Caro, ignoring the invitation, waves her arm to indicate the whole of the spick-and-span flat. 'Can you deny that you've been putting your affairs in order, as they say?'

Lady Ainslie smiles at her affectionately. 'I know it's not done to talk about the possibility of one's own death,' she says. 'One of the odder taboos of our society. I haven't been fibbing to you, darling. What I told you is precisely what Toby – Mr Mallinson – told me. This is elective surgery. No crisis. No emergency. But *any* operation presents a risk to someone of my age, just from the general shock to the system. If I consider the possibility that in a week's time I may be dead, it doesn't distress me. But if I also had to envisage you and Martin struggling to sort out a confusion of draft speeches and committee minutes and bank statements and letters and bills, *that* would bother me a lot. So.' She makes clear her wish to change the subject. 'Whose lunch are you cooking today?'

Caro hesitates for a second before giving an ostentatious sigh of acceptance and picking up her cup.

'A firm of lawyers in Lincoln's Inn. Immensely stuffy and respectable. They specialize in family trusts. Once a year they invite all their richest clients round for a gorge – presumably to make sure that they're still alive.'

'And how will the new hair-do go down in Lincoln's Inn?'

'The cook is expected to remain invisible,' Caro points out. 'Phil and Kate do the front-of-house stuff. You know, Nanna, I'm shocked to find you growing so conservative in your old age.'

'No you're not. Horrifying the elderly is one of the pleasures of the young. I can remember bobbing my hair for precisely that reason. And I often think that I'd never have managed to stick so many years of medical school if my parents hadn't made it so clear that they disapproved. You would have been thoroughly disappointed if I'd pretended not to notice. Now we should go.'

'You're always too early for everything,' Caro grumbles, finishing her coffee. 'Why did you choose Freddie's anyway, out of all the hospitals in London? It could hardly be further from West Hampstead.'

'When Dr Fanshawe wanted me to see a specialist she asked which hospital would suit me best. And Dame Freda's is handiest for the Lords. Of course, at that time I was only thinking about tests. I didn't expect them to lead to an operation.'

'And it will be handy for any of your noble friends who decide to drop in,' Caro recognizes.

23

'I don't want visitors,' Lady Ainslie says, more sharply than she intends. 'You, of course, and Martin if the poor boy is ever allowed to stop pounding his beat for a moment. But I haven't told anybody else that I'm being admitted.'

'Why on earth not?'

'It's a hangover from the past. No one in politics ever confesses to ill-health. The faintest doubt about your stamina and that telephone call from Number Ten or Buckingham Palace will never arrive.'

She laughs at the ridiculous thought. More than twenty years have passed since she accepted a life peerage and in so doing automatically debarred herself from further promotion. The newspapers at the time wrote gossipy paragraphs about the effective retirement of someone who might have been Britain's first woman prime minister, but that was never a possibility. A future leader of the Labour Party should not make her first appearance in a stately home and boast a recorded pedigree going back to the Conquest.

As she goes to fetch her overcoat Caro carries the tray back to the kitchen and can be heard washing up. Lady Ainslie looks down at the three battered diaries which last night she was too tired to consider.

About two of them, so unusually identical in the creasing and doodling of their dark green covers, she is still uncertain. Perhaps she should keep one – but which one? Annoyed with herself for postponing such a decision to the very last moment, she pushes them both into the handbag, as large as a briefcase, which she always carries.

To throw whichever of the two she decides to reject into a waste paper basket here in the flat will be to risk Caro's curiosity when she lets herself in, as she undoubtedly will, to turn on the heating ready for her grandmother's return. In hospital, though, cleaners will tip trash into plastic bin liners without a second glance and send it off to be incinerated. She has been a doctor for long enough to know that she will not be trundled straight into an operating theatre. There will be tedious hours of waiting; plenty of time in which to dispose of something which is not only the record of a long-forgotten quarrel, but its cause.

About the third of the diaries, though – the pretty one whose cover imitates an embroidery sampler – there should never have been any doubt. It must be put out of the reach of any curious reader. Taking a plastic carrier bag from a kitchen drawer, she drops in the notebook and folds the wrapper into a neat parcel.

Five minutes later, following Caro down the stairs, she rings the bell of the Jaffreys' flat. It has already been arranged that she should leave her keys in case there should be an emergency of fire or flood in her absence. She presses the carrier bag into Mrs Jaffrey's hand.

'This should have been in the box I gave you,' she says.

Lady Ainslie is an unsentimental woman, not given to sighing over decisions or events of the past. But, as she watches her neighbour lay the small parcel on top of the box which has been pushed under the stairs, she gives an involuntary sigh. How different the course of her life would have been if she had never met Gil Blakey again!

Four

An unexpected caller this morning. Gil Blakey, the swineherd's son. Out of all the village children of my sort of age, the only one who 'got away' – joined the army young and never really returned to Kingsgelding.

He seemed to know all about me; disconcerting. Asked me out to dinner and told me a bit about himself in return. Apparently he runs (edits? owns? not clear) a magazine called The Investigator. *Haven't ever seen it myself, but remember it being in the news when it revealed one of the honours-for-sale scandals. Must be doing quite well if he can afford Harley Street fees. He didn't come to see me just in order to gossip, of course. His wife has a problem.*

At eleven o'clock on Friday, 15 July 1936, Dr Ainslie Dangerfield pressed the footbell beneath her desk. All her appointments for the morning were with patients she was seeing for the first time. Her smile would need only to be one of welcome, not of recognition; but it changed to surprise as the door opened.

The man who paused for a moment in the doorway was tall and powerfully built, with corn-coloured hair and bright blue eyes. His broad smile suggested that he found enjoyment in startling her.

'You won't remember me,' he said. 'But we knew each other, in a way, when we were children. In Kingsgelding. Gil Blakey.'

'Of course I remember you.' Ainslie held out a hand to be

26

shaken. 'I won't pretend that I recognized you, though, after so many years.'

'You seemed rather taken aback.'

'That's because I always expect my patients to be female. Do sit down. What have you been doing all these years?'

She was genuinely curious. His voice, abrupt in its phrasing, had lost the broad vowels of the village; it was that of a man who was well educated, although not at a public school or university. He had gone to grammar school, she remembered, before joining up. Everything about his dress and his ease of manner suggested that he had done well for himself since the end of the war.

'I'll be glad of a chance to tell you sometime. I don't imagine you want to waste your consultation hours on that kind of chatter, though. I've known rather more about what you've been doing, I should say. I give a bit of money from time to time to that clinic of yours in Bethnal Green. The birth control one.'

'I didn't know —'

'I never put a name to it. Just put it in an envelope and shove it through the door. Because I watched my mother bring up so many babies. One every year, and the only way she ever stopped it was by telling my dad to keep his distance. You do a good job down there, Dr Dangerfield. It's a pity that not all doctors are so brave; or so generous with their time.'

'It's other people's money that I'm generous with. I charge the women who come to me here at Harley Street through the nose, so that I can have time for the others.'

'Ah, the Robin Hood system. Well, let's get down to why I'm here.' He put an attaché case on the desk and opened it. 'I want to find out if you can help my wife.'

'Why hasn't she come to see me herself?'

Gil lowered the lid of the case so that he could look straight into Ainslie's eyes.

'She had a miscarriage ten days ago,' he said. 'The sixth miscarriage in four years. This time, she'd been promised that everything was going to be all right. We'd waited, after the last one, to make sure that she'd got her strength back. We did everything we were told. And yet . . . She's been crying for a

27

week. She wants a baby, and I do too, but I'm not going to let her put herself through this again. I don't want her hopes raised unless there really is a hope.'

'Is her doctor willing for me to see her?'

'Didn't see why it should be *his* decision. I didn't ask him if it would be a good idea to go to a consultant; I told him. He wrote out a kind of timetable of all the miscarriages for me to show you, but I wasn't sure whether that would be detailed enough, so I got hold of his notes on her. Thought you might be able to tell from them what's going wrong and whether anything can be done about it. She'll come soon enough, Jessica, if she thinks you can help her.'

He opened the case again and passed over a folder of papers.

'What do you mean, got hold of her notes?'

'Stole them,' said Gil matter-of-factly. 'Seemed to me they ought to be our property anyway. It's Jessica's body they're describing.'

Ainslie refrained from comment as she turned over the pages. 'How far into the pregnancy was she this last time?' she asked.

'It wasn't one of the worst. She's been further on before, and had more pain with it. It's the disappointment that's making her cry. Sixteen weeks, I think it was.'

Ainslie made a note. 'We call it an abortion when it's as early as that. A miscarriage is something that comes later in a pregnancy. But most people get the terms wrong.'

'Thought abortion was a dirty word.'

'It is when it's induced by a human hand. But Mother Nature performs abortions all the time, unfortunately. There's no law which can protect society against that.' She patted the sheets together. 'I wish she'd come to me earlier.'

'Should have done, I see that now. But it was tricky. I married, you might say, well above myself. Rich county people. There's a family doctor who's been there for ever. Brought Jessica into the world, so of course he knows best what to do with her now. It's not easy, when your wife feels ill and wants to go home to Mummy for a bit of woman-comfort, to tell her that the local quack is incompetent. It'll be all right this time, he said – every

28

time. Just bad luck before. Who were we to know better? But this one's the last straw. She'll do anything I suggest. Only reason why I've come ahead to scout it out, so to speak, is that I'm not prepared to raise her hopes for nothing.'

Ainslie nodded her understanding.

'After six miscarriages – especially since I see that one of them was at twenty-seven weeks – there's a possibility of internal damage,' she said. 'She ought to be examined in any case. You could explain your knowledge of me just by the fact that we knew each other as children. I'll make sure that the examination, and the questions I ask, are very thorough. After that I'll give you my opinion and you can talk it over with her when you feel she's ready. But Gil.'

Ainslie paused. She had not intended to use his Christian name. It was, after all, a very long time indeed since they had played together. But to amend it now to 'Mr Blakey' would be too pointedly formal. 'Even if I feel I can help, there's a warning I shall have to give her, and I'll give it to you first. These spontaneous abortions she's been having. As often as not, it's Nature's way of saying that there's something wrong with the baby, the foetus. So there's a danger, you see. If I succeed in getting your wife to full term, I could be helping her to produce an imperfect baby. You'd both need to be quite clear about the risk.'

'I asked around before I came to see you,' said Gil. 'They told me you were always honest with your patients. Thank you.' He hesitated for a moment before continuing to speak. 'They also told me you didn't believe that any child should have to go through life unwanted or badly handicapped and that you had the courage to act on that belief when necessary.'

Ainslie was startled into standing up and Gil also rose to his feet. She stared across the desk into his eyes and seemed to see in them a touch of menace. But perhaps she was only imagining it. She met both his gaze and his insinuation with courage.

'I don't know who "they" may be, but they've given you quite the wrong impression. I'm not a complete innocent. I know that there are a few midwives, and perhaps even some doctors, who will look at a baby they've just delivered and decide that for its own sake it shouldn't be allowed to draw breath. I'm not one of them. You need to be clear about that as well.'

Gil's smile broadened. 'Something I discovered long ago. Make somebody angry and you learn the truth at double speed. *In ira veritas.*'

The realization that he was deliberately testing her was unsettling. In her own consulting room, as a rule, she was the one in control. But, sitting down again, she continued calmly.

'It's perfectly true that my work divides itself into two parts. I've always found it tragic that there are so many women who long for a child and can't manage to produce one, whilst so many other women who've had enough babies already desperately need to be sure that they won't have any more. I try to help both kinds, and while I'm trying my duty is to my patient, the woman herself. But the moment she gives birth, I have a second duty, and that's to the baby. So if you and your wife, Mr Blakey, have any hopes that you can take a gamble and then expect me to help you evade your responsibilities if the gamble doesn't come off –'

Still standing, he interrupted her.

'Your position is noted.' The nature of his smile changed, becoming mischievous, boyish, recognizably that of the swineherd's son. 'You called me Gil a moment ago. Please don't take a step backwards. I'm going to Lady Lucy's six o'clock tonight. May I take you with me, and then on to dinner afterwards? So that I can truthfully tell Jessica that I've met you and learned about your work in a social setting. I earn my living by telling the truth and I like to keep the habit going at home.'

It was amusing that May Blakey's son should apparently be at home in the world of aristocratic soirées whilst she, the Honourable Ainslie, had no idea who Lady Lucy might be. But more than amusement led her to accept the invitation. She was curious as well. Exactly how did Gil earn his living?

He told her, in a surprisingly straightforward manner, over an expensive dinner. Ainslie liked to believe that she was not a snob, but she needed to control her surprise at the easy familiarity with which her host greeted the head waiter, made recommendations from the French menu, chose and tasted the wine. She

30

must stop thinking of him as a village boy who had once poached on her father's estate, and instead get to know this new acquaintance, a man of the world.

'You said you earned your living by telling the truth? How?'

'Have you ever heard of a magazine called *The Investigator*?'

'I've heard of it, yes. I've never read it, though.'

'No, you wouldn't. Circulates mostly amongst politicians, money men, socialites. People who want to know what's going on. Its function is to expose scandals. Print things that somebody would prefer to keep secret.'

Ainslie's face must have expressed distaste, for he explained more fully.

'Don't mean *really* private stuff. If Joe Bloggs in 35 Jubilee Avenue has a bit on the side, that's between him and his wife. But if the king of England is flaunting his fancy piece all round the world and no one in his own country has got the guts to mention it, that's a different matter. A matter of state, you might even think. Devaluing the monarchy. There's trouble coming, and *The Investigator* is the only place you'll learn about it.'

'The king? Honestly?'

'You see! You didn't know, and how could you, if no one tells you? Conspiracy of silence in Fleet Street. Because they hope the trouble will go away, or because all the proprietors are sweating on their titles? Well, we don't very often get juicy bits about kings, of course. More down to earth usually. Honourable City gentlemen who have private information about how the market's going to move and don't see why they shouldn't cash in on it. Workers' leaders who'll sell their members short for the sake of a holiday for themselves and wife, all expenses paid. Members of Parliament with business interests, who happily despatch a shipment of arms to a government that they voted to censure twenty-four hours earlier. Why have you got that quizzical look on your face?'

'I'm surprised at you telling me all this. I'd have thought you'd want to keep quiet about what you do, so that you can worm people's secrets out of them without their realizing.'

'Other chaps do that. There has to be one front man. All our best exposures start with informers. The underpaid clerk who

31

wants to get his own back on the boss who's living it up on dirty money. People like that need to know where to come.'

'You must have a lot of enemies.'

'Yes. And while they're busy hating me, they don't notice the others who are quietly beavering away. Of course, to start with, our victims always assume that we're in the blackmail business. I'm not sure that it isn't the greatest shock of all, finding that they can't buy us off.'

'Never?'

'Never. Sometimes they pay without being asked. That's where the money comes from that arrives in places like your clinic. I don't want to keep it, but I don't see why I should give it back. Doesn't do them any good. Mind you, sometimes they can *talk* us out of publishing. There was a charity, a couple of weeks ago. Fellow who ran it had embezzled three thousand pounds. No doubt about it. We told the trustees before we printed, and they put up a case. If the public lost faith in the charity, it would hit the beneficiaries, the children of the unemployed. They promised to sack the manager and make up the money from their own pockets and we spiked the story.'

Ainslie felt dazed as the conversation continued. How had a village boy like Gil managed to acquire such knowledge and power that he could make her feel so unsophisticated? She needed to remind herself that she had her own expertise. It was her experience and success in her own sphere which had provided the occasion for this conversation. However powerful and feared Gil might be in his working life, he was in need of help, and she was the one who might be able to give it.

Five

Pickets are blocking the main entrance of Dame Freda's Foundation, their slogans painted in thick red letters on what look very much like hospital sheets. Caro takes a quick glance and continues along the road without stopping.

'I'll take you in through the kitchens,' she says. 'Then you can go up by lift inside the building. I can say I'm making a special delivery.' She has been to the market at Nine Elms early that morning and the back of the estate car is stacked with the fruit and vegetables which she needs for her catering work.

'No,' says Lady Ainslie sharply.

Caro brings the car to a halt. 'I thought you probably wouldn't want to cross a picket line.'

'I shan't be crossing it to work. And I'm not going in as a private patient. The pickets have the right to explain their case to me peacefully and of course I shall listen. But they're striking against the government, not against the patients.'

'Oh Nanna, darling!' Caro sighs at the naïvety of someone who has been a politician long enough to know better. She does a U-turn nevertheless and returns to the front of the hospital. The sloping approach reserved for ambulances has been blocked by parked cars, but there is a lower road leading to the bottom of a wide flight of steps. Caro drives as far as the chain which has been stretched across it and turns off the ignition.

'Leave me to handle this,' she pleads. 'I wouldn't want to destroy your illusions. But if you could bring yourself to accept just the tiniest of terminological inexactitudes, it would help if

33

your admission could be a matter of life and death. Your operation absolutely urgent.'

Lady Ainslie sits quietly in the car and watches as Caro begins to argue with the picket in charge. She does not appear to be having much success. He shakes his head and, as Lady Ainslie winds down the window of the car, she hears him repeat a refusal. 'I don't care who she bloody is.'

'But don't you realize –' Caro, it seems, is losing her temper – 'that she's always been on your side? If it weren't for people like her, the National Health Service wouldn't exist to be mucked about with by people like you.'

Lady Ainslie sighs, wishing that she had forbidden Caro to mention her name. Her right to be admitted to Dame Freda's Foundation is no more and no less than that of anyone else. She notes that the chain does not extend across the pavement, so that no athleticism on her part will be required. Moving carefully, she gets out of the car.

Someone else has intervened in the argument – a tall and very thin young man wearing large spectacles and an earnest expression. 'Remember, Pete, the eyes of the world are on you.'

'You can take the bloody cameras away,' growls the picket.

'No.' The young man speaks firmly. 'You asked us to come here instead of to Guy's, so that you could get some. publicity and see yourselves on telly. We've come and we're staying and we're filming. Now. Don't forget that TV-am had that story about the woman who died in a police van because your people wouldn't pick her up. If there are too many cases like that, you'll lose public sympathy. It's your choice. What you decide is none of my business. But it will be a public decision.'

As the man hesitates, Lady Ainslie walks towards him. Good posture was a gift imposed on her in childhood by Nanny Frensham and a backboard, so she holds her head high now not out of any spirit of defiance but because it is her habit to stand up straight. She smiles at the pickets but says nothing except 'Thank you' as they silently part to let her through. Caro, she hopes, will be allowed to bring her suitcase.

The twenty wide stone steps which now confront her have no

handrail. After tackling the first six slowly, she finds that she can go no further.

'Damn,' she says, furious at her own weakness. Anger almost brings tears to her eyes. She takes three deep breaths, hoping that by some magic these will restore her strength. A hand slips gently under her elbow.

'May I help you?' It is the tall young man who has been talking to the pickets. Even as he speaks, Caro comes running up the steps with the suitcase to join them. Slowly, with their aid, Lady Ainslie attains the entrance hall. Half a dozen bright orange chairs, fixed to the ground in a straight line, offer themselves for a moment's rest. Lady Ainslie sits down to wait for the erratic beating of her heart to subside.

'Thank you very much,' she says to the young man. 'May I know your name?'

'Carrington. Daniel Carrington.' His expression is as earnest when he smiles as when he is arguing. He appears to be about the same age as Caro, although his fair hair has already begun to recede. 'I hope everything goes smoothly for you now, Lady Ainslie.'

She watches as he runs down the steps two at a time and then turns to Caro.

'Would I be right in supposing that Mr Carrington was not entirely motivated by sympathy for a poor old lady? That more to the point is his admiration for a beautiful young lady?'

'You wouldn't be *quite* right. Daniel has excellent manners and a proper respect for his elders and betters. He's also a fanatical student of twentieth-century history, so meeting someone like you is a big deal. But if you mean, is he a friend of mine, the answer is yes. Quite a close friend.'

Lady Ainslie nods. Then another, unwelcome, thought occurs to her. 'He told the pickets that the cameras were running. Was that true? He wouldn't surely – not on television – Caro, dearest, would you ask him, make sure that he doesn't –' Realizing that she has been flustered into incoherence she takes a grip on her speech and starts again. 'I don't wish the fact that I'm in hospital to be announced to the whole nation on the television news.'

35

'I'll tell him. He works on documentaries, not for ITN. He'll have plenty of incidents to choose from, and your bit of film will be the first to be cut out just because he appeared on it himself. What's the objection though, Nanna, to being seen sticking up for your principles? I don't mean crossing a picket line, but turning up for an operation as an ordinary NHS patient?'

'It's a question of privacy,' Lady Ainslie asserts. 'In any case, I worry about the logic of my principles. If there really is a shortage of nurses and resources, it could be argued that I'd serve the NHS better by paying my own way. But . . .'

'Old loyalties die hard, is that it?'

'That's it. A gesture of my faith in the system.'

'Then the more publicity the gesture gets, the better for the system.'

'Oh dear,' sighs Lady Ainslie. 'If my own granddaughter out-debates me, how shall I ever dare return to the House of Lords? I can only say that I have a distaste for publicity and I rely on you to convince Mr Carrington of that. Now then, where do you think I have to check in?'

'Wait here while I find out.'

She sits for a few seconds without moving, conscious that an inexplicable limpness is affecting not only her body but her mind. She is perfectly well able to explore the building for herself. It is curious that the mere fact of crossing the threshold of the hospital should rob her of initiative as well as energy. During the past few days she has made all her arrangements in a responsible manner. Why should she suddenly now expect to be looked after even before the process of handing her body over to doctors and nurses has begun? Indignant at her own weakness Lady Ainslie stands up and, with her usual briskness, hurries to catch up with Caro.

Thanks to the strike the in-patients' reception area is compara-tively uncrowded. It is presumably those who most urgently need the hospital's services who are finding most difficulty in making their way there. With Caro at her side Lady Ainslie presents her letter of referral and admission card. She confirms that she is who she is, noting with interest that her age absolves her from having an occupation. Rather than spell out her son's distant and complicated address she gives Martin as her next of kin. She signs a form which will permit the surgeon to attack her body in any way which takes his fancy. She is taken into a small room where her finger is painfully punctured by a gadget resembling a tin opener in order that a phial may be filled with her blood. Then she is directed to take a seat.

'I hope you think this is worth it,' says Caro as the waiting time extends itself. 'Queuing for everything, when under a private insurance scheme you could have been whisked into something looking like a luxury hotel. Or even on to the private floor here at Freddie's, where you'd have a room to yourself and the consultant of your choice.'

'You mean instead of being carved up by a medical student and dumped in a ward full of snorers and chatterers? You're not being very tactful, dear, to a nervous old lady.' She smiles, unworried. Her old friend Toby Mallinson has promised that he will personally carry out the operation. 'I have to confess that Toby has promised me a room to myself.'

'One of these – what are they called – amenity beds?'

'No. As free as any other. Every ward has one small separate room at the end, and that's what I've been offered. If someone arrives who's either dying or breastfeeding I shall have to move out, but otherwise I can stay on my own. There's not a great demand for privacy, I'm told. Most people prefer to be ill in company. But you mustn't wait any longer, dear. You've got your lunch to prepare.'

Caro looks at her watch. 'Yes, perhaps I ought . . .' She goes over to speak to the receptionist and returns looking pleased with herself. 'You can go up to the ward and wait there,' she says. 'Riverside Six.'

A nurse, smiling in welcome, comes forward to take the suitcase as they step out of the lift on the sixth floor.

'I'll be back this evening to see that you're settled in,' says Caro. 'In the meantime, a small present.' She feels in her handbag for something she has not bothered to wrap. It is a notebook whose cover appears to have been designed by Jackson Pollock in drips of red and black. 'So that you can keep a hospital diary. I wouldn't like to think of you suffering from withdrawal symptoms.' She gives her grandmother an affectionate hug. 'Look after yourself.'

A most inappropriate remark, thinks Lady Ainslie. She is just about to hand over control of her body to others. From now on doctors and nurses will be doing all the looking after. The plastic identification bracelet which has been clipped round her wrist relieves her even of the responsibility of remembering who she is. Sitting down beside the central desk in the ward, she submits to another session of form-filling.

'Your operation will be at twelve o'clock tomorrow,' the nurse tells her, slipping all the papers into a file.

'Did I need to come so early, then?'

'Oh, there are a lot of checks to be made. Blood pressure, weight, allergies, that sort of thing. And we have to make sure that you starve overnight. Dr Cameron, who'll be your anaesthetist, will need to examine you this afternoon; and Mr Mallinson said he'd be calling in to have a word. He's asked us to put you into the single, and we expect to be able to do that when you come out of theatre. But for the moment it isn't free. I'll settle you into a ward cubicle for the time being. You can use the day room, of course, as long as we know where to find you.'

The day room is heavy with smoke and loud with television. The ward is crowded with curious and garrulous women, anxious to discover what her problem is and to give her a point-by-point account of their own operations. The headphones of the radio, donned as a defence against conversation, prove to offer only the raucous din of Radio One or the well-meaning but uninteresting chatter of the hospital's own service, and Lady Ainslie is a Radio Three person.

She finds herself more annoyed than she likes to admit that the room which ought to be ready for her should be occupied by someone else. Toby had promised. Surely it could have been made ready in time. But she reminds herself fiercely that this is not a hotel and that she has always been opposed to privilege, whether of birth or money. It is illogical to believe that old age or a love of privacy should entitle her to expect special treatment.

Time passes. She has been asked to take off her day clothes in order to simplify the anaesthetist's examination of her chest.

Wearing nightdress, dressing gown and slippers, like all the other patients, she makes her way to the end of the ward and stares for a moment through the diamond pane of glass into the single room which should be hers.

Propped up by pillows, a young black woman lies motionless. On one side of the bed tubes sprout from her nose and arm. On the other side a man kneels on the floor, in despair rather than prayer. All that can be seen of his head is curly black hair, for his mouth and nose are pressed down into the bedclothes and his arms are crossed over his forehead.

Staring, even from the far side of a door, is an invasion of privacy. No longer impatient, Lady Ainslie returns to her own cubicle and tries to concentrate on one of the books she has brought with her. To hope for her own selfish and trivial reason that someone should be quick about dying would be unforgivable.

At two o'clock the house surgeon, Mr Graham, comes to ask again all the questions which she has already answered several times. She repeats the information patiently, remembering the period when she was in his shoes, always with too little time and too many responsibilities.

The surgeon himself arrives soon afterwards; tall and good-looking, wearing an air of confident authority and an expensive suit. There is nothing to indicate his medical status except the deference with which he is greeted by the ward sister.

Lady Ainslie puts down her book and smiles. She and Toby Mallinson stand on opposite sides of the political fence, but have been friends for thirty years. As a young man he championed the cause of overworked registrars against both the government and the senior consultants, but always in the interests of an efficient health service. Now he is one of the top surgeons himself, but his loyalty to the system is unchanged.

'I'm sorry that we've had to start you off here,' he says, after they have discussed the timetable for the next day. 'But it will only be for another hour or so.'

'That's all right. You warned me that if anyone was dying . . .'

'She's dead already to all intents and purposes. We've been keeping her on the ventilator for a little while to give her husband time to come to terms with it. That's why we moved her out of

Intensive Care and up here, so that he could have her to himself. He can't believe . . .' Toby sighs. 'A nasty case. Two days ago a gang of blacks, four of them, raped a white fifteen-year-old girl. Yesterday the girl's brother and some of his mates, all white, went out on the street and just beat up the first black woman they saw. She was seven months pregnant. We operated last night, hoping to save the baby, but it was no good. There was never much hope for the mother. We shall have to turn the machine off soon. Well.' He stands up. 'I shall see you tomorrow, although you won't see me. Have a good night's sleep. You're not worried about anything, I hope.'

'Just one thing. If this lump proves, when you get at it, to be less benign than you think, and if you find metastasis, I don't really want, you know, to spend the rest of my life feeling sick from chemotherapy or radiotherapy. There's nothing left that I need to do. It's always seemed to me that the most agreeable way to die is to feel a prick in the arm before an operation and simply never wake up again.'

'What a selfish woman you are! Am I to sacrifice my reputation as a surgeon for your convenience? And find myself accused, for good measure, of political assassination because we've been known to disagree? It's well known that any doctor's least favourite patient is another doctor. It would serve you right if I washed my hands of you on the spot.' He smiles down at her affectionately. 'I've been telling you the truth about your tumour, you know. I have absolutely no reason to believe that there'll be any unpleasant surprises. Surgeon now retires hurt. Patient had better grovel.'

'I grovel. Sorry, Toby.' But she is not sorry. She has wanted to put her feelings on record. There is a phrase for what can happen in hospitals when sudden emergencies arise. She wants no heroic measures in her own case.

Another hour passes. Most of the other women in the ward have visitors by now, and the danger of unwanted conversation has diminished. In the ward sister's office a different kind of conversation appears to be in progress. Two hospital porters have been summoned and are being given instructions.

Sister moves out of sight. Within a few moments there is a

40

sound which brings every conversation in the ward to a halt. It is a roar in which pain and rage are combined, followed by a furious shouting. The words can not be distinguished; but as the two porters, receiving some signal, move towards the room in which the dead woman lies, Lady Ainslie knows what is happening. She has heard a sound like that before.

Six

Too stirred up to write this yesterday, and I'm not sure that I'm calm enough yet. Unprofessional, to get too involved with a patient. But I've been treated unprofessionally. Need to let off steam.

Jessica Blakey. Came to see me twelve months ago. Nice woman. Too thin and highly strung, but anxious to please. To please Gil primarily, of course, knowing that he desperately wants a son. But to please me as well if I could help her provide it. Dutifully provided samples and endured tests and passed on instructions to Gil about when he shouldn't and should try to start another pregnancy.

Confession of more unprofessional behaviour. On the date when I'd told her she could go ahead, I found myself identifying with my patient. As though I could actually see Gil undressing, advancing, very large and strong. Found myself wondering if he'd be gentle or forceful, whether he'd lose control or whether the special importance of the occasion would make him anxious. Disgraceful to think like that. And disgraceful, having thought it, not to record it in my diary at the time. Sorry, Edward.

Anyway. Hormone treatment did the trick, with bed rest for a week every month. At thirty-six weeks, everything going well: baby the right size with a strong heartbeat. J.B.'s blood pressure erratic, but not dangerous. Bed booked at the Wimpole Street clinic, with their top obstetrician signed up for the delivery. Weekly checks arranged for the last month.

Yesterday, a fortnight before full term, Mrs Blakey didn't keep her appointment.

I didn't think too much of it at first. London is stinking hot, so her parents' country house must have seemed tempting. I'd told her not to travel, but I suppose an hour in a chauffeur-driven car wasn't much. I phoned to check, though, and found the household in a fluster. Doctor, midwife and monthly nurse already on the premises; baby expected at any moment.

I phoned the clinic. Dr Janes was just about to perform a Caesarean and wouldn't be free for several hours. So I drove myself down, worrying all the way. Why hadn't they phoned me or Dr Janes instead of chasing around for a monthly nurse? J.B. could have been back at the clinic in an hour, and I'd told her how long labour usually extends with a first baby. I could smell a rat from miles off, though I didn't identify it till I got there.

Gil was standing beside the cradle when I arrived, looking down at his daughter. He'd pulled the shawl open and was using one finger to touch each hand and foot in turn, letting her kick against it, or clutch it with her fist. A pretty sight, just for the moment.

He looked across at me with an odd sort of smile. Half friendly and grateful. Half proud. Half ashamed. Too many halves there. Perhaps I was imagining one of them. 'Perfect,' he said. And then I knew.

All new parents worry, of course. They all ask the same first question, make the same first checks. But I'd given Gil and Jessica more reason than most to worry and they – well no; only Gil, I'm sure – had worked out a way to deal with it. Have the baby delivered at home by a sympathetic doctor, and never mind that he may be incompetent. If anything proves to be wrong, there'll be no officious medical staff and equipment on hand to make sure of survival. They must have had it all lined up for weeks.

I was so angry that I hardly noticed when Gil went off to see his wife. It makes my blood boil again just to remember it – although now, of course, knowing what came next, I'll never be able to express my feelings anywhere but here.

While I was alone with the nurse, I asked her when Mrs Blakey's labour had started. Was told that it had been induced. Two weeks early, in a case where there could be no possible doubt about dates! I asked her to tell the doctor I was here and that I'd be glad of a word with him and a chance to see my patient. Formal politeness to cover *seething fury. Maybe Gil hadn't realized the risks, but even a country doctor . . .*

Long pause. If I'd been in charge, the baby would have been in her mother's arms now. Frustrating, being kept at arm's length. In the end, I set off to look for the delivery room. Big house, so it took a minute or two. Went up a flight of stairs, along a corridor, round a corner. Another corridor; but the atmosphere stopped me in my tracks, like a wall. Not just anxiety: panic. No one to be seen, nothing to be heard, but panic somewhere.

And then this sound. More than a sob, more than a groan; a roar of disbelief and anguish.

In the past ten years I've had to break bad news to a lot of men. Some cried, one fainted, most merely stared, incredulous. I've never before heard a sound like Gil's cry yesterday. Shan't ever forget it.

Seven

Ashamed of her curiosity but unable to control it, Lady Ainslie leaves her cubicle and walks down the ward until she can see, although not hear, what is going on in the single room, whose door has been hooked open. The young husband – or rather, the widower – is struggling with manic strength to remain at his wife's bedside. The two porters, each almost as black as he is, restrain him with an impassive sympathy. Sister waits quietly for the moment when he is forced to stop and gasp for breath. When she speaks, it is undoubtedly with kindness, but her high white headdress, symbol of authority on her own territory, distances her from the man's distress. He shakes his head, unwilling to listen to whatever she is trying to say. It is always too soon to talk about formalities: death certificates, personal effects.

For a few moments his raging struggle continues. He is a powerful man, capable of wrecking a ward, knocking down a nurse, picking up his wife's body and carrying it away. But abruptly the fight goes out of him. Sister touches his arm, indicating that he should follow her. Flanked but no longer gripped by the two porters, like a prisoner who on his way to execution knows that there is nowhere to run, he moves out of Lady Ainslie's sight. Already, behind his back, the body of his wife is being lifted on to a trolley.

The trolley is pushed towards a lift and the room becomes a scene of bustle. A cleaner swabs the floor and wipes the bedside locker with a disinfected cloth. Orderlies strip and remake the bed. A nurse wheels away the steel gallows from which tubes now ineffectively dangle. Within a few moments the room will not only belong to its next occupant but will seem always to have done so. The hospital exists to cure people, and maintains silence about its failures. None of the nurses will mention to Lady Ainslie the woman who has just vacated her bed.

She turns away and walks back through the ward, pausing on her way to look down from a window. There is a view of Lambeth roofs, Lambeth streets. Somewhere out there a man will soon be walking, pacing the pavements because no building is large enough to contain his grief. But there is nothing she can do to help him. She will never see him again. Back in her own cubicle, she sits down in the chair beside the bed and reads patiently until a student nurse comes to lead her to her new quarters.

Now the room is hers. The high white bed is hers. Best of all, the view is hers. Surprised and delighted, Lady Ainslie looks out of the wide sixth-floor window and sees the Palace of Westminster – her workplace, her second home, for more than forty years. How many times has she gazed southwards across the river from a committee room or the terrace, watching the lights come on in the windows of Dame Freda's and wondering who is lying behind each window; what pain and fear the rooms hold. Now, looking north, she imagines instead the leisurely activity of her noble friends, the noisier bustle of the Commons, but sees it all with the same detachment with which before she studied the hospital; it has nothing to do with her today. More real is the pleasure steamer which appears under Westminster Bridge. A band is playing, balloons bob, people are drinking and dancing, someone is giving a party. She smiles, sharing the gaiety, and then sets to the task of laying out her possessions.

There are not many of them. Books and toilet articles take up little space. The clothes in which she arrived are already packed in the suitcase, to be taken away. She hesitates over the new notebook which Caro has given her, wondering whether to embark at once on the record of the day, and finds herself curiously reluctant to do so. What is the point, when no one is ever to see it? It is a question she has not asked herself for more than seventy years and she finds disquieting the answer which presents itself. For the moment, when she has climbed into the

46

high bed, she is content to sit without occupation, propped up by pillows and a sloping metal backrest, absorbing the ambience.

There is a ghost in the room, the ghost not of a dead woman but of a live one. Only just alive, perhaps: it is the intensity of the husband's refusal to let go which has so charged the atmosphere that it attacks Lady Ainslie's confidence in herself. Is it really her elderly white body which is occupying the bed? She puts out a hand to hold back the student nurse who has been sent to check that she is comfortably settled in.

'What's your name, dear?'

'Tricia.'

'Tricia, can you tell me the name of the patient who was here this morning? The one who died.'

Tricia hesitates, but although she has probably been told not to introduce the subject of the room's previous occupant, she can see no reason to avoid a direct question. 'Mrs Barnaby.'

'Thank you, Tricia.'

Mrs Barnaby. An odd sort of name. Did some plantation owner in the West Indies once give each of his slaves a Christian name, and did one of them later celebrate his freedom by adding the Mister as a mark of personal dignity? But she is allowed no time to consider this further, for Caro has arrived, carrying with anxious care a bowl piled high with fruit.

'The left-overs,' she announces, setting the bowl down before bending to kiss her grandmother. 'By the time they've chopped at the cheese and made pigs of themselves on the puds, the lunchers never have any appetite left for fruit, but we're expected to produce it all the same. Sometimes I'm tempted to invest in some wax replicas. But today I chose everything with you in mind. And your visitors, of course. I know Martin's always hungry.'

'It's beautiful. Delicious as well, I'm sure, but beautiful anyway. Something I could never manage, making food look as good as it was supposed to taste. You're a talented child. And talking of beautiful, take a look at my view.'

'Oh yes!' Caro sighs appreciatively as she takes in every detail of the wide panorama. 'This should knock days off your convalescence. Nothing like a river for healing power. And – oh, brilliant!

You've got the whole of the Establishment stretched out in front of your eyes. Did you realize, Nanna?'

'The Houses of Parliament, you mean?'

'That's only part of it: state power in stone. There's Westminster Abbey and St Margaret's, and those pink stripes must be Westminster Cathedral, for the church. The white domes of the Foreign Office for administration. Come and look. What are you doing in bed, anyway? There's nothing wrong with you yet.'

'It seemed the simplest thing. They want you to take my outdoor clothes away when you go.' But she is happy to join her granddaughter at the window and join in the identification of the mainly floodlit buildings. 'That dark dome is the Middlesex Guildhall. Local government.'

'The chateau spires of Whitehall Court and the National Liberal Club stand for male chauvinist domination.'

'No, I can't let you have that,' protests Lady Ainslie. 'But the Tate Gallery for art.'

'The National Westminster skyscraper for the City, and the Post Office Tower for technology.'

'And people. People walking over Westminster Bridge to represent the purpose of everything else.'

'That's what *you* think.' They are both talking for the sake of talking, on a topic which will not remind either of them that this is a hospital, in which unpleasant things may happen. Now Caro pulls a chair from beside the bed to join one which is already near the window so that they can both sit as they look out. 'Now then. Visiting. Martin phoned to tell me his shift times. He won't be getting off till six this week. He'll try to drop in at about seven. Will that be OK?'

'Not tomorrow. I'm bound to be dopey after the operation. No visitors tomorrow.'

'Sure? Okay, then, I'll tell him. We'll phone up to make sure that all is well. I'll be along the next day. And Nanna.'

'Yes?' asks Lady Ainslie as the pause extends itself.

'Would you mind if Daniel came along with me one day, when you've got to the state of feeling bored? He's longing to talk to you. About the setting up of the NHS, that sort of thing. A very serious-minded chap, Daniel. Daniel Carrington, you know. The one who was with the telly camera crew this morning.'

'Yes, I remember. By all means bring him along.' She glances quizzically at her granddaughter. 'Close friends, you said before. More than that, perhaps?'

Caro makes a sound something between a laugh and a sigh.

'It's odd, isn't it, how it hits you? I mean, I've got lots of friends, men friends. Some have asked me to marry them. Most of them make passes sooner or later. It's always been easy to say No if I wanted to. The AIDS business has made everyone more careful anyway, in the last couple of years. Chastity is back in fashion. But now this chap comes along and I can hardly keep my hands off him. When he looks at me, I – oh!' Her sigh this time is no longer amused. 'It's humiliating, sort of. The feeling that he'd only need to whistle and I'd start to dance. And yet at the same time I feel pretty sure that I have the same effect on him, and that's exciting.'

'All very natural,' says her grandmother briskly. 'Nature's honey trap to ensure the continuation of the species. The important thing is to be able to step aside for a moment, even when you're dizzy with desire, and ask yourself whether you *like* him. Whether you'd want him as a friend and companion even if you didn't love him.'

'Did you do that with Grandfather before you married him?'

'Yes.' The answer is honest. 'But as a result of learning from a time when I didn't do it, if you see what I mean.'

'Nanna! Are you going to tell me all about your secret love life?'

'No, I'm not. But I shall be very pleased to meet Mr Carrington again.'

Like most deliberate changes of subject, this one fails to run. The conversation continues as a chat about matters of no importance. When Caro stands up to leave, she is careful to make her parting embrace as casual as it is affectionate, so that there shall be no suggestion of any fears about the outcome of tomorrow's operation. She leaves her grandmother still sitting by the window, still staring at the river.

The tide, now at its lowest, is turning. The first ripples of movement are gentle, but soon they surge in more strongly, fragmenting the reflection of the bridge and checking for a moment the passage of a piece of driftwood carried down with the current. It tosses in indecision, rocking forward, pressed back. Lady Ainslie watches, but does not see. She is remembering the moment which she has already mentioned to Caro: the moment when a tide of passion swept her almost beyond the reach of common sense. She is thinking of Gil.

Eight

Friday, 10 September 1937

Gil Blakey arrived at the flat this evening; no warning. Could see I was dressed to go out (expecting Richard to pick me up for a first night in half an hour), so stood there, not saying anything. Such a large man and such an air, somehow, of desolation. Asked him in.

He seemed unable to speak, so I enquired after the baby. Called Greta, doing well with nurse and Jessica's parents. Then it all spilled out. He'd come to apologize to me, confirming what I'd already guessed, that he wouldn't have allowed a deformed child to live. Wanted to know if Jessica's life could have been saved if she'd been in the clinic. Obviously hadn't come hoping for bromides, so told him the truth: top obstetrician, skilled nursing, best monitoring equipment, longer and more gradual labour at the proper time — all bound to offer better chance.

Gil nodded. Needed to hear someone tell him the truth. Everyone else — naturally — full of sympathy. Then he burst into tears.

Very odd feeling, to watch someone so big, strong, sobbing loudly, wanting to be comforted like a baby. Even odder to find myself doing that; rocking him in my arms, his head pressing into my neck.

Well-known aphrodisiac: the more powerful the man, the greater the effect of his weakness. Careful, Ainslie.

51

Thursday, 16 September 1937

Dinner with Gil at Rules. Delicious game pie. Gil made it clear why he wanted my company. He feels a hypocrite with everyone else, likes to think that he and I can be honest with each other.

Another well-known aphrodisiac: village boy made good, finding himself on level terms with daughter of the 'big house'. Careful, Gil.

Sunday, 19 September 1937

Usual tennis foursome at the Cumberland. Richard asked me to be his partner at the end-of-season ball again. I shall need a new dress: how I hate shopping! Found myself wondering whether Gil plays tennis. A matter of no importance. The height of bad manners, to think about one man while talking to another. Richard is civilized, good-humoured, easy. Gil the reverse of easy – forceful, determined to get his own way, probably unscrupulous. More need to prove himself, I suppose, than a Winchester and New College barrister.

Thursday, 23 September 1937

Dinner with Gil. Long talk about The Investigator. *I was curious about how he got going, from unpromising village start.*

He joined the army under-age in the war; I knew that. Was still only eighteen when made part of a firing squad to shoot a 'deserter' – a boy of his own age who'd broken down after four months of shellfire and ran away screaming when a grenade killed the next man to him in the trench. Officers had breakdowns too, Gil said, but were quietly transferred to base.

He collected details of three executions, reckoned they were all cases of medical (nervous) collapse, uncontrollable, not true cowardice; needing hospital treatment. Believed that civilians would be shocked to know of executions. Wrote an article (anonymously) and spent a whole day of next leave pushing a copy through the door of every paper in Fleet Street. None of them published it, but it must have been passed around; eventually appeared in obscure magazine, The People's Voice.

After being demobbed, he called on the editor of The People's Voice, *revealed authorship of article, was taken on as general factotum, later allowed to dig for stories. Eventually took the mag over, changed name, built up circulation.*

Big gap which he's clearly never going to fill. How did he get his hands on the necessary funds? Jessica's parents obviously rolling in money, but surely the sort who'd expect a son-in-law to have made a pile for himself before requesting their daughter's hand. Would his own life stand up to exposure in his own magazine? He claimed earlier never to blackmail, but I wonder. I imagine he could be frightening to anyone he was hunting down. Perhaps that's why I find him exciting, because he's trying to please me, not to expose me, but could change at any moment.

Agreed to go to Lady Lucy's six o'clock with him next week.

Wednesday, 29 September 1937

To Gil's new place for dinner. He's given up his house, taken rooms in the Adelphi; recognizes that he'll have to let Greta be brought up by her grandparents.

Curious moment when I arrived. We didn't shake hands. As though a kind of electric current would have linked us if we'd touched, and we weren't ready.

Gil is in love with me. Not that he says, but I know. Less than two months since Jessica's death, and he loved her deeply; no doubt of that. But instead of being numbed, it's as if his emotional nerves are exposed. Sorrow begets lust; I read that somewhere. I think he wants to drown himself in me. But I might drown, as well. Be swept away.

I tried to think out why I've always felt so sure that I could do without a man. Rebellion against my mother's continual talk about 'a good match'? Something to do with the climate of opinion when I was coming out of the schoolroom? Not enough men of the right age left after the war to provide husbands for all my generation of girls, so wouldn't it be more dignified not to compete at all?

No, that's only part of it, a petty part. Much more because of wanting to be a doctor. Such a long, hard training. It would have been terrible to waste it by getting married. No regrets about that.

Then there was Michael. Not a fair test, I suppose. Experiment without commitment. Curiosity. The need to be sure that if I chose medicine rather than marriage I'd know what I was missing and wouldn't regret it. Neither of us – both still medical students – ready to be tied down to anyone else. Almost clinical on my part – the feeling that I ought to know how it felt before discussing the subject with patients. Perhaps that was why I didn't enjoy it much. But because I didn't enjoy it, there never seemed any need to repeat it.

Why should I be so sure that it would be different with Gil? Not a matter of commonsense argument, that's why. Body speaking to body. But I must hang on to commonsense if I can.

Sunday, 3 October 1937

The Cumberland Ball yesterday. The new ball gown a great success: Richard obviously approved. As well as dancing, we talked a lot about ethics in the legal and medical professions. He specializes in divorce – shocked me with descriptions of subterfuges to get round the law, perfectly well understood by judges as well as lawyers. Doctors could never get away with that sort of thing.

As he was taking me home, he said he felt sorry for women who didn't work, had nothing interesting to talk about. A compliment, definitely.

Sunday, 10 October 1937

Just back from house party at Lady Lucy's country place. Turns out that she has a husband, Mr Staignton. He only likes country life, leaves her to do the London season alone, comes into his own now with the shooting.

I don't shoot. Lady Lucy hardly knows me, and Mr Staignton not at all, so why was I invited? And why didn't I ask myself that question before accepting? Because I guessed the answer, I suppose. Gil wanted me there. Bedrooms on the same corridor. Gil had asked for that as well. Hostesses take such arrangements for granted.

I locked my door on Friday night. Heard him trying the handle,

54

tapping with his fingernails, but pretended to be asleep. Needed to talk it out in the open, daylight. But spent the whole night wishing he were there; imagining.

Saturday morning I rode with Lady Lucy and two of the other women. Went down in the brake to join the guns for lunch, stayed to watch the afternoon shoot. Gil got one of the best bags. Funny to remember that he started his sporting life poaching on my father's estate.

We walked back to the house together, paused in the woods. Not much talking after all, only kissing, clinging.

Told him, though, that my bedroom door would still be locked that night. I think Gil would like to flaunt possession. A muckraker probably realizes that a secret can't be exposed if it never is a secret. I prefer my private life to be private. Besides – sordidly prosaic detail – I haven't been carrying a cap round with me for the past twelve years 'just in case'.

I left by train after Sunday tea. Odd, all the men leisured and the one single woman, me, the only guest with working appointments to keep on Monday. Perhaps, though, for Gil these gossipy house parties are working territory.

He'll come tomorrow night, I'm sure. It's exciting, the wait, as if for a wedding night. Wise? No, not wise. But it's out of control; no half measures possible. If everyone has only one great love in her life, this is mine. I love him. I love him.

Nine

On the morning of her operation, Lady Ainslie awakes to find herself part of the hospital system. No longer a gypsy, wandering the ward; no longer a stranger, apparently healthy. She has a place now. Her charts are clipped to the end of her bed. Her name is known to the nurses; she is on their lists.

A rattling trolley approaches and a cup of tea is set down on her locker. The nurse draws the blinds and Lady Ainslie discovers to her delight that the view which gives her so much pleasure can be seen even from the bed.

Another pleasure is that the room has its own facilities behind a sliding door. There is no bath, but she is able to perform the rest of her morning toilet at leisure and in privacy. She is just returning to bed when a second trolley, no doubt carrying breakfast, is pushed past her door without stopping.

A cheerful Irish nurse, Kathy Corcoran, offers her a bath as though it were a special treat instead of a compulsory item on the pre-operation agenda, and afterwards checks her fingers for rings and her mouth for false teeth and helps her tie the tapes of the special theatre gown. She is a state enrolled nurse; it has not taken Lady Ainslie long to identify the hierarchy of the ward from the colour of belts, the elaboration of headdresses, and the uniforms whose shades of blue deepen from the washed-out orderly up to Sister's navy.

'Sorry you had to miss your breakfast today,' Kathy remarks in a chatty voice as she performs her duties.

Lady Ainslie cannot resist the temptation to tease.

'That's all right,' she says, equally cheerfully. 'My granddaughter brought me all this lovely fruit last night, so I haven't starved.'

'But – you don't mean that you've *eaten* any of it? You're Nil by Mouth.'

'Am I? Nobody told me.'

'But you knew. I mean, everyone knows, before an operation. Because if you vomit, you might choke.'

'I've never had an operation before.'

'I won't have you frightening the nurses.' Toby Mallinson, on his way to theatre, has called to give a last word of reassurance. 'It's all right, Nurse. She was only joking.'

'Is that right? You didn't eat anything?'

'I didn't eat anything,' repeats Lady Ainslie dutifully and truthfully – but then, after the nurse has withdrawn to leave the surgeon with his patient, she adds, 'But the fruit should have been taken out of the room last night.' She knows the routines.

'It should have, yes. But remember, it was your lot which kicked up all the fuss about authoritarian regimes in hospital. Matrons who wouldn't allow visiting outside one hour a day. Sisters who insisted on a daily bowel movement and didn't care about anything else. Surgeons who thought they were gods. You were always especially hot about the god-like surgeons. Patients are people, you said. They have the right to know what's happening to their own bodies, you said, and to change things or complain. No one was ever to say "Doctor knows best" again.'

'We were right,' says Lady Ainslie, nettled by the lecture. 'So I should have been informed that I ought to starve, and why. They didn't know that I knew.'

'Of course they did. You have letters after your name.'

'I never use them now.'

'I put them on your notes, all the same. Sister has as much right to know who her patient is as you have to know your surgeon. Ninety-nine patients out of a hundred who come into hospital have a perfectly simple attitude. They want to hand their bodies over to a team of professionals and be given them back again in better shape. It makes them feel safe just to do what they're told. Someone with your history is likely to be in the other one per cent. However, we can develop that argument

57

tomorrow. For today, I am the god-like surgeon and I have anaesthetics on my side to keep you under control.'

He takes her hand for a moment and squeezes it. Then he leaves to put on the drab and unbecoming garments that his patients never see. Lady Ainslie continues to think about what he has said, and decides that there is a compromise position. She is prepared to do what she is told, but only if she is told why. She is prepared to regard a surgeon as god – for has she not recognized that Toby could bring her life silently to an end if he chooses? – but only when he has her own authorization to play the role.

These thoughts occupy her mind for longer than she realizes, so that the next event on the timetable takes her by surprise.

'Pre-med.' It is the staff nurse who has appeared, carrying a tray covered with a cloth. 'Just a prick. It won't hurt.'

Her arm is swabbed, pricked, pressed. It doesn't hurt.

'Stay in bed now. You'll begin to feel woozy soon; it comes on very quickly.'

Order and explanation. Lady Ainslie nods in approval although not in obedience. The two green notebooks, forgotten since she unpacked her possessions, are waiting in the wardrobe for her to make up her mind. She begins to slip her legs over the edge of the bed. But the wooziness is arriving far more quickly than she could have expected, unless a few half-dozing moments have already passed without her being aware of them. If she tries to walk, she will spin and fall. Staff Nurse knows best.

And what does it matter, after all? If she survives the operation, she can think about the diaries again. If she does not, they will mean nothing to anyone else. Caro may be puzzled to see that they appear to cover the same period; but the period is more than fifty years ago. Who cares? She allows herself to sink comfortably back on the pillows, already half asleep.

Has time passed? She is comfortably cocooned in pillows and only half awake. The room seems to be darker, as though the blind has been drawn. There are shadowy figures moving about the room. To turn her head and watch them is too much effort; she can hardly even keep her eyes open for more than a second at a time, and so catches only glimpses. One of the figures is that of the Irish nurse. Another has a black or dark brown face. Once she thinks that the staff nurse has returned, is perhaps asking a question. But she cannot make herself hear or speak, and drifts back into sleep.

Waking again, it seems to her that the operation must have been cancelled. She is too comfortable; too cosy. She moves slightly, intending to wriggle herself lower in the bed. An arrow of pain shoots through her body. No, the operation has not been cancelled. A little at a time she becomes aware that her throat is sore and that one of her arms is strapped down so that tubes may drip their contents into her veins. Anyone looking through the diamond peephole of the door now would see a white woman as helpless as the black woman was yesterday.

No. That's not true. She can blink. She can breathe. And as if the movement of her eyes is a signal, the dark-faced nurse – she is Indian – bends over her.

'I'm putting the bell here on your pillow. If you want to call us, just press it. Any time. Now, would you like something to drink? Or eat?'

'Sore throat.'

'It's the tube from the anaesthetic does that. I'll get you some ice cream.'

She feels herself being spoon fed, like an infant. The first mouthfuls are painful, the next are refreshing. Her head begins to clear. So Toby has refused to take her hint. He has condemned her to live more years which have no particular purpose, until the arrival of some other illness which will have to be endured before it provides release. Selfish Toby, putting another tick on his list of successful operations! Once again she abandons herself to sleep.

In the twilight of her mind she is aware when the atmosphere in her room changes. There is a moment when she need no longer be kept under continuous observation; she has passed some milestone of recovery. Quiet figures pause in the open doorway from time to time, and then pass on. Night is falling. Soon it will be time for a normal sleep, from which she will

59

awaken next morning in a normal manner. Only one odd thing causes her to frown in a vain attempt to focus her eyes and pierce the dusk.

There is someone sitting in the shadows. In the chair next to the window. Not a nurse, whose white headdress would catch the light from the door. Not Caro, who would have made her presence known with a touch. Someone invisible, and yet surely solid, taking up space. Not a ghost, then. But she lacks the strength to solve problems, and once again allows her eyes to close.

A sound awakens her. The someone who is not a ghost has risen from the chair and is moving past the end of the bed and round beside it. Through half open eyes she sees a black-skinned hand, its fingers pointing stiffly towards the splint to which her arm, and the tubes which feed it, are bandaged. The fingers flex but are still stiff. Although Lady Ainslie is only half conscious and would not have thought herself capable of rational thought, she knows at once what is happening.

The widower has returned to the place in which his wife was last alive. Twenty-four hours earlier, perhaps not realizing that death had already occurred, he must have watched a nurse unclip what seemed to be a lifeline. Now he is tempted to take his revenge on life. But his fingers have scruples of their own and are refusing to take orders from his anger.

The cable of the electric bell is touching Lady Ainslie's cheek. It will be painful to reach it, but not impossible. Even if the tubes are detached for a moment or two before a nurse comes running, she will not die of that. But she does not move, seeming instead to be watching the scene from outside her own body. Left alone, this stranger may perform the favour which Toby has refused. A peaceful slipping away.

For her, but not for him. He will go to prison. His life will be ruined. Only she can save him. Suddenly awake, she opens her eyes wide for the first time since the pre-med took effect and stares up at the intruder.

He steps backwards, startled by her gaze. Did he think that she was dead already? A bell rings, but not to raise an alarm or call a nurse; it is merely the signal that visiting time is over. The widower walks out of the door and joins those others who are leaving the main ward.

There is something incomplete about the encounter. As she drifts back into sleep, she feels certain that her uninvited visitor will return.

Ten

On the day after her operation Lady Ainslie, wishing only to drowse the day away, finds herself subjected to an almost sadistic programme of activity. She is roused and propped up in bed at a ridiculously early hour in order to drink a cup of over-sweetened tea. Instead of being offered a bedpan, she is helped on to a commode. The movement is not as painful as she has feared, but makes her so conscious of her weakness that all she wants to do afterwards is to sleep again. But Mr Graham appears every two hours to check her chest, Toby Mallinson calls in to boast laughingly of what a good job he has done on her, and a physiotherapist arrives to teach and supervise breathing exercises. It is all very hard work.

Since Toby has given the game away, there is no point in trying to conceal her medical background. Too exhausted to pretend that she is joking, Lady Ainslie complains to Staff Nurse in a faint and husky voice.

'In my day patients were left in peace to recover from their operations.'

'And died like flies from embolisms or pneumonia. You'll be grateful to us later. But if you eat up your lunch like a good girl, we'll leave you to rest this afternoon.' Luckily, she does not linger to check that her instructions are observed, for her patient has no appetite and still finds swallowing uncomfortable.

Caro, arriving promptly at the two o'clock start of visiting time, is quick to appreciate the situation.

'I'm not going to stay long. I just wanted to make sure that all was well, and Sister tells me that you're doing magnificently.'

'Nice to know.'

'You don't have to talk to me if you don't feel like it. I can chatter on indefinitely without help, as you're well aware.'

'Throat's still a bit sore.'

'I've got just the thing for you. To restore the tissues with special reference to throats and taste buds. Made it last night. The Caro Johnson special.' She sets two bottles down on the bedside locker.

'What is it?'

'Mostly blackcurrant, with a few little extras. You can amuse yourself by trying to guess what they are. Bung full of Vitamin C. Have about an inch in a glass and fill up with the soda water to give a bit of sparkle. Now, Nanna, tell me what you'd like Martin to do. He was planning to call in after he comes off duty, about half past six. But you look to me like someone who'd appreciate an early night. Would you rather he waited till tomorrow?'

'Yes please. If he doesn't mind.'

'I'll let him know. Visitors are hard work, aren't they?'

'Not you.' She pauses, gathering her strength for the next sentence. 'Caro.'

'Yes?'

'Lucky to have you. Some old ladies, quite alone.'

'People have what they deserve.' Caro bends down to kiss her. 'You had to bring up my father without anyone around to help you. Only fair that you should be rewarded by enjoying the company of such a delightful granddaughter. I'm going to pour you a glass of the elixir and then I'll be off. Back again tomorrow.'

'Thank you, darling.'

She sips the blackcurrant soda, which is as refreshing and soothing as Caro has promised, and then slides down in the bed, glad that she need not expect any further visitors that day.

Supper arrives on a tray at half past six. She is not accustomed to eat so early in the evening, but has taken no food except ice cream for the past forty-eight hours and finds that she is hungry. Just as she raises the soup spoon to her lips for the first time she becomes aware of a very tall, very thin young man standing uncertainly in the doorway.

'I've come at a bad time,' he says. 'Please don't let me interrupt your meal. I'm Daniel Carrington.'

'Of course I remember you, Mr Carrington.' Time and blackcurrant juice have healed her throat, so that she can speak normally again. 'If it weren't for you I might never have got inside the hospital. I was most grateful for your assistance.'

'I hope you don't mind me coming to see you.'

'Caro mentioned that you might do so. But she's already been here and gone today.'

'Yes, I know. I was due to turn up with her in a few days' time. But something happened – I felt I ought to have a word with you alone first.'

'Do please sit down.' As he has suggested, she continues with her meal.

'I hope very much that Caro will marry me one day. That's not a secret. I mean, she knows that I hope it, and I think . . . She enjoys doing her work, having her own life. As long as we both understand each other's feelings, waiting doesn't seem to matter.'

Lady Ainslie listens patiently. On the basis of her very brief acquaintance, she likes the tall young man, but she would not in any case dream of interfering with her granddaughter's choice.

'Caro has talked about you, of course, as being her grandmother. That's the only way I'd thought of you, as her grandmother. I'd never given any consideration to your life and what you'd achieved in it.'

'Why should you?'

'Well, I'm employed in television as a researcher. I ought really to have my curiosity on permanent alert. But it was only that remark which Caro made, about people like you being responsible for the health service, which set me thinking at last. The least I could do was look you up in *Who's Who*.'

It is a great many years since Lady Ainslie has bothered to add to, or even to read, the proof of her *Who's Who* entry which is sent to her once a year. If something in it has surprised her visitor, he will have to tell her what it is.

'I knew that you were a life peer, of course, and realized that you must have chosen a new name when you became a baroness.'

'Ainslie was my Christian name. It's one of the awkwardnesses of being made a baroness that you suddenly find you're expected to sign even your most personal letters with what feels like a surname. I just decided that I'd like to go on being recognizably myself.'

'And before that, with Caro's father, your son, being Leonard Johnson, I naturally thought of you as being Mrs Johnson.'

Sooner or later, Lady Ainslie supposes, he will come to the point of what has worried him enough to bring him here alone. She moves the empty soup bowl away and pulls forward a plate of fish pie and vegetables.

'There was no reason, you see,' he says earnestly, as though trying to excuse himself for some inadequacy, 'why I should have wondered what your maiden name was.'

'It's hardly a matter of much interest, I should have thought. But you've now discovered it?'

'I did at last – I mean, yesterday – do a little research on your career. I'm immensely impressed. You must be very proud of everything you've achieved.'

'You didn't come here tonight to say that.'

'Well, of course, reading the *Who's Who* entry, I found that you'd started out in life as Ainslie Dangerfield. And I discovered that you'd qualified as a doctor. That was something Caro had never bothered to mention. Dr Dangerfield.'

He pauses as though she should be able to guess what he is driving at; but she, puzzled and not yet interested, can only wait to discover the point of his remarks.

'Dr Dangerfield is a name that's been familiar to me ever since I was a boy. My grandfather owns a whole set of books called Famous Trials. They were published in the Thirties; you probably know them. Popular, chatty sort of stuff. They didn't only set down what went on in the courtroom. They gave the background, and the consequences. The beginning and end of whatever quarrel was being resolved.'

Lady Ainslie sets down her knife and fork in order to give the conversation her full attention. 'I can guess which trial you're referring to,' she says.

'Yes. Please don't misunderstand me. The thing that's worrying

65

me is nothing to do with you, not with you as you were then. It's me. I didn't want to come along with Caro under false pretences, in a way. I thought you ought to know in advance. The reason why I was always interested in this particular Famous Trial. Sir Gilbert Blakey is my grandfather.'

'He can't be.' The supper tray begins to slide dangerously off Lady Ainslie's knees and she hardly notices when her visitor rescues it. 'I knew your mother – well, only as a baby, but I kept an eye on what happened later. She married someone called Peters.'

'My mother married four times,' says Daniel ruefully. 'I'm the son of Number Two. An Australian who didn't last long. She brought me back with her to England and married a German baron. My current stepfather is American, but I've never met him. The steady element in my life has been my grandfather. His house was the only settled home I had as a child. He's very rich and very successful – well, you'll know all about that – but the one thing that he wanted and didn't have was a son. I think he's felt that a grandson is the next best thing. I'm very fond of him. I wanted to – well, to put that on the table, so to speak. So that if you're going to hold my parentage against me, you won't explode in front of Caro.'

'I wouldn't do that.' But Lady Ainslie is disturbed by a thought as unwelcome as it is sudden. Her young visitor has read pieces of paper and believes that he understands the whole of an old quarrel. There is a good deal, however, which has never appeared in print. The author of the relevant volume of Famous Trials would not have been aware of the fact that is worrying her now. She waves a hand to indicate that she no longer has any appetite for the meal, and Daniel obediently removes the tray.

By the time he turns back towards her, her anxiety and indecision are too great to be concealed. Should she tell him? No, she mustn't. Should she tell Caro? Does it matter? She can feel her heart beating too fast and her breath is pumping itself out as though each gasp is necessary to relieve the pressure in her chest.

'Lady Ainslie?' Daniel moves quickly, leaning across her to press the call bell. She, for her own part, closes her eyes and retreats from the situation into faintness or sleep, although she is aware of a murmur of voices, a finger on her pulse, a rearrangement of her body in the bed.

'Swallow these, dear.' She is being offered tablets and a drink to wash them down. She dislikes being called 'dear' and is strongly averse to taking pills which may prove to be habit-forming; but tonight she lacks the energy to argue. She does, however, have just enough determination to keep herself awake for a few moments after the blinds are closed and before the pills take effect, for there is a decision to be made.

Her thoughts are interrupted by the movement of a dark figure across the room; so silently, so invisibly, that only a displacement of air tells her she is not alone. It is the black man, of course. She has expected his return. But she ought not to think of him as the black man. He has a name, if she can remember it. The effort is considerable, for the tablets are beginning to take effect, but she is successful in the end. Mr Barnaby.

A nurse appears in the doorway. Mr Barnaby has been seen to arrive and is about to be told that he no longer has the right to visit the hospital. Lady Ainslie manages to raise a hand in a gesture of permission. If it gives the young widower comfort to sit by her window and think about his wife, she has no objection. But she cannot spare him her attention now. Her concentration must be applied to a simple question. Should she tell her granddaughter what her son, Caro's father, has never known?

Eleven

Friday, 18 February 1938

*Five days overdue. Too early yet to use the laboratory toad for a test,
but I'm sure already – was sure in the moment when it happened. If
I'm right, the baby should arrive on Guy Fawkes Day.*

*How my friends will tease! Physician, heal thyself; birth controller,
control thyself!*

*Gil won't tease, though. He'll guess that it wasn't an accident and
he'll try to work out the reason. Does she expect me to marry her? If
she does, do I want to? If she doesn't, what the hell is she playing at?*

*I'm not sure of the answer. I only know that I'm excited and happy.
Is that because it will be Gil's baby, or only because it will be mine?
Mine, I think. The child of someone who's thirty-three years old and
can't afford to wait much longer. But there couldn't have been any
other father. It had to be someone I love; it had to be Gil.*

*Do I want to marry him? If he asks me, I shall say yes, because a
baby has a right to two parents. It will be all right because I love him,
although I don't approve always of what he does. But if he doesn't
ask me that won't be a tragedy. I don't intend to stop working in any
case. I might go through an adoption process with the baby, so that
he, she, won't have to go through life 'illegitimate'. Nosy parkers could
think that I'd taken pity on some tiny scrap after his mother, one of
my patients, died. But I'd always tell him the truth, that I was his
mother. About Gil, I suppose I'll have to keep quiet if he turns his
back on me. It would be amusing to see the investigator's own life
investigated in the gossip columns; but unfair.*

Gil always says that women can't keep secrets. Rich, coming from him, the professional sneak. Pregnancy proclaims itself, so I shan't be able to get away with that. And I shall tell him, because he has the right to know. Not straightaway; that might seem as though I were forcing him towards a shotgun marriage. I'll wait till the baby quickens, so that he can put his hand on my skin and feel it. If he doesn't want to be a father again, then he needn't be afraid that it will ever get out. A secret between me and this page.

A happy secret.

Twelve

On the second day after her operation Lady Ainslie is already awake before the distinctive rattle of the tea trolley approaches. The sharpness of her hunger suggests that the effects of anaesthetics and drugs have worn off, whilst the pain caused by every movement tells her that she is inhabiting her own body again. It is no longer merely a lump in the bed to be lifted and turned by other people. Her mind, though, is less securely under control. The state of confusion in which Daniel Carrington left her the previous evening has been slept away, but a great effort of concentration is required before she can sharpen her thoughts to a fine point of accuracy.

Eventually, however, she is able to reach a conclusion. Although it has come as a shock to learn that her granddaughter is in love with and may marry the grandson of a man who did his best to ruin Lady Ainslie's life, there is no need for Caro ever to learn that that man is her own grandfather as well. True, there are good arguments against the marriage of first cousins. But these two young people, with different grandmothers, are only half cousins; and there is not, as far as she knows, any hereditary illness on either side to which children of their union might be exposed in a double dose.

Nor has any past relationship been distorted by the deception, since Caro was born many years after the death of her grandmother's husband. No lies have been told, because no questions have been asked.

The problem which seemed so heavy on the previous evening fades away as rapidly as the darkness of night. Lady Ainslie stares

70

from her bed at the view framed by the window, watching as the Victoria Tower emerges from the darkness and the scene changes from monochrome to colour. The sky flushes with a pink which is reflected in the water of the river and red double-decker buses carry the earliest commuters over Westminster Bridge. The sun, rising, glints against the windows of the House of Lords, whose halls and chamber and committee rooms are no doubt throbbing with the sounds of vacuum cleaners and scrubbing machines. Another ordinary day, full of light and empty of secrets, is beginning.

It is a day to be endured, not enjoyed. Time must pass in order that her battered body may cease to protest at its condition. There are some people, Lady Ainslie supposes – invalids, hypochondriacs, adolescents, voluptuaries – who are perpetually conscious of their physical condition, but except for the short period of her pregnancy many years ago she has never been one of them. Her life is in her head, which regards her body as an essential but uninteresting adjunct, to be neatly clothed and sparingly fed but not otherwise allowed much of its attention.

On a morning like this one, though, even her mind – after its brief effort of clarity and decisiveness – appears to be fuddled. Big Ben strikes the hours: eight, nine, ten, eleven. In one of the committee rooms just across the river her note of apology for absence is being read out and noted in the minutes. At this time last week she was contributing to the discussion, thinking of herself as a working woman. Now it is hard to believe that she will ever again have either the physical or the intellectual energy to resume such a routine. Withdrawing her attention from the world, she allows more hours to pass, neither thinking nor moving except as bidden by the nurses. In the afternoon, however, Caro brings her a welcome offering.

'I took your clothes back to your own flat,' she tells her grandmother. 'They'd get a bit of a culture shock if they found themselves in my wardrobe. I thought you might like this, since you're not in a ward where other people can be disturbed.'

She is carrying Lady Ainslie's own bedside radio. No longer now will the only entertainment on offer be the chatter and cacophony piped through the headphones. Thoughtful in small

71

matters, Caro also provides a copy of the *Radio Times* before leaving; but the type swims in front of her grandmother's eyes. Exploring the wavebands, she enjoys an hour of Beethoven and Mozart, but all too soon one concert ends and another begins. Harrison Birtwhistle now. She is too old to come to terms with Birtwhistle. Earlier in her life she has made her gesture towards the twentieth century by learning to enjoy Mahler and Britten, but can go no further.

Moving along the waveband to Radio 4, she allows words of no interest to tap at her ears without gaining admission. She does not wish to grow prize leeks or build up a portfolio of shares. Even the news describes a world in which she feels little interest.

Worried but also defeated by her apathy, she makes an effort to chat with the nurse who brings her supper tray, and to enjoy the meal. By then she has had enough of the day. But there are still rituals to be observed. A menu will be brought so that she may choose by a series of ticks what she would like to eat next day. The night sister will come in to look at the charts clipped on to the end of the bed. A hot drink will be offered. And, last of all, the drugs trolley will make its slow approach, carrying the nightly ration of painkillers and sleeping tablets. So there is no point yet in trying to sleep.

The radio has been placed on top of the bedside locker at supper time. Carefully, since to stretch is uncomfortable, she reaches out to switch it on and finds herself listening to a writer who is being interviewed about his most recent book – a biography of someone chiefly famous for the number of times he is mentioned in the memoirs of his contemporaries. Clues to the identity of the subject come quickly. It will be interesting to see if the writer's name also can be guessed before it is revealed in the final 'Mr So-and-so, thank you very much.' Sliding down in the bed, she closes her eyes in order to listen.

The door of her room opens, although she has heard no footsteps approaching. Turning her head and distancing her attention from the radio, she sees that last night's shadowy visitor has returned; but now the light is on, so he can be clearly seen.

As before, he is dressed entirely in black. Black jeans, black training shoes, black tee-shirt, black leather jacket. He is in his middle twenties – younger than she had thought at first sight; and his face, now that it is no longer distorted by grief, is a handsome one, strong-boned and smooth-skinned. People passing him in the street would see him as an ordinary good-looking young man – until they noticed his eyes. Bloodshot, expressionless, they introduce a disquieting element into his appearance, like those of a horse advancing on a trespasser in its field; perhaps to seek company or sugar lumps, but more probably to bite or kick.

'Good evening, Mr Barnaby,' says Lady Ainslie.

There is no change in his expression; no surprise that she knows his name or friendliness because she uses it. Instead, he stares at her for a moment with hostility, not prepared to utter even the most formal politeness in response to her greeting. He is angry because she is not his wife; because she is alive and his wife is dead. She makes no further attempt to impose herself on his attention as he sits down in the chair nearest to the window and stares out at the river.

The radio interview has come to an end during this distraction. Now she will never know who it is who believes that a biographer's duty is to his readers and not to his subject, and that he should feel free to disregard any requests that private papers should be locked up or destroyed. Instead of the high-pitched, self-justifying voice, another news bulletin is beginning.

Could she ask her visitor to turn off the radio to save her stretching? Even as she decides against it, the door opens again and she smiles to see her grandson.

'Martin, darling. How lovely!'

He bends to kiss her. 'How are you?'

'All the better for seeing you. Turn off the news, will you?'

Martin starts to move round the bed and then pauses as he sees that his grandmother already has a visitor. Mr Barnaby rises to his feet and for a moment the two young men stare at each other. Martin is puzzled, Mr Barnaby is contemptuous – for Martin is wearing his constable's uniform. Still without speaking, Mr Barnaby walks out of the room.

'Who was that?'

The radio is switched off and, with two oppressive influences

73

removed at the same time, the room is once more her own. She explains to her grandson what has been happening.

'I expect he feels that he can be close to his wife here, whilst she may be slipping away from him everywhere else. Quite understandable. I don't mind at all.'

Martin frowns at the story, but makes no further comment. Instead, sitting down, he asks about his grandmother's progress. Realizing how quickly talking tires her, he describes the excitements and frustrations of his own day.

During the past six months, the intellectual disciplines of his three years as an undergraduate have been replaced by a form of discipline less easy to accept. While he recognizes that his superiors are experienced in the workings of the criminal mind, he has discovered that many of them are stupid and that others are inarticulate, unable to formulate principles with the clarity which his university life has led him to expect. These two years in which he is expected to pound the beat, explore human nature and do what he is told may be necessary but are not likely to be enjoyable.

It is almost certainly because of Daniel Carrington's revelation of the previous evening that Lady Ainslie finds herself looking at her grandson in a new way. With surprising success she has managed to expunge from her memory for all these years the fact that Martin, like Caro and like Daniel, is Gil Blakey's grandchild. Now the resemblance shrieks at her. Martin is as tall as Daniel, but instead of being thin is broad-shouldered and muscular. This is Gil's powerful frame, and the short-cropped fair hair is Gil's as well. The way his forehead creased in a frown as he noticed the intruder, the narrowing of his eyes as he considered his grandmother's explanation, both these gestures are familiar to her memory. So too is the manner in which the frown is transformed into a smile – the smile which fifty years ago was able to make her heart beat faster and her body flush with love. What fools young women are! Her grandson's nearness naturally has a less devastating effect, but in a surge of affection she holds out her hand for him to squeeze.

Too soon, the eight o'clock bell rings for the end of visiting time and Martin stands up.

74

'Just before you go, darling, there's a carrier bag in a drawer in the wardrobe. Could you put it down where I can reach it?'

Smiling, and without showing any curiosity, he lays the bag on the bed, kisses her goodbye, and leaves. But within only a few minutes he is back again.

'I've been having a word with Sister about this black chap. I gather she was a bit unhappy about allowing him in last time, but left it to you to decide. She gave me the same story that you heard from Mr Mallinson. I don't like the sound of it. It could be, you know, that he's brewing up a great hate – and perhaps not just against the louts who battered his wife, but anyone white. He might decide to take a revenge on anyone who happens to be handy.'

'There are an awful lot of perhapses in that train of thought. I don't think –'

'You can't tell. His wife seems to have been a random victim, so he could pick on somebody equally at random. I wouldn't want it to be you. Obviously I can't prove what his state of mind is. And unless he's threatened you, there are no grounds for arresting him.'

'Certainly not! He's unhappy, that's all.'

'Well, he has no right to be here. You don't have to be alone with him and I don't think you ought to be.'

'Would you say that if he were white?'

'Yes, I would. He's not behaving rationally. The fact that there may be an understandable cause doesn't make it any safer. I'll try to come earlier tomorrow night. But it's difficult. If we're in the middle of something at six o'clock we're expected to hang on until we've dealt with it. So Sister has promised to see that he's not admitted. Be a sport and back me up on that. Otherwise I shall spend the whole of the next week worrying.'

Lady Ainslie's smile expresses gratitude for his consideration, which he perhaps mistakes for agreement. But she is not really interested in Mr Barnaby and after Martin has left for the second time allows her thoughts to linger once more on the resemblance between the young policeman and his grandfather.

It has never previously occurred to her that even Martin's choice of career may have been influenced by heredity. His

75

ambition is to become a detective and to investigate fraud. If he succeeds, his discoveries will appear in court records instead of in the pages of a scandal sheet, but the motive and the drive may be the same as were Gil's fifty years ago.

And even the methods . . . this too comes as a new idea. As a detective Martin will certainly make use of informers. From time to time he will take on a new persona in order to insinuate himself into someone's confidence, with the intention of betraying it. He will search waste paper baskets for discarded notes and, with the authority of a court order, will read private papers, listen in to private telephone calls. The difference is that he will be defending the established order, with the weight of the law on his side, whereas *The Investigator* was always seen as subversive. In much the same way, Lady Ainslie supposes, spies are always heroes in their own country and scoundrels in every other.

That is a lesson which she learned from one of the two books which are lying on her bed at this moment, its pages written when she was naïve and trusting and very much in love. She slides both the dark green notebooks out of the carrier bag, studies them briefly and then puts one of them away again.

The other she considers for some time. Fifty years have passed since she doodled on its front cover, outlining the letters which spell 'Exercise Book' with baroque curves and filling one corner with a pattern of tulips and precisely-veined leaves. Another corner is crumpled. On a third there is a splash of tea or coffee.

Without needing to open the notebook she can remember what its pages contain. A series of dates in March and April of 1938 and, innocently recorded beneath them, the treasure sought by every spy or detective: the unguarded, unembellished, dangerous truth.

Thirteen

Monday, 7 March 1938

First 'patient' this morning was a man. So rare, this, that I found myself remembering Gil's appearance here, and smiling. The smile surprised 'Mr Green' into thinking I'd recognized him; and after a moment or two I did. His photograph was at the top of a charity appeal which came at Christmas. Homes for orphaned children. He seemed from the appeal literature to be a figurehead president of the charity as far as I remember, presumably chosen for extreme respectability – peer of the realm, chairman of a bank, lay member of the Church of England Synod.

Hadn't come to ask me for money, though. Instead, wanted assurance that everything would be confidential. Said his thirteen-year-old daughter was in the waiting room. He believed she might be pregnant as a result of rape. Didn't want to discuss it in front of her, since she's young for her age, and innocent; no suspicions herself. Mother ill in Switzerland (sanatorium? asylum?); no female relatives in England to give advice; only one aunt, in Kenya.

Rape details – gardener's boy – sounded fishy. Not reported to the police; why?

Asked receptionist to bring M. up and examined her in anteroom. Extraordinarily beautiful girl; long blonde hair, rosebud complexion. Early puberty; breasts developing. Not just young, but mentally retarded. I chatted as I examined her. Had anyone ever hurt her down here? Or bounced on her tummy? She'd been told not to tell anyone. It was a special secret. She wasn't supposed to talk about that part of her body.

Assured her that she could tell me because I was a doctor and that was why her father had brought her here. So she did. Father Christmas had hurt her there on Christmas Eve when he brought her stocking into her bedroom. She didn't mind; she knew that Father Christmas was really Daddy dressed up.

Had it happened again since then? Yes, lots of times, but never hurt as much as the first time. Was she frightened of her Daddy? No, she loved him more than anyone else in the world.

Took samples for testing, sent her down to the waiting room while I talked to 'Mr Green'. Told him exactly what I thought of him. He expected that, of course.

Test needed, to confirm pregnancy. Any baby likely to be an idiot. Incest always carries this danger, and M. is already sub-normal. Asked if her mother had mental illness; yes.

He asked me to terminate if the test was positive. No choice with such a victim, but I wasn't prepared to operate and then put M. straight back into his clutches. Instructed him, if he wanted my help, to make a legal guardianship arrangement by putting M. in care of female relative. He agreed to ask her aunt to undertake her upbringing for the next seven years.

Fourteen

On the third day after her operation Lady Ainslie becomes aware of a new briskness in the attitude of the nurses. She has been successfully cosseted through the after-effects of surgery and now their aim is to restore her to a normal way of life as rapidly as possible.

'We want you out of bed for part of the time today,' says the staff nurse, delivering a short lecture on the need to get the circulation going and keep the chest clear. She summons Tricia, one of the student nurses, to help the patient into a chair. The position is uncomfortable and Lady Ainslie says so.

'We'll find you an air cushion. You can go back after the bed's made if you want to. But try walking around the room for a few minutes first.'

'Surely I'm allowed to feel ill for a little bit longer,' she complains, only half joking. She has been a hard-working woman for the whole of her life and this is almost the first time she can remember when she has wanted to do nothing but flop back in bed and doze the time away.

'Sorry. It's one of the differences between medical and surgical. On a medical ward very often things have to run their course. But here, once the surgeon has done his stuff, your willpower is almost as important as our nursing in getting you back to normal. Right, Nurse?'

'Right.' Tricia, only six months out of school, is eager to learn. In an effort to make herself look older she has pinned her fair hair into a French pleat, but her shinily-scrubbed enthusiasm gives her age away.

'What you mean is that you want the bed for someone else as soon as possible.'

'That too,' agrees Staff, laughing. 'But this is all for your own good. I'm sure you know about the dangers of thrombosis. And a little gentle exercise now will reduce the shock of returning to normal life when the time comes, as well as keeping your joints and muscles in working order. Besides, what's the good of having a private washroom if you can't get yourself to it?'

She has a point there. When Tricia returns half an hour later with Jean, a nursing orderly, to make the bed – and to notice if she should fall – Lady Ainslie makes her way cautiously and painfully towards the lavatory. She belongs to a generation trained to be regular in its morning habits and made anxious by failure, but finds herself inhibited today by the fear that too great an effort may tear at her stitches. By the time she abandons the attempt she feels as exhausted as if completing a marathon and is grateful to be helped back into bed.

It would be pleasant to sleep again, or at least to lie with her eyes closed, but a programme of distractions makes this impossible. The pulse check, the mid-morning drink and the visit of the house surgeon, Mr Graham, are all regular items in the day's routine, and to these visits is added Toby's appearance – not on this occasion as a friend dropping in but as the consultant surgeon making his ward round.

A newspaper seller arrives with a clutch of shrieking headlines and promises to reserve something more to her taste next day. The physiotherapist calls again, this time giving instructions on how to tighten and relax muscles while lying in bed. Lady Ainslie has taken no regular form of exercise since 1939 and has no intention of changing her ways at the age of eighty-three. But she believes in accepting the advice and instructions of those whose medical help has been requested, and dutifully continues for a little while to squeeze her buttocks together, or raise them a few inches above the mattress.

More startling is the appearance of a large lady, unwisely dressed in purple, who opens the door half an hour before lunchtime to demand – as though challenging her to a duel – 'Pistols or hearts?'

'I beg your pardon?'

'Oh, sorry, dear. Of course, you were in theatre last time I came round. I'm the library trolley. Romance on one side, crime on the other. If you tell me which you prefer, I'll push the trolley in with the right side facing you.'

'I don't really read novels, thank you very much.' She has brought her own choice of books with her to the hospital, although since the operation she has found her eyes to be dimmer than usual, reluctant to focus on small print.

'Can I offer you one of our special selections instead, then? It won't take a moment to fetch it. Natural history, the royal family, history and biography –'

'That would be very kind.' It is clear that the volunteer librarian does not intend to leave until she has suited her customer. 'History and biography, then.'

Within five minutes she is presented with a neat contraption which looks like a suitcase but opens and adjusts to reveal the spines of twenty substantial books. Biography in modern times is a long-winded art – and so, since the invention of the tape recorder, is autobiography. She studies the titles, her concentration interrupted by the purple lady's non-stop recommendations.

'These are the memoirs of a footman at Buckingham Palace. Little titbits about the royal family, I suppose, as well as what went on in the servants' hall. Crawfie died the other day, did you notice, dear, though Mrs Something-or-Other she was by then, of course. And then there's that policeman. Stalker. Such an appropriate name, don't you think? Or if you like the heavier sort of thing, there's another set of memoirs somewhere here, from an ex-cabinet minister. Yes, there we are.'

'I don't approve of that kind of tittle-tattle.' Lady Ainslie sounds more severe than she intends, because she is too tired to phrase herself tactfully. 'Breaches of confidence ought not to be rewarded. Publishers should refuse . . .' She checks herself and points a finger. 'What's this one?'

All the books on the trolley and in the special collection have been published within the past few months: except one. *Anthology of Armageddon*. A small, fat, shabby book, its torn and faded paper cover looking out of place amongst the glossy artwork of the modern biographies and the metallic gold and silver titles of the romances. Its price, eight shillings and sixpence, is printed on the spine with the boldness of a time when both inflation and decimalization were still in the future.

'That ought not to be there,' says the purple lady. 'But I hadn't the heart, not in front of their eyes. It belonged to a patient, a very old patient, who died last night. Nothing contagious,' she adds hurriedly, since the book is already in Lady Ainslie's hands. 'Just old age and pneumonia. He'd brought the book into hospital with him. His daughters were collecting his effects this morning and said they'd like the hospital library to have it as a gift. Well, what could I say except thank you very much. But it's not the sort of thing –'

'I'd like to borrow it.' Lady Ainslie has been turning over the pages as the explanation proceeds. It is an anthology of writings about the Great War, taken from contemporary books and letters and published while the survivors of that war were still alive.

The library lady's face expresses a surprise which she is too polite to put into words.

'I'll just write it down, then. *Anthology of Armageddon*. You can take more than one book if you like.'

'No, that will do for the moment. I brought some of my own with me.'

'Well, I'll be back in three days, in case you want a change.'

'Thank you. It's very kind of you to give up your time for this sort of work.'

This gesture of politeness is misconceived, since it causes the trolley to pause on its way towards the door.

'Well, to be honest with you, dear, I think a lot of the books that are borrowed are never even opened. People don't read nowadays, do they, not unless it's something that's been on TV already? What they really like is someone to stay and chat with them for a few minutes without seeming to come specially to do that, if you see what I mean.'

It is all too clear what she means, but a weary closing of the eyes provides an adequate defence for an elderly invalid on this occasion.

For a little while after her visitor has left, she remains motion-less, considering the titles she has just been studying. Is her distaste for the current wave of self-revelation justified?

Like the elderly ex-spycatcher whose recent memoirs have caused even greater controversy, the policeman presumably holds a sincere belief that what he is saying needs to be known; and that nobody but himself is qualified to tell the story. In the past – or so she has always believed – there have been rules to control such disclosures: DORA once upon a time, the laws of treason, the Official Secrets Acts, contracts of employment, D notices to editors, covenants of confidentiality. Have they never been anything more than Chinese walls, to use the City phrase currently in vogue? Cabinet leaks, civil service leaks – it would seem that the state has lost the fight to plug the holes in its bucket, leaving the struggle to preserve any kind of secrecy in the hands of businesses threatened by industrial espionage.

If *The Investigator* were still in existence today, it would have a rival in every newspaper. Gil Blakey has been haunting Lady Ainslie's memory ever since his grandson's visit, and she recalls now that during the first months of their love affair in 1937 he was obsessed by the need to search out the names of British Fascists who might be expected to collaborate with the Nazis.

How hard he worked at it: weekending in the country, guiding the gossip over after-dinner port, encouraging young men to drink too much and betray their own fathers, charming women into indiscretions about their husbands. None of this would be necessary these days, for almost certainly one member of such a group would publish his memoirs and list his comrades. In such a case, exposure would be approved by the authorities and the public, if not by the comrades concerned. If there are proper and improper subjects of secrecy, who is to decide what they are?

On any normal day, taking her accustomed place on one of the red benches in the House of Lords, Lady Ainslie would have no difficulty in answering such questions, but her mind is still dulled by the operation on her body. Shaking her head, as though the movement will shift the cobwebs, she puts on her spectacles and is about to open the anthology when the arrival of lunch on a tray saves her from any further intellectual effort.

Caro's visit that afternoon is only a brief one, for she has to move almost without pause from a directors' lunch to the preparation of a banquet for forty to celebrate a ruby wedding. But she exclaims in congratulation on discovering her grandmother seated in a chair and not in bed, and can stay long enough to hear about the library lady.

'I've been trying to clarify my views on biography,' Lady Ainslie says. 'There was one book I was offered this morning that I wouldn't want to read at all. The biography of a musician, written by his wife. I only know what I've seen in the reviews, of course, but I get the impression that it's largely devoted to accounts of how he chased after every woman in sight. If that were true, the description of the man might well spoil my enjoyment of his music. It oughtn't to have that effect, but I fear it would.'

'Perhaps that was the lady's intention. A posthumous revenge for her husband's infidelities.'

'There ought to be a set of rules of fair play for the subjects of biography. Once you become a historical figure, a century or so dead, you're fair game, I suppose; but don't you think there should be some protection for those who are shopped by the friends and relations almost before the wreaths have withered on the grave?'

'It's your question. What's your answer?'

'That people should be judged by their achievements. So that a biography of a musician, for example, should describe his life in terms of the music he creates. A writer should be judged by his writing.'

'But suppose his writing – or his music – is influenced by the availability of women's bottoms to pinch or young men to be picked up in public lavatories. Don't those facts become part of his work as well as of his life?'

'Not necessarily. The biographer could still confine himself to the work that emerged.'

'But then he'd only be writing lit. crit. or music crit. Won't wash, Nanna. And just think of tackling some chap who's devoted his whole life to molecules or genes or something and has ended up with a Nobel prize. How could you possibly make

84

his life sound interesting to a general reader if you leave out all his private affairs?'

'The answer is that you don't have to write the book. The important thing is what he's discovered, not whether he likes two eggs for breakfast.'

'You're being too purist, Nanna. A biographer presumably considers his work to be an art form on its own. Designed to entertain as well as to instruct.'

'But if the subject objects, or would have objected if he were still alive . . .'

'Did you know that there's a movement in America now to give rights to foetuses at the expense of their mothers?' asks Caro with apparent irrelevance. 'There are too many claims to rights flying around in my opinion.'

'I thoroughly agree with you, but what has that to do –?'

'If you start offering rights to the dead as well, the living will find themselves without any of their own. Anyone who sincerely doesn't want to be biographized can cover his tracks while he's still alive. But I suspect that most people secretly long to be thought important enough.' Caro stands up. 'You said I could bring Daniel with me one day. Perhaps I ought to warn you that his great ambition is to write biography. Don't put him down too hard, will you? I must go now, Nanna. I'll be able to stay longer tomorrow.'

'About Daniel. Before he comes . . .' But Lady Ainslie bites back the words. With Caro in a hurry to be away, this is not the moment to talk of past history. 'Thank you for coming, darling,' she says instead.

Will there, she wonders, be a second visitor today. Lacking the strength to walk as far as the cubicle from which the ward is supervised, she asks the orderly who brings her supper to find out whether Sister could spare her a moment. But it is Lesley, the Australian SRN, who arrives.

'Can I help you, Lady Ainslie? Sister's not here at the moment. But if you'd rather wait –?'

'There's a Mr Barnaby, whose wife died here. I believe my grandson asked Sister last night not to let him into this room if he came back again.'

85

Lesley nods. 'There's a note about it.'

'He didn't say that at my request, and I haven't any objection. In fact, if Mr Barnaby finds it helpful to return here, I think he should be allowed to.'

'I'll tell Sister. If he turns up again, one of us could come in to see whether you still feel that way.'

'Thank you very much.' He will come, she is sure of that. But her certainty is wrong. Evening arrives and passes, and she remains alone.

Fifteen

Sipping her early-morning cup of tea next morning, Lady Ainslie struggles to shake off the intellectual lethargy which has overcome her since the operation. Stretching painfully to open the drawer of the bedside locker, she takes out a Biro and the notebook which her granddaughter has given her.

Saturday, 12 March 1988

Time to open Caro's Jackson Pollock diary; haven't felt up to it until now. Eyes still wuzzy, but it's easier to write than to read. Easier to concentrate on writing, too. I'd forgotten, or never knew, what a restless place a hospital is. Even here, insulated from the traffic of the ward, the door opens every few minutes. So many different faces! Hard to believe that in the world outside – newspapers, television, parliamentary debate – a shortage of staff in the NHS is the topic of the day.

By now I can put names to most of the faces. Always Christian names, except for Sister. It's just about allowable to say 'Nurse', but 'Nurse So-and-So' would be considered formal and unfriendly. An odd modern habit, this, addressing strangers with such intimacy. In return, they tend to call all patients 'dear'. Saves them having to remember names that are constantly changing, I suppose. Only Lesley, the Australian SRN, calls me Lady Ainslie. Perhaps she disapproves of titles. But it could be a recognition on her part that stuffy old ladies aren't used to being offered instant friendship.

Names are facts. It's amusing to apply a little fantasy, inventing futures for each nurse; helps to differentiate them.

Sister's way of life probably settled. She's in her forties, calm and firm. Home and friends and family no doubt organized in the way she's chosen for herself. Most of the others, though, are much younger. There's a certain restlessness; a sense of only temporary presence. Possibilities of choice and change only just below the surface. Anything might happen.

Fairly predictable choices for Tricia, the more earnest of the student nurses. She'll work conscientiously to qualify, rise to become a staff nurse, marry a doctor and have children as studious and well-scrubbed as herself. Heather, though, the student on night duty, shows signs of feeling the strain of study and responsibility. She may give up.

Staff Nurse: Sue. An interesting personality, Christian seriousness beneath a cheerful smile. I can imagine her leaving England while she's still unattached and under thirty, to work in a refugee or relief camp.

Someone else might also go abroad, for a different reason: Ginetta, one of the SRNs. Impression of fragility and discontent. Even stronger impression of resembling a film star. Forgotten her name. The French Lieutenant's Woman. Ginetta will succumb to the lure of the salaries and myths of American private medicine one of these days.

Some will go, some have come. Kathy is from Ireland, Mercy from Jamaica. Kind, comfortable, unambitious, the two of them; state-enrolled nurses, happy to have got so far.

Mahandra is different. Parents born in Uganda and came to England when the Asian community there was evicted. Her own accent is Birmingham, but she's trying to change it. She not only asks me questions but listens to the answers, copying my vowels, moving her voice towards standard English. A very intelligent young woman – ten O-levels and three A-levels; she could have gone to university. But she's chosen the career she wants – an SRN already, and I can see her as a Sister Tutor in a few years' time. Will she be able to resist family pressure for an arranged marriage?

Lesley is also from overseas. Born in Sydney. Harder to invent a future for her. Positive personality which might become abrasive if not kept under control. In her work – she's on the afternoon and early evening duty – she's decisive, inspiring confidence; but there's an impression of personal doubt beneath it. Is she finding it hard to decide whether to return to Australia or stay in England? Perhaps she has a boy-friend in the country she wouldn't otherwise choose. To ask would be an impertinence.

88

'Impertinence!' exclaims Lady Ainslie aloud. Luckily there is no one in the room to hear. 'What *do* I think I'm doing?'

She rips out the pages which are covered with her handwriting and tears them into little pieces, tutting as she does so. It is one thing to put down her opinions of people in the privacy of her home, knowing that she can lock the diary away where no one will see it. But to do the same thing here, when at any moment she may fall asleep or be taken from the room for some purpose, is unforgivable. It is putting temptation in the way of young women who will be ashamed of themselves if they succumb to it, and angry with her for making personal remarks about them. Her brother was right, all those years ago, to tell her that frankness was only possible in circumstances of privacy.

Her expectation that at some point she will have to leave her room unguarded is quickly confirmed, for all the nurses today have one common piece of information to divulge.

'You'll be having your stitches taken out today, dear,' says Kathy, bringing breakfast.

'Your stitches come out today,' says Tricia, making the bed.

Mr Graham, coming round with Sister to inspect progress, gives the necessary instructions. 'I think we could get rid of those stitches today.'

Even the cleaner pauses as she pushes a damp mop over the floor. 'Stitches out today, is it then?' It begins to sound like some kind of initiation, and Lady Ainslie is almost surprised when the newspaper seller refrains from commenting on the subject. When the staff nurse arrives in her room at eleven o'clock, she is able to get in first with the news.

'You're going to take my stitches out!'

'Right first time. We'll do it in the treatment room.'

Tricia is at hand to help her out of bed, steadying her while she slips her feet into bedroom slippers and puts on her dressing gown. The three of them move slowly towards a small room containing little but a high bed and a trolley.

'Check the trolley,' says Staff to Tricia. The student nurse bites her lips with concentration as she counts off swabs and instruments, steel receptacles and sterile dressings. Meanwhile Lady Ainslie is being arranged in the correct position and, with a curious regard for modesty, covered with cloths which leave only the necessary area of her skin exposed. With a cruel-to-be-kind swiftness, the plaster which holds a dressing in place is ripped away.

In her time Lady Ainslie has both stitched up lesions and removed the stitches. She expects now to hear a gentle snip at the knot and to experience briefly a slight discomfort as each piece of thread is pulled out. But instead she finds herself attacked with pieces of steel. Something presses hard down; something else – it is out of view – levers painfully up.

'Is this the first time you've taken out these clips?' asks Staff.

'No,' says Tricia. 'The second.'

Lady Ainslie gives a protesting laugh. 'Don't you think that conversation should have taken place while I wasn't listening?' But in fact the psychology of the exchange is effective. It means that for the young student's sake she feels obliged to refrain from grimacing as the probing and pulling go interminably on. The staff nurse chatters away with the obvious intention of distracting the patient's mind, but Lady Ainslie closes her ears to the words. She adheres to the school of thought which believes that pain can be made endurable by concentrating on deep breathing, and puts her belief into practice now.

Success does not dissuade her from registering a complaint when the process at last comes to an end.

'What an appalling system! What were you doing? Those weren't stitches.'

'No. I don't know why we go on using the word. Most of the surgeons now use these clips.'

She is handed one to see. It is a miniature man-trap with three saw-like teeth on either side. 'Good gracious!' she says faintly.

Although her own part in the struggle has been passive, she is exhausted by it and is humiliated to find that she needs a wheelchair to take her back to her room. The metal bedhead is adjusted to support her in a half-sitting position, and she stares out of the window without the energy even to read. Often in the past twenty years she has joked that she is an old woman; it is no longer a joke but a fact.

Caro, visiting her at tea-time, finds her depressed, managing to describe the removal of the man-traps as though it were a funny incident, but then sighing.

'What sort of a day is it whose chief excitement is half an hour's pummelling in a treatment room?'

'Nonsense,' says Caro briskly. 'Your chief excitement is the visit of your darling granddaughter. Who would like to suggest a double visit tomorrow, with Daniel coming as well.'

'Caro, have you ever met his grandfather?'

'Sir Gilbert? No. He lives in Jersey, I think. Went there for tax avoidance reasons originally and settled down so well that even the Thatcher regime couldn't tempt him back. After all, he's immensely aged now.'

'He's four years older than I am,' says Lady Ainslie precisely.

'Sorry. How do you know?'

'We were born in the same village.'

'Kingsgelding? Go on!' Caro has never been inside Kingsgelding Hall, which was sold to pay death duties before she was born. But she and Martin have been taken to the village as children to study the tombs of their ancestors in the church and exclaim at the size of the house in which their grandmother was brought up. Both they and their father appear to feel relief rather than regret at being freed from the responsibility of a crumbling and unheatable heritage. 'So you knew each other as children?'

'Yes. And then we met again later. And quarrelled. Quite severely. I think perhaps you should ask Daniel how much he knows about that quarrel.'

'Why don't you tell me?'

Lady Ainslie shakes her head. 'It's of no importance to me. I'm not suggesting that there's any kind of living family feud. Not on my part, at least. But Gil, Sir Gilbert, might feel differently. If any kind of ghost is going to float between you and Daniel, it would be as well to blow it into the daylight straight away. If he has expectations under his grandfather's will, for example, it might –'

Caro hoots in delight. 'What a marvellous word. Expectations! No one has expectations these days, Nanna. This is the look-after-yourself generation. Selfish and mercenary we may be, but we don't sponge or suck up. This all sounds very mysterious. I rather fancy myself as Juliet. If I do ask Daniel, you must promise to tell me your side of the story afterwards.'

Lady Ainslie refrains from promising anything and the conversation moves on to other subjects. Only just as she is leaving does Caro ask a pointed question.

'How did you know that Daniel was Sir Gilbert's grandson?'

'He came here without you, specially to tell me. He thought I ought to realize. I don't suppose your generation talks about honourable intentions any more than about expectations, but I have the impression that Daniel's feelings about you are serious.'

'So the quarrel really was serious too?' Caro is no longer joking. 'You mean, he thought *you* might tell *me* not to tangle with a Blakey descendant.'

'I'm sure he realizes that I don't give you orders. He just doesn't want there to be any secrets, that's all – and he had sufficiently good manners to ask my permission before bringing them into the open. So ask him.'

'Right. Till tomorrow, then.'

The visit has cheered Lady Ainslie. She feels strong enough, after a little while, to leave her bed and sit in the chair by the window; and is still there, staring at the river, when her second visitor of the day arrives.

'Mr Barnaby!' She is startled at first, and, then pleased. 'I thought – you didn't come yesterday.'

'It was the funeral.'

The words come as a second shock, for this is the first time he has spoken in her hearing. And his deep voice is not what she would have expected, although she silently rebukes herself for assuming that it would be rough and ill-educated. Can she excuse herself with the argument that she has judged him by his clothes and the lack of restraint in his extremity of grief? No. She has allowed his skin to colour her assumptions, and is ashamed of herself. This man is more than simply well-spoken. He has a beautiful voice.

But she must not make a second mistake and allow his accent to persuade her that he will necessarily behave in a civilized manner. This is still an angry man.

The door of the room opens again and Sister looks in.

'It's all right, Sister. Thank you very much.'

She nods and retreats, but leaves the door wide open.

'You want them to turn me out, is that it?'

'No. My grandson felt that I ought not to have visitors whom I didn't know, and he had a word with the nurses. But after he'd gone I told them that I'd be glad to see you again. Would you like to bring up the other chair?'

'Your grandson. The pig? What did he think I'd do to you? Take an eye for an eye? A life for a life? Yes, of course he did. And what makes you so sure he'd be wrong?'

He is still standing, towering above her, his fists clenching only a few inches from her head. Instinctively she glances towards the call bell which hangs – out of reach – at the head of the bed, but at once regrets the movement.

'I've frightened you now, have I?'

'No.' The answer is only partly untrue. 'I'm an old woman. You can't rob me of more than a few months. But think of the price you'd have to pay, just for the sake of making a gesture. They know who you are.'

'Why should I care?'

Lady Ainslie tries without success to think how she can console him. She would like to take his hand, or to stroke it in an attempt at comfort, but knows that he would snatch it away. They have no relationship within which she can offer friendship. Only time can heal his wound, and that is not something which the wounded ever believe.

'You don't understand. Comfortable ladies like you. You don't understand.'

'Everyone has to face bereavement at some time, even comfortable ladies.'

'Not like this. Murder, it is, and no one getting punished for it. No one even looking for them. Getting away with –' His lips form the word 'bloody' but refrain from pronouncing it. She is sure that in any other company he would at this moment spit out a string of expletives, and would like to tell him that this is a good way of relieving his feelings and that she would quite understand. But what she does understand is that he has been

93

brought up not to swear in front of women and that any lapse will increase his anger.

'Getting away with murder,' he says through clenched teeth. 'Well, you don't have to worry. I wouldn't touch you. Not your fault. But *them*! If I ever catch up with *them*!'

His hands, strong and pink-palmed, unclench to grip an invisible neck in a stranglehold; they quiver with strength and venom. 'You don't know, do you, what it is to hate someone, hate, hate, hate, and not know what to do about it?'

That is an easy question. She looks into the fixed stare of his eyes.

'Oh yes,' she says – and the quiet force of her answer surprises him into silence. 'I know how it feels to hate.'

Sixteen

Monday, 2 May 1938

Still shaking with shock and fury as I write this. Try to keep it calm.

Arrived at Harley Street this morning to be told by receptionist of gentleman waiting to see me without appointment. Apparently he'd had some difficulty remembering what his name was, but came up with Mr Green eventually. Claimed extreme urgency.

Naturally feared that M. had suffered some bad reaction after the operation, so agreed to see him at once.

'Mr Green' stood in the doorway of the consulting room; unable, it seemed, either to speak or move. Ainslie walked across to close the door, smiling at him to conceal her anxiety on the child's behalf.

'How is Margaret?'

Finding his voice at last, he stepped forward towards the desk.

'Margaret is in Kenya with her aunt, in accordance with your instructions. I assume that she is well, since no one has informed me otherwise. I have kept my side of our bargain. You have not, however, done the same.'

'What do you mean?'

By now he had set his attaché case down on the desk and was opening it. He took out a magazine and held it out.

'Are you acquainted with this filthy rag?'

It was *The Investigator*, Gil's magazine. Even as she stretched out a hand to take it, Ainslie's pulse quickened in alarm.

'I'm aware of its existence,' she said cautiously. 'I haven't seen this one.'

'It's the May number. Came out on Friday. To judge by the phone calls I've had, half the population of London grabs it as it comes off the presses. The half that matters, anyway. Page 18.' His voice squeezed through a tight throat, as though to speak naturally would release the emotions which he was for the moment suppressing.

Ainslie opened the magazine at the page he had indicated. As she began to read, she sank down into her chair behind the desk; not consciously, but because her legs would not support her.

Charities which devote themselves to the care of orphaned children deserve our sympathy and our money. When one of them chooses for its President a man of unquestioned financial acumen and probity, a respected elder of the church, this should qualify it also for our respect and trust.

But society hands over more than merely money to such a charity. It entrusts it also with the lives of vulnerable young children. So what are we to think of the standards of an organization whose President is apparently unable to keep his hands off even his own daughter?

Sexual assault within the confines of the home is notoriously difficult to prove, except when its consequences reveal themselves in the body of the unfortunate victim, and Lord I***** no doubt hopes with some confidence that he may escape criminal prosecution. But we should spare a thought for the innocent thirteen-year-old who might, given the choice, have preferred to have, like the orphans, too little paternal love rather than too much.

'I don't believe it.' Ainslie's whispered reaction was the truth. She could not believe that the words she had just read had been printed and distributed for all the world to see. 'Excuse me, please.' The pregnancy sickness which she had endured every morning for the past few weeks was as a rule under control by the time she arrived in Harley Street. Her retching now had a different cause. Luckily there was a washbasin in the anteroom used for examining patients.

There seemed no further need to continue the charade of calling her visitor Mr Green. She had checked her guess at his identity after the first consultation and knew that *The Investigator* was correct in identifying him, beneath the asterisks, as Lord Impney. He remained standing after she returned; but Ainslie, drained of energy, needed to sit down again.

'The first thing I asked of you, Dr Dangerfield, was an assurance that you would respect my confidence. You gave me that assurance, but you have betrayed my trust.'

'I promise you –'

'How can you expect me to believe your promises? My unfortunate daughter needed your help. I told you of my suspicion that she had been interfered with by the gardener's son, taking advantage of her youth and innocence. That was not actually any of your business. All that needed to concern you was Margaret's predicament. I should have had cause enough for anger if you had allowed the facts of the case as I reported them to become public knowledge. But that you should dare, should dare –' His face went purple with rage and breathlessness prevented him from completing the sentence. His hands grasped the back of the chair which was provided for Ainslie's patients, and he rocked it furiously forwards and backwards as though he could only just restrain himself from smashing it to pieces.

'I assure you, Lord Impney –'

'You can assure me of nothing. How else could this preposterous story have come into being except through unjustifiable gossip on your part? I would hardly be likely to invent such a libellous accusation about myself. You have a great deal to answer for, Dr Dangerfield. I shall be interested to hear how you propose to explain it.'

'Please sit down, Lord Impney.' Ainslie was frightened – not so much frightened of what an angry man might do to her if he lost control of himself, but frightened of having to accept, and perhaps even to admit, what in her heart she knew must have happened. But she forced herself to keep calm while she tried to extricate herself from responsibility. 'What Margaret told me, she may have told other people.'

'What did she tell you? Nothing which could possibly justify

97

this filth. She's a child, too inexperienced to distinguish between the lust of a boy who'd been a childhood playmate and the natural affection of a father. In any case, what she told you is of no importance. You had no right to divulge to anyone at all even the fact that she had attended for a consultation.'

'Nor did I. I understand your anger, Lord Impney, but be kind enough to consider my position for a moment. If this matter is investigated and my connection with it is made public knowledge, it will have a serious effect on my livelihood. *All* my patients expect confidentiality. And that's not the end of it. You asked me to perform an abortion on your daughter, and I did so. That was an illegal act, and both of us knew it. Whoever has written this is almost certainly aware of the end of the story, although he has chosen not to mention it. If the full facts come out, your reputation will be damaged, but I shall go to prison and be stripped of my right to practise. This is as serious for me as for you, Lord Impney. Whatever story you may wish to produce for the outside world, there's no point in pressing it on me when you have already acknowledged privately that my understanding of the situation was a correct one.'

'It remains my impression that only some indiscretion on your part can be held responsible for this scurrilous attack. You realize that it will be impossible for me to let it pass without taking action. Whether I want to or not, I shall have to sue the author for libel. No doubt he'll prove, whoever he is, to be a man of straw. But I shall ask for heavy damages, and expect him to offer an apology and retraction in settlement. I need to know from you that I shall have your support. And I also need to know what words or documents have put this idea into the writer's head, in order that my lawyers can think how best to discredit them. I will leave you to give that second matter your most careful consideration, Dr Dangerfield. And for the first —'

Ainslie stood up. Her sickness a little while before had left her trembling with cold; now her blood seemed to have turned to ice. She recognized what must have occurred. How could Gil do such a thing to her? Pretending to love her, but betraying her trust. Had he intended right from the start to use the key of her flat, offered to him in love, as the means to search out secrets?

It was unforgivable, and she never would forgive him. Her anger was quite as great as that of the man who faced her.

'Yes,' she said. 'You will have my full support.'

Seventeen

Startled by the bell which announces the end of visiting time for the day, Lady Ainslie finds herself shivering as she recalls how much she hated Gil Blakey fifty years ago. Does she hate him still? The question is not an easy one to answer. Perhaps it is only the memory of hatred, and not the original emotion, which has caused Mr Barnaby's question to make her pulse beat faster – but if so, it is a powerful memory. Until today she has continued to picture Gil as she last saw him, as a man in his late thirties, physically strong and mentally ruthless. It will take a little time before she can replace this image with the one suggested by Caro: of an eighty-seven-year-old man hugging his fortune in the Channel Islands.

Has she dozed or fainted in this moment of remembering? She is still sitting in the chair by the window, but Mr Barnaby no longer stands beside her. He has brought a second chair from beside the bed. Taking no notice of the bell, he stares, as she does, out of the window, looking across the river to the Houses of Parliament.

To her the building is more than her place of work. It is the home of liberty, which has flourished here for centuries. She is tempted to make this comment aloud, but restrains herself. The man beside her may see Parliament only in terms of the stop-and-search powers it has given to the police. But she feels it to be a good sign that he has started to talk to her, and hurries to break the silence.

'Were you born in this country?' she asks.

There is a long pause while he makes up his mind whether to

100

take part in this different kind of conversation. Polite small talk may be too bland to suit his mood. But in the end he nods his head. 'My father was in the High Commissioner's office.'

'Where did you go to school?'

'Holland Park Comprehensive.'

'Did it do you well?'

'Eight O-levels. Two A-levels.' He shrugs his shoulders as he speaks, indicating his indifference to academic achievement.

Lesley, the Australian nurse, appears in the doorway of the room.

'Visiting time is over, Lady Ainslie.'

'If we could have just ten more minutes.' It's important, she feels, to keep a conversation going – if possible to the point at which his wife can be mentioned. She turns back to him as soon as Lesley has left.

'So what did you do with your A-levels?'

'Nothing, not then. I wanted to be an actor.'

She nods approvingly. Yes, he has an actor's voice, pleasing to the ear, a musical instrument capable of playing a wide range of notes. The way in which he has changed its tune within the past few minutes testifies to his control of it. He is a good-looking man with strong features and a tall, powerful body. Presence; that's the word. He has presence.

'I should think,' she begins, but he cuts off the compliment she has in mind.

'It was easy when I was a kid. Children's television, they're always looking for black boys who can talk like white boys. And older kids can get hired as sort of street furniture. Leaning against a lamp-post, looking as though a riot's just about to start. Musicals, too; they don't mind your colour if you can dance. But real acting; no chance. I didn't care about that till I met Darleen. But there's no way a black actor can support a wife and children.'

'Not many white actors can do it either unless they have a sideline of some kind. It's a question of being in an insecure profession, not the colour of your skin.'

He grunts, not attempting to conceal his disbelief.

'A white actor can hope that he'll get lucky one day. Someone will see him in something and give him a break. Hope and luck, that's what you've got to have. But someone like me –' His voice changes in imitation of an agent or producer. '"One of these days, in twenty years or so, you're going to be an absolutely brilliant Othello, Duke my boy." How am I supposed to live for those twenty years? And then I shall find that Othello is still being played by a white man in black paint. No problem about that, but it wouldn't do for a black man to play Hamlet. "Who ever heard of a black Dane, for Christ's sake?"'

'So?'

'So I went to the poly. Got myself a degree and a job as a maths teacher. No difficulty there. Every London school's desperate for someone to teach maths, and looking to fill its quota of blacks as well. Would have been better still if I were gay, but they can't have everything. They'll promote me faster than anyone else, just to show they're not discriminating. And then they think they're not racist!'

'Are you complaining about that? You'd have blamed your colour, I suppose, if they *hadn't* appointed you or if they *don't* promote you.'

'I'm complaining because I did all that, all that time studying, with Darleen waiting and working, so that I could get a mortgage and a home and see my wife sitting at home bringing up my children. And now –'

He is near to breaking down again and she remains silent for some time before risking the most dangerous question. 'Will you tell me about your wife?'

He does not answer at once. When he does, the anger has gone out of his voice, which is soft and sad.

'Darleen? She was a beautiful woman. A good woman. We taught Sunday School together. She took the little ones. I had the big boys. And she had this lovely voice. It made my heart ache for happiness, thinking how it would be, listening to Darleen singing lullabies to our baby. And then those bastards –' He stands up and punches at the back of the chair, knocking it over. Lesley, who must have lingered nearby, hurries in to make sure that no one is hurt and is pushed aside as he leaves. She looks seriously at Lady Ainslie.

102

'Your grandson may be right, Lady Ainslie, about this being unwise. Having this man in here.'

'He thinks the whole world's against him – and who can blame him? I'd like him to feel that there's one person who isn't.'

Lesley makes no comment, her silence implying that she hardly feels an elderly white woman to be the most effective comforter. This is not the first time that Lady Ainslie has noticed a certain coolness in the attitude of this particular nurse, who perhaps thinks that a titled patient should be paying for her accommodation in the private wing.

The conversation has been a strain. Lady Ainslie begins to stand up, staggers a little and falls back into the chair. Whether or not Lesley disapproves of her, she is quick to move, helping her to stand and to return to bed. It is only half past eight, but the day has been long enough.

An early night leads to an early awakening. Even before the morning cup of tea appears Lady Ainslie opens her eyes to consciousness of discomfort. At first she thinks that the removal of the surgical clips must have caused soreness, but then locates the trouble more precisely. Cautiously she makes her way to the lavatory, but has no success there.

She raises the subject after breakfast with Sue, the staff nurse.

'I've had no bowel movement since the operation.'

'It often takes a little time to get back to normal.'

'But five days!'

'If it worries you, I'll find you something to help.'

It seems a surprisingly casual attitude, but within a few moments Kathy comes in with two tablets and a glass of water. Since the morning when she was teased for not removing the fruit bowl she has been meticulous in doing everything by the book, and waits to watch that the tablets are swallowed immediately.

With the arrival of the newspaper man half an hour later comes the discovery that it is Sunday. Lady Ainslie, who prefers not to keep altering her regular delivery order at home, takes the opportunity now to make a selection of those Sunday papers which she does not see as a rule. This 'tasting' leaves her badly shocked – not just by triviality and nastiness, but by the possibility that some readers may never know anything but this about the world outside their own experience.

Sunday offers other small changes in the hospital routine. Ginetta is having a weekend off, so it is her replacement, an agency nurse, who brings details of morning service in the hospital chapel and offers help with an arm or wheelchair; but it is a long time since Lady Ainslie went to church on any but the most formal occasion. She declines with thanks, refraining from mentioning to someone so temporary that the laxative pills have had no effect.

In the afternoon Martin arrives to visit her at two o'clock. Caro – who has probably arranged the timetable with her brother – comes later, bringing Daniel with her. He is content to sit quietly at first while Caro chatters, but is drawn into the conversation by direct questions. Lady Ainslie learns that he is an Oxford graduate whose first research job in the television world was a temporary one. Now he is on the permanent staff and the ideas which he researches are his own. He has just finished working on a programme about the National Health Service and on Monday will embark on a new subject: the effects of late marriage and more frequent divorce on housing requirements.

'Gracious!' exclaims Lady Ainslie. 'How very well informed you must be about modern life!'

'There's never enough time. And the subjects are important. I mean, they seem to be about huge organizations or wide principles; but if they have any effect at all, the effect is on individuals. We ought always to remember that and get it right. But racing against the clock, it's hard to be sure. What I really enjoy is researching things properly. Taking time.'

'What kind of things?'

'Well, not things at all, actually. People. Did Caro tell you that my real ambition is to be a biographer?'

Lady Ainslie nods. 'Of any special period?'

'Oh, definitely of people who are still alive – or at least have friends left alive. I like asking questions and getting answers, not having to dig everything out of books. I look at someone like you, Lady Ainslie, with a long life of activity behind you, and extraordinary social changes – some that you've endured, and some that you've caused – and I don't see you as Caro's grandmother, recovering from an operation. I see you as a mass of answers to fascinating questions.'

'How quite horrible! You make it sound like maggots!'

'I'm sorry. But one day when you're back home again, would you allow me to ask the questions?'

She shakes her head. 'Anything that's of interest is on record, in Hansard or wherever else that matters.'

'You shouldn't be so secretive, Nanna.' This is Caro coming to Daniel's support. 'I mean, this libel action that Daniel's been telling me about. You've never breathed a word.'

'Because that's not interesting either.'

'Interest is in the ear of the hearer. You can't possibly judge it yourself, Nanna. I think it sounds fascinating.'

'It was a very unpleasant experience. If I were ever to write a book of Lord Chesterton-type letters of advice to my grandchildren, letter number one would tell you never to find yourself in a law court. I've no wish to talk about it.'

'But just for a moment,' Caro insists. 'There seems to be something about that libel action that doesn't make sense.'

'I don't suppose a popular book of Famous Trials bothered too much about getting the details right. Anyway, I really don't remember much about it. It was fifty years ago.'

'There's a transcript of the trial,' says Daniel softly. 'The record taken at the time. If you'd like to read it –'

'No, thank you.'

Caro is still worrying away at whatever it is that has surprised her in the summary of the trial. 'It seems odd that you should have been called to give evidence without anyone knowing what you were going to say.'

'I believe the rules have changed now. Both parties have to give statements of what points they propose to prove. Though even now – there was a libel case not too long ago brought against *Private Eye*. They believed that they had a witness ready to give evidence for them, and only found out at the last minute that he wouldn't.'

'But the way it happened. In your case, I mean. Had you had some sort of quarrel with Sir Gilbert?'

'He wasn't Sir Gilbert then.'

'Well, Mr Blakey, then.'

'Yes,' says Lady Ainslie. Her voice is cold. She changes the subject with a firmness which makes it clear that this is to be the end of this topic of conversation. Daniel and Caro, polite young people, follow her lead, chatting inconsequentially about skiing and the avalanche which has almost claimed the life of the heir to the throne. But the other matter, the old history, hangs in the air. They have asked a question and received an answer, definite and truthful. Yes, indeed there was a quarrel. But that – she is well aware – does not tell them what they would like to know.

Eighteen

Tuesday, 3 May 1938

What sort of world is this to bring a baby into? Bombs falling in Spain, Austria invaded, Czechoslovakia likely to go too. But would I even have asked myself that question if it hadn't been for Lord Impney? No. When I woke up yesterday morning I was happy. Not noticing the rest of the world.

Lay awake all last night wondering what to do about the baby. Not too late to get rid of it; and tempting, because the thought that some part of Gil has invaded my body made me sick. Actually sick, as though I could vomit the child out of the womb. But I came to terms with it in the end. It's my child, not his. I shall be responsible for it alone. I shall love it alone. Gil is never going to know, never.

Thank God I hadn't told him already. The only good thing about this mess is that the reference to Lord I. came at the beginning of a new notebook. No mention of pregnancy in the one Gil must have got at. I've read it through to make sure.

Lying sleepless, I reminded myself of the slim chance that he learned the information somewhere else, but couldn't make myself believe it. He must have read my diary, must. Letting himself in with the key I gave him – how could I have trusted him with that! Ferreting around, looking for dirt. A thief, stealing secrets. Oh Edward – it didn't occur to someone decent like you that even locking a diary away in a bureau would be no protection from someone who was trusted but underhand.

That's what hurts. He's got me into trouble with a patient and before all the dust has settled he may get me into trouble with the GMC. I could even be sent to prison. If it was an enemy who'd done *it I'd be angry in an ordinary way. But I was in love with him. I thought he was in love with me. It's not just theft, but betrayal. I must have known, if I'd ever thought about it seriously, that this is the way he sniffs out all the stuff he prints. Didn't think he'd do it to me, that's all.*

This evening, we'd already fixed to go to the theatre. Pregnancy not visible yet, thank God. I tried to behave ordinarily. Determined to make him raise the subject first – and knew he'd have to if my suspicions were right.

As usual, he paid off the taxi, saw me up to the flat, waited, smiling.

'Nightcap?' asked Ainslie as she unlocked the door.

'If you're not tired.' ·

'I am a little, as a matter of fact. A late night last night. But come in for ten minutes.'

The hints that lovers give to each other. How, wondered Ainslie, do married couples make subtly clear their wishes to approach or retreat? Pouring his whisky and water, she watched Gil show by lighting the gas fire that he was as much at home here as in his own rooms. Her own glass contained only tonic water, although she moved the gin bottle as though pouring from it. He prowled restlessly for a moment. Each was waiting for the other to speak first, and Ainslie's silence was stronger.

'Another libel writ coming my way, I was told today,' Gil said, his tone of voice as casual as though this were an everyday occurrence.

'It must be an occupational hazard for a magazine like yours. I'm surprised you don't spend your whole life in the courts.'

'There's a lot of difference between a writ and an action. People think they can bully me and pick up a tidy sum in damages. They soon back down when they realize that I always defend. All they'd be doing is bringing their skeletons even further out of the cupboard, for the whole world to inspect. And this chap's skeleton is a particularly nasty one. Rape and incest. The gutter press would have a field day.'

'That wouldn't be much fun for the victim of the rape.'

'No. That's why he won't press the action. He needs to be

able to tell everyone that he's bringing a case, but it will all fizzle away.'

'Good.'

'I have to give my lawyers a sort of dossier, of course. The stronger the defence, the more quickly the plaintiff retreats.'

'Another whisky?'

'No thanks. You know this chap, as a matter of fact, Ainslie. Lord Impney.'

'Do I? No, the name doesn't ring any bells.'

'I expect he tried to keep his real name quiet. In fact, it was you who put me on to him. Only indirectly, of course. Something you said in your sleep.'

Ainslie set down her glass in order that it should not reveal how her hand was shaking. Was this the moment to explode? It was interesting that he should feel sufficiently ashamed of what he had done to lie about it. Should she force him to admit the truth? He had come to sit on the arm of her chair, his fingers riffling through her hair. Two days earlier her body would have thrilled to the touch, but now she was only pleased that he could not see her face as she pretended to laugh.

'Doesn't sound a madly likely story. In the middle of the night I suddenly make an announcement. "Mr Smith, or whoever, has committed rape and incest." And you carefully note the fact and decide that Mr Smith is really Lord something different. No, I don't think so.'

Gil's caressing hand on her head was still. He was considering, almost certainly, whether to come out with the whole truth. At any other time Ainslie might have been pleased that in a curious way he was proving how much he loved her, recognizing that she would never forgive what he had done and for that reason being anxious to conceal it. But he could not change the subject. She was too important to him for that.

'I think you'll find, when the lawyers give you the details, that you do know about the man and the incident,' he said. 'And what you know will be quite enough to make sure that the case never comes to court. That's what's best for everybody – especially, as you said yourself, for the victim, the child. It was the child who was your patient, not the father.'

'How do you know?'

'I've been following the case up, digging things out. I've got my own ways of doing that.'

'If all this is true, you know that I can't possibly talk about my patients.'

'A court is a privileged place. And in any case, you'll only need to talk to the lawyers. The action will collapse.' He stood up and walked round the chair to face her. 'Oh my darling, I do love you so much. I shouldn't have mentioned this when you're tired. You know, don't you, that I'd never ask you to tell a lie. You're the most honest person I've met in the whole of my life, and that's one of the things I love you for. I just want to be sure that you'll tell the truth, that's all. And I *am* sure.'

Ainslie stood up, no longer concerned to conceal her anger. 'You haven't given much thought to *my* reputation in your effort to destroy someone else's, have you?' she demanded. 'Pillow talk. Not exactly what's expected of either a doctor or a single woman.'

'As long as the case never comes to court, no one outside the lawyers' office will know you had any part in it.'

'I don't admit that I do have any part in it. I'm touched that you think so highly of my truthfulness. But I can keep silence. No one can make me talk if I don't want to.'

'A judge can. And if you let it go as far as that, it will all be out in the open. *Everyone* will lose.'

'Then everyone will have to lose. You must see that I can't possibly volunteer the kind of information you seem to want. The only way I can talk is under orders that can't be disobeyed. It's not just a question of professional etiquette. It's my self-respect.'

'I see. Yes, I do understand your attitude, although it's not quite what I hoped for. And a mistake from your own point of view. Well, you're tired. I'll be –'

'I'd like my key back.' She found it extraordinary that he had not expected that.

'Ainslie, darling –'

'I'm not your darling. I'm just a possible source of scurrilous information. I was a fool ever to think anything else.'

'That's not true. I love you.' He stepped forward, towering

110

above her as he pulled her roughly into his arms. Did he think he could shake her back into loving him? She twisted away, allowing her scorn to show in her eyes.

'When I first met you again in London, I admired you for the way you'd pulled yourself up. Out of the mud of a swineherd's cottage. But at least your father could wash his skin clean of the muck at the end of every day. I don't think you've come so far after all.'

She held out her hand and Gil took the key from his pocket and handed it to her.

'I've upset you, and I'm sorry. I'll be in touch. When you've had time. Goodnight, Ainslie.'

Standing motionless as he let himself out of the flat, she gave a quick laugh, bitter but triumphant. She had allowed just enough of her sense of betrayal to show, but not too much. He still trusted her to be honest in spite of her anger.

Girls always tell in the end. He expected her to reveal a secret, and took it for granted that she would do it truthfully. It had not occurred to him that he too could be betrayed.

Nineteen

Lady Ainslie is weeping. Tears trickle from her cheeks and are channelled into the grooves which run from each side of her mouth. She dabs at them with paper tissues, alternately green and yellow, tugged from a box given to her on the previous day by Martin. There is no waste paper basket within throwing distance: her bed becomes littered with damp crumpled paper, as though she has been trying to make paper primroses in the rain.

'Is something the matter?' The nursing auxiliary who brings in the Monday morning breakfast is a new face, but her voice is as solicitous as though she has had this patient in her care for weeks.

'Nothing at all, thank you.' The words emerge with a normal clipped briskness, because they are true. Nothing upsetting has happened overnight; there has been no change of any kind in her life. She feels, in fact, reasonably cheerful – but still the tears continue to run.

Ginetta comes after breakfast to take her pulse and temperature.

'You're looking very sorry for yourself today. What's the trouble?'

'Nothing, thank you. I appear to be suffering from incontinence of the tear ducts, that's all.' She is trying to make a joke of it, but presumably the words fail to carry conviction, for it is not long before Sue, the staff nurse, arrives in the room.

'What can we do to cheer you up?'

'I'm perfectly happy. I just can't stop crying. But you could do something about my constipation. A week!'

The words emerge more snappily than she intends. Although she is certainly aware of an increasing discomfort, it is not that but her inability to stop crying which has made her irritable. But someone ought to be keeping an eye on her condition. They are treating her as though she should be looking after herself, as though her body has already been handed back into her own care after the operation; and she is not ready to receive it.

Sue accepts in silence what is very nearly an order. Within a few minutes Tricia arrives wearing thin plastic gloves and carrying a tray on which two glycerine suppositories and a small bowl of water are arranged like a plate of nouvelle cuisine. Throughout the undignified routine which follows, Lady Ainslie forces herself to make light conversation. Resisting the temptation to ask whether this, like the removal of the clips, is something which the young student is doing only for the second time, she enquires instead about the weekend.

'I haven't seen you for a day or two, have I?'

'No. Free weekend. Prized above rubies. Am I hurting you? Terrible choices to be made. It's tempting to rush around, catching up on one's social life. Dances and things. But equally tempting to go home to the Aged Parents and have a properly cooked meal and fall into bed on Saturday night knowing that I can stay there till lunch – or all day – on Sunday.'

'Which did you choose?'

'Combination. Best of both worlds, really. My mother was a nurse, so she's sympathetic. She let me invite my boy-friend home with me. Not *that* sort of boy-friend, I don't mean. So he drove me to Sevenoaks after the disco. I fell asleep at three in the morning and didn't need to surface again until the smells of roast beef and Yorkshire pudding started wafting upstairs. There. That should put you right.'

'Thank you, Tricia.' She lies without moving for a few moments after the student has gone and then gets out of bed with what has become a regular caution, in case she should need to move swiftly towards the lavatory. For a little while she walks up and down the room like a prisoner, dabbing her eyes at every turn, for she is still weeping.

113

This inability to control her tears makes her angry, but she is intrigued at the same time. Her life has in most respects been smooth and happy, even privileged, but like any human being she has suffered bereavement and tragedy. She knows, in other words, how it feels to express emotions through tears – and remembers, too, that crying of that kind, which has a cause, can almost always be controlled if necessary, although as a rule it is more therapeutic to let it run its full course. How extraordinary it is, then, that it should be completely beyond her power to check this unjustified wateriness.

She sits down beside the window and once again finds enjoyment in the view of river and Parliament as she waits for the suppositories to take effect. But time passes without any sign of internal disturbance. Her head still feels as though she is being poisoned and her abdomen is still heavy with pressures in the wrong places. The discomfort breeds a pointless anger as she raises her handkerchief to her face with the regularity of a wound-up automaton.

Sister is standing in the room. Her approaches are always silent, her appearance always immaculate. The other nurses from time to time look hustled or crumpled, but Sister is invariably unhurried, with a newly-pressed uniform crowned by the ridiculously elaborate headpiece. 'I hear that this is your crying day,' she says. It sounds like the title of a song.

Lady Ainslie is reassured by the casual remark. 'Does it happen so regularly?'

'Oh yes. Almost always after an operation. Sometimes straight-away, sometimes later, like you. If there's anything *really* wrong, do please tell me.'

'No, nothing. Although it's beginning to make me cross that I can't stop.'

'What I always recommend is a really bad book. The sort of old-fashioned detective story in which everything depends on the 3.30 from Paddington arriving five minutes late one day. You know the sort of thing I mean? Concentrate madly on something like that, and you'll be fine in a couple of hours. In the meantime – I came to say that it's Mr Mallinson's teaching round today. He'll have half a dozen medical students with him. You have the right to say that you'd prefer not to have them in here, and I imagine –'

Lady Ainslie, who has been a medical student herself and knows that not everything can be learned from cadavers, shakes her head. 'Let them all come. Presumably they need to learn about the existence of crying days, as much as about tumours.'

'Are you sure? Let me help you back to bed then, before the hordes arrive.'

They crowd into the room half an hour later, filling the atmosphere with respect for the man who is Mr Mallinson, the eminent surgeon, rather than Toby, her friend. Odd, thinks Lady Ainslie, trying to distract her mind from herself, how surgeons are always eminent, although an adjective like 'skilful' might seem more appropriate.

'What's all this about?' It is Mr Mallinson who speaks, but Toby's eyes which express anxiety and compassion.

'A special exhibition for your benefit.' Her mouth widens in a genuine smile even while her chin continues to tremble with the effort to control her tears. 'An example of post-operative something-or-other for you to explain. Does it affect men as well? I shall listen with interest.'

Mr Mallinson accepts her invitation, but moves across the room as he speaks so that the students have to turn away from the bed in order to keep their eyes on him. When he has finished, he leads the party out without making any attempt to expose the site of her operation for general scrutiny, leaving her tears to flow unobserved.

'Sing!' That was what Nanny Frensham always used to say. 'You can't sing and cry at the same time.' Nanny Frensham has been dead for sixty years, but some of her confident assurances have stood the test of time. Quietly, lest she find herself recognized as eccentric, she obeys Nanny's command.

'This is my crying day.' She has remembered the tune suggested by Sister's phrase. 'This is the day I shall remember the day I'm dying.' The absurdity of such an idea brings her abruptly to a halt. 'Oh, really!' she exclaims aloud, and surrenders to her infirmity.

And now, as though in justification of her tears, she remembers

115

that she has been apologetically warned by Caro not to expect a visit today. At this moment her granddaughter will be driving north towards a stately home whose kitchens for the past ten years have been used only to produce dainty teas but from which tonight will issue a banquet for a party of touring Americans and the earl who owns the house but does not live in it. She has made a joke of the need to take with her every grain of spice or cooking utensil that she expects to need, causing her grandmother to shake an admiring head at the thought of so much detailed planning before the actual cooking even begins. What an enterprising and hard-working young woman she is – and how much her visit will be missed!

Lady Ainslie has no regrets about the decision to conceal her whereabouts from her friends, but that is mainly a matter of pride. They think of her, she hopes, as a brisk and businesslike woman, neatly and sometimes even smartly dressed, with the waves of her short white hair well brushed and soft with cleanliness.

None of those adjectives is true of her now. Her night clothes are unglamorously sensible, her mind is lethargic and undisciplined, her hair feels lank and is certainly tousled from rubbing against pillows. She has no wish to display herself to old friends and colleagues in this state.

Caro is different. Caro has seen her at her lowest ebb and so can exclaim with honesty each day how much better she looks. If Caro were likely to arrive, it would surely be possible to make these ridiculous tears cease to flow. The fact that she is not coming today makes her grandmother feel lonely and neglected. All this is quite unreasonable and completely out of control.

An unexpected ally arrives. Ginetta, the blonde, willowy SRN whose lop-sided smile resembles – Lady Ainslie has remembered the film star's name – that of Meryl Streep. She has not until now made much impression on her patient, doing whatever is necessary with apparent competence, but little warmth. Today, however, in the period after lunch when the nurses usually hope to sit down briefly while their patients rest, she appears smiling in the doorway.

'Would you like me to wash your hair for you? There is a

116

hairdresser on the ground floor if you feel up to that; but if not, I could at least get it clean.'

'How very kind.' Even when she is in good health, only an urgent need for a trim can persuade Lady Ainslie to visit a hairdresser. But it is tiring at the best of times to keep her hands at head-height while she shampoos and dries her hair, and to that now has been added the fear that she will tear something if she stretches.

While the hairwashing is in progress, she keeps a cold flannel pressed against her eyes, pretending that it is to protect them from the shampoo. By the time she removes it, she is cured and is able to sit dry-eyed while Ginetta goes to work with a hair-drier. She feels her hair being lifted by a comb, rather than turned on a brush, until at last the nurse steps backwards and gives her Meryl Streep smile.

'Very nice. You're lucky to have such a strong natural wave.' She brings a mirror, and is thanked sincerely. Even such a small difference in appearance and cleanliness cheers up the spirits. The crying has come to an end.

To ensure against its return, she looks around for occupation. Today the river view which has so much delighted her during the past week reminds her only that she is a prisoner, unable to walk along its bank. Her swollen eyes make the thought of reading unattractive. Doubtfully at first but increasingly tempted, she stares at the bright drip-and-blot cover of the notebook which Caro has provided for a hospital diary. As long as she is careful to avoid her earlier mistake of including personal comments on the nurses, there is no reason why she should feel inhibited. She reaches for her pen.

Monday, 13 March 1988

Why am I writing this? Because sooner or later Caro will ask whether I've made use of her gift, and I don't want to hurt her feelings. Quite the wrong reason for keeping a diary.

And why have I left the first pages blank? So that later on I can write in again what I've already torn out? That won't work. First impressions change with every day that passes, and one can't ever

117

dismiss later events or discoveries from the mind. Whatever date one puts on a diary entry, it can only be a true statement about the day when it's actually written.

Unless one sticks to facts without opinions. Caro came at four, fish pie for supper, that sort of thing. Not worth the effort of writing. Boring, boring, as Caro would exclaim. But then, most days are boring in the sense of merely repeating previous activities. What would have been so exciting about spending today in the Lords, debating business education? Looked at from that angle, it's odd that I should choose a time of change and new experiences to break a habit of seventy-one years. Seventy-one years! Gracious!

Raises a lot of questions. Has it been only habit? The feeling that having gone on so long it would be a pity to break the thread now? Or the wish for a memory-jogger, so that an incident can be recalled at the turn of a page? No, not that, because I so rarely reread, except perhaps to check a date.

Merely a habit, then. An addiction, rather, because just meandering on about nothing like this makes me feel calm, rested – and still alive. A day recorded is a day experienced.

But nothing to record about this morning except that I couldn't stop crying, Ginetta washed my hair, and I'm still constipated. That disposes of today!

Why don't I write about Mr Barnaby, then? Unlike the pages I had to scrap before, this isn't ever likely to be read by its subject.

To start at the beginning.

It is like writing a short story, with the added interest of not knowing in advance how it will end. There is a problem, though, in that she is not at all clear what kind of man she is describing. Sister probably sees him as one of the many bereaved and distressed relatives to whom every year she has to give bad news. Martin undoubtedly thinks of him as 'a black' who has become both the victim and the possible instigator of racial violence.

Lady Ainslie's picture is a more complex one. She believes him to be, almost certainly, a decent man. A Sunday School teacher, he said. She sees him as a boy not only working hard at school but sent by God-fearing parents to Bible Study classes. Hit all the harder because of that background by something which no good God should have allowed – spun from New Testament meekness back into Old Testament revenge – but decent beneath it all.

Yet she is not quite sure. Is she allowing her assessment of his character to be affected by the fact that he is an educated man doing a useful job? There is not the slightest trace of social snobbery about Lady Ainslie, and she has devoted herself from childhood to helping those who find it hardest to cope with the complexities of modern life. But like everyone else she has her own criterion for choosing whom she will respect, and is aware that she probably over-values paper qualifications. Whilst suspecting that Mr Barnaby's true talent may be for acting, she is judging him by his degree and his job as a schoolteacher.

Well, there is no need to set down opinions when the facts known to her provide quite enough material. Her handwriting – as neat and legible as if she had never been a doctor – flows over the pages. No longer is the day a lonely one. She is writing to herself in her accustomed way. Yes, this diary-writing *is* an addiction. Like alcoholism; one sip and she is off again. But why not? It is surely the most harmless of drugs.

Twenty

Resolute in mind and even more uncomfortable than before in body, Lady Ainslie on Tuesday morning summons Sister to attend her. The request, naturally, is politely phrased but is still recognizably a command. Sister not only promises further action on the state of her patient's bowels but, unlike her juniors, returns at hourly intervals to enquire after its effectiveness. As Big Ben strikes noon on the far side of the river, Lady Ainslie is seated on her private lavatory groaning aloud with effort and pain.

The sound is loud enough to bring Tricia running.

'It's all right.' One final groan is followed by a shuddering of relief. She buries her head in her hands for a moment before smiling up at the student. 'Remember this if you ever have a baby. Most of the time you can stifle pain with deep breathing. But there's always a moment when what helps most is to yell. A great mistake to be dignified all the time.'

Certainly she does not feel dignified now as she asks if she may have a bath, confessing that she needs support, and is helped into and, later, out of the water. Back in bed, she shivers with weakness and emptiness and, after lunch, sleeps for two hours. Then at last that particular problem can be put behind her.

Later, as she makes her cautious way to the chair beside the window, her mind and her eyes are both clear. When she opens one of the books she has brought with her, the pattern of black on white divides itself into intelligible words instead of presenting itself as an incomprehensible smudge. This small relief raises her spirits; yet almost at once she puts the book down to contemplate a greater pleasure.

Caro, forced to miss yesterday's visit, is certain to come today and the mere thought of her arrival adds a sparkle to the atmosphere. Lady Ainslie tries to remember herself as she was at the age of twenty-four. Did she have the brightness about herself then that she so much enjoys in her granddaughter?

'No,' she says aloud, shaking her head ruefully. At a time when she should still have been young, she was swamped by the long hours asked of a hospital doctor, by the fear of making mistakes and the strain of continuous appraisal by her superiors. Young men in the same position, she recalls, took refuge – as their successors still do – in rowdy high spirits. But she and the other young women who had chosen a medical career, carrying the flag for their gender, retreated into sober earnestness, moving straight from carefree childhood into mature responsibility. She has no memory of regretting this at the time; it is only her granddaughter's exuberance which tells her what she has missed.

And here comes Caro now, bubbling with all her usual vivacity.

'I say, I say, I say! What has been going on in my absence? Your eyes are shining. Your hair looks stunning. Are you about to enter a Glamorous Grandmother competition?'

'If we're going to talk about hair, am I allowed to say how glad I am that the spikes have disappeared?' Caro's hair has reverted to its natural blondeness. Its usual length can not, naturally, be so speedily restored, but instead of the upward-pointing spikes a mass of tight short curls suggests that she has just had her first permanent wave.

'You weren't the only one to be rude about them. But you merely thought they were hideous. Daniel said they were old-fashioned. I can't live with *that*.' She gives her grandmother a hug before bringing the second chair across to the window and sitting down.

'How did you meet Daniel?'

'I met him for the first time a few years ago on a skiing holiday. That is, *he* was having a skiing holiday; I wasn't. Do you remember, after I'd finished the Cordon Bleu course, I went off to be a chalet girl in Austria. My very first customers were a bunch of Oxford undergraduates. Eight of them.'

121

'I remember you writing about them. They arrived for Christmas, didn't they?'

'Yes. Had to take their holiday in the university vacations, poor things. Hopeless, really. There's hardly ever enough snow before the New Year. The first four days it rained, and they spent a lot of the time sitting around in the chalet, playing madly intellectual games. They wanted me to join in, so I introduced them to a few silly ones for a change. Then the snow came, overnight. They were all mad to get out on the runs. And Daniel – I hadn't particularly sorted him out from the rest till then – made them all stay and help me wash up breakfast first, so that I could get out to ski for a bit. It was my job to clear up; I knew that. But he said it would take me an hour and the rest of them only five minutes. Wasn't that nice?'

'Very. But I thought you said you hadn't known him long.'

'Not really known, no. I mean, there was that fortnight, but then it ended. He was taking his Finals that year, working really hard. I didn't expect to see him again. But about a year ago the eight of them had a reunion and asked me along. And they fixed up, all of them who could get time off, to make up another party this January, including me. To ski, not to cook. They all wanted to take girl-friends or wives this time. Everyone seemed to have a partner except Daniel. He asked me if I had a boy-friend that I wanted to invite. And when I said "No," he said "Good." So I suppose that was when it started.'

'I see.' Lady Ainslie had known that Caro's most recent holiday was with a party, but had not enquired into its history.

'Skiing's never been one of your things, has it, Nanna? Well, I can tell you, it's a terrifically good way of getting to know someone. You see them when they're fed up because they've fallen over, or absolutely exhausted after a long day, or being teased because they look so comic, doing things wrong – I'm talking about ordinary near-beginners like Daniel and me. If they can still laugh and be good-tempered after all that, it suggests that they might be quite amiable people to live with. I started off by *liking* Daniel. And then, I suppose, I fell in love with him.'

'The right way round,' says Lady Ainslie approvingly. 'And as well as being amiable, he seems very intelligent.'

122

'Oh, frightfully. He got a First. And he really works hard, digging out his subjects. He's a bit like Martin, I sometimes think. I mean, you know how Martin wants to be a detective and spends all his time on the beat making deductions from what he sees, just for practice. Daniel has the same sort of attitude – treating even the most ordinary fact as though it were the clue to a mystery. But he doesn't seem to mind me being a featherbrain outside the kitchen.'

'You're not –' begins Lady Ainslie. But Caro is not fishing for compliments.

'How did you first meet Grandfather?' she asks. 'Isn't it odd, that one doesn't know these things.'

'Not so odd when you never met him.' Lady Ainslie thinks back fifty years. 'Richard and I belonged to the same tennis club. Oh yes, you can laugh. You can't imagine that your decrepit grandmother was once a demon at the net, can you? Just remember that one day you may talk to your own grandchildren about a meeting on the ski slopes, and see them snigger.'

'I wasn't sniggering. In fact, I was feeling rather sad. Because you're right – it *is* hard for me to imagine you dashing around in a short white dress, and it oughtn't to be.'

'They weren't *so* short in those days. You'd probably think of it as being too long for a mini.'

'Anyway, you played together there?'

'Yes. We were both about the same standard and became partners in competitions. Had a regular doubles game every Sunday morning through the summer. People were more conscious of seasons then, as well as wearing longer dresses. Tennis was a summer game. So I didn't see much of him in winter. He'd ask me out to a theatre from time to time, just to keep in touch. And the tennis club had a rather grand ball once a year; we went together to that.'

'So you were a bit like me and Daniel – getting to like him first?'

'That's right.'

'What happened, then? To jerk you out of only liking, I mean?'

'Actually,' says Lady Ainslie, 'it was connected with that libel action you were talking about on Saturday. I needed some help.

That's to say, I didn't realize for myself that I needed help, but Richard did. He was a lawyer, you see, before he became a Member of Parliament. I think, dear, if you don't mind . . .' She has been a widow for more than forty years. It is absurd that the memory of her husband should bring tears back to her eyes now. It must be the after-effect of the operation that once again makes it necessary to dab her cheeks.

'Sorry, Nanna. I didn't mean to upset you. Let me tell you all about yesterday. An enormous success. Your noble friend even came down to the kitchens at the end of the evening. First time he'd ever penetrated that far, to judge by his expression. Said some very nice things about how he'd lived in the house for seven years before his father inherited and this was the first time he ever remembered having a good meal there. It was the jam roly-poly that got him. I remembered what you said about the House of Lords being fixated on nursery food.'

She chatters on until the end of her visit, aware that her grandmother is not listening to the details, but content to fill the room with words. After she has left, Lady Ainslie continues to stare out of the window at her river view. She is remembering the evening when her liking for Richard changed its course.

Wednesday, 18 May 1938

An astonishing evening. Haven't quite taken it in yet.

Out to dinner with Richard. Expensive restaurant, private alcove, orchid corsage, candles, champagne, superb meal (rather wasted on someone with no appetite). Talked a little about tennis, but mostly about politics and his ambitions.

Politics first. Rearmament, appeasement, Fascism, social reform. Mostly in agreement. I knew he was a Labour supporter (shameful secret in Cumberland Club circles, but he realized my sympathies lay the same way). Now he proposes to fight a by-election after the approaching death of a Conservative MP. Believes that the Popular Front has genuine hope of allying Labour and Liberal voters against Chamberlain. As a barrister he's used to making speeches.

After dinner he drove me home, came in for a nightcap. Until then had talked mainly about his own plans. Now switched to mine.

'I hope you won't think that I'm speaking out of turn,' Richard said as Ainslie set a brandy down beside him. 'I want permission to be your champion. I point my lance, hoping that my lady will toss her ribbon upon it and allow me to joust in her colours. In other words, will you let me represent you in the case of *Impney* v. *Blakey?*'

'I'm not the defendant,' said Ainslie, surprised. 'I don't need a lawyer.'

'If you really think that, then by God you need a lawyer! Blakey is proposing to defend himself against a charge of libel by pleading justification. In other words, that what he wrote was true. Just about the biggest gamble that anyone can take in a law court. If he fails to convince the jury, he'll have made matters so much worse that they'll quadruple the damages against him.'

'That hasn't got anything to do with me.'

'I understand that he's proposing to subpoena you as a hostile witness. That is, as someone who is in a position to give evidence supporting his case, but may be unwilling to do so. I presume from that – knowing your occupation – that he must have got on the scent of the story through you. Presumably he originally hoped that you'd volunteer to back him up. Presumably also – I'm having to make a lot of presumptions since I don't really know anything about the case – you've given him to understand that you wish to maintain professional silence.'

'He can't make me say anything I don't want to,' said Ainslie.

'Yes, he can. There's a nasty little thing called contempt of court. If the judge orders you to answer a question and you refuse, you could even find yourself in prison. And that's only half of it. Let's do some more presuming. Let's say for the sake of argument that this chap *did* bring his young daughter to you and that you *did* help her out of a hole. I expect it could be proved. Private detectives flashing bank notes around would soon find a nurse who liked the thought of a little pin money. And then you're likely to find yourself in trouble not only with the law but with whatever council it is that strikes doctors off registers.'

Ainslie considered this in silence, knowing that the danger was real. Recognizing her anxiety, Richard pressed the point home.

'Once you're under cross-examination, you see, there's no reason why a hostile lawyer should stick to the one case which is the subject of the trial. He'll ask you whether you've ever done this, that or the other. How often? Why? I'm sure you've helped a good many women out of a tight spot in your time, and I think all the better of you for it; but can you put your hand on your heart and swear that you've never broken the law? Of course you can't. Nor can other doctors, no doubt; but most of them never have to stand up to cross-examination in court.'

'Gil warned me about all that. I thought he was trying to blackmail me into saying whatever he wanted.'

'And so he was. But the nasty thing about a blackmailer is that his starting point is usually the truth. The only unusual thing about this case is that the price to be paid is also the truth. Why does he hate you so much, Ainslie?'

'Is it hatred? I don't think so. Something colder than that. He's angry at the moment because I won't play his game and he'll fight me ruthlessly for as long as he must. But if he wins, well, I think he'll expect to be friends with me again, as though nothing has happened.'

'And it's not like that?'

'I don't care whether or not he hates me, but I hate him. Passionately. When I think about him my heart beats too fast and my hands tremble and my whole body feels as though it's on fire and I can't think straight about anything except the fact that I loathe him. I'd like to tear him to pieces – I mean, really I would.'

'Except perhaps for that last remark, you appear to be describing the symptoms of a woman in love.'

'Oh no!' exclaimed Ainslie with a force which must have carried conviction.

'What did he do to you? Betray a confidence?'

'I don't want to talk about it any more.'

'But you must. I've convinced you, surely, that you need a lawyer.'

'Yes, you have. But not you.'

'Well, there's a slap in the face, if ever I felt one! I admit that libel isn't a speciality of mine. But it's very often the case in the divorce courts as well that someone not directly accused needs to have his interests defended. A watching brief. I hope you don't think I'm an incompetent lawyer!'

'Of course not. I didn't mean –' Ainslie stretched out a hand in apology and was comforted by the firmness with which he gripped it. There was a long silence in which she was aware of him checking through all the possible explanations and reaching a solution.

'I think I see it. You intend to fib in court. You don't expect to enjoy this much, and feel you can only get away with it if even your own lawyer doesn't know what you're doing. So you'll first of all have to lie to your lawyer. But you don't want to lie to a lawyer who is also a friend: me. Possibly because I may have told you in the past that a lawyer is part of the machinery of justice, with a duty to the court to bring out the truth. Possibly because you fear that if the truth emerges at a late stage you could get me as well as yourself into trouble. But probably, I think, because you know that I admire and trust you and you don't want to disturb my trust. That's what I'd like to believe, anyway.'

Ainslie burst into tears. She had no warning, and could think of no reason for it. 'Stupid!' she said, searching for a handkerchief. 'I just feel a bit low, that's all.'

'Not stupid at all,' said Richard. 'Very natural. You can't deal with something like this alone.' He hesitated, and then added another possibility to those he had already listed. 'I suppose it could be that you've trusted someone – Blakey – with a secret, and he's let you down, so now you don't feel prepared to trust anyone ever again. But you need to talk about it. Forget I'm a lawyer, if you'd rather. I am a friend, aren't I? Come on; tell me all about it.'

This time it was Ainslie who was silent for some moments. But what Richard said was right. She needed a friend; and if she now refused to trust him with the truth there would always in the future be a barrier between them.

'I've never passed on other people's secrets to anyone,' she said. 'Certainly never to Gil, who lives on exposure. Not even a hint. He stole this one. Forced a lock, like a burglar.'

'So the story, as he printed it, is true?'

'Yes. And of course you're quite right. They'll track down the clinic. They'll be able to prove that the child had a gynaecological operation and that I performed it.'

'Can it be proved precisely what operation it was?'

'As you said, they could try to bribe a nurse. But she'd lose her job.'

'Could you provide an alternative explanation for the operation?'

'Yes. That's what I intend to do. You were quite right to guess that I'm going to lie about it. The child deserves protection. And even the father . . . There's nothing good to be said about him except that he might have gone to some back street abortionist who'd never know who he was. He came to me because he wanted the best possible treatment for his daughter. He had the right to expect me to keep his confidence. He'll lie, of course. Even if I told the truth, he'd deny it. As for the girl, she never knew she was pregnant.'

'The clinic records?'

'The owner of the clinic knows as well as I do what is illegal and what just scrapes inside the law. You could say he has his own code book. I know what the words mean, and so do the nurses. But the official translation gives a different picture. I don't *want* to lie about all this, Richard. I believe that the law is cruel and I'd like to stand up and say so. It's a law made by men who have absolutely no idea of the desperation a woman feels when she finds that her body's been invaded by an unwanted child.' She checked herself. This was no time to make a speech.

'They'll dig out as much as they can about your past work,' Richard warned her gravely. 'If they can't prove the details of this particular operation, they'll try to build up a picture of regular abortions, under whatever excuse, in order to suggest the likelihood that this was one of a series.'

'I don't do so many. But I understand what you're getting at. Whatever happens in the libel case, I shall almost certainly be struck off the medical register afterwards.'

'I don't wonder that you feel like tearing Blakey into pieces.'

That was, as it happened, only a minor element in her rage,

128

although it was bound to grow in importance when she had to face the fact of losing her vocation and her livelihood. For the moment she had enough to worry her without that.

'Still,' she said, 'if Gil's lawyer produces a list of my old cases, presumably I can put in another list, to show the ways in which I've helped women to *have* babies and to suggest a different kind of likelihood.'

'Of course. Anyway, as regards this particular case, you feel reasonably confident that you can't be attacked through the clinic records or staff – or your own case notes? In that case, it will rest on a straight confrontation: your word against Blakey's. There's no other evidence, is there, which might support Blakey's defence?'

Ainslie hesitated before replying. Yes, there was one more piece of evidence. The diary. This whole disastrous episode had started with the diary. Richard didn't know it existed, but was nevertheless warning her that anything of the sort should be destroyed. It would be easy enough to do that. But there was another possibility. The diary could be used as a boomerang. She turned round to smile at Richard.

'No,' she said. 'Nothing at all. If this case goes to court, I'm bound to be a loser, in one way. And that poor girl will be a loser as well. But Gil Blakey is not going to win.'

'Good,' said Richard. 'And now there's something else. We've got all that straight between us, haven't we – that I know you are about to perjure yourself and I don't care.'

'Yes, I'm glad. You were right earlier on. I didn't want to fib to you. Until now, I'd have said that I never lie.'

'You may need some help, then. It's not a habit to be lightly taken on by an amateur. It needs confidence and strong nerves and careful preparation. But I want to change the subject.'

Ainslie waited; but instead of continuing, Richard stood up and walked across to the window, standing with his back to her. 'Yes?' she said.

'Not easy. You were half ashamed, weren't you, to make a confession to me? Now I'm half ashamed as well, although – no, it's stupid. You're a doctor, after all. And this is your speciality. My wife was one of your patients once.'

129

'Your wife? I didn't know you were married.'

'I'm not now. I'm talking about some years ago. Before you'd attained the dizzy heights of Harley Street – when you had a fertility clinic at the Royal Free. She came to see you because she'd been married for three years and was longing to have a baby, lots of babies, and nothing seemed to be happening.'

'I don't remember . . . I didn't realize . . .'

'Why should you? We didn't know each other then, and Johnson is a common name. The only contact you had with your patient's husband was the little bottle I had to leave at the clinic one morning. It turned out to be all my fault for having mumps at the age of seventeen. Nothing to be done about it. If Rosalie wanted children, she'd have to find another father for them. The hard thing was that I wanted to have a baby in the family as well. I wouldn't have minded . . . Still, naturally enough, she preferred to have everything legal. So off she went.'

'Why are you telling me this now, Richard?' asked Ainslie.

'Obviously I can't ever ask another woman to marry me without warning her. But I still have this hankering to bring up a child. Not caring who its father was, not wanting to know. Just loving the mother and reckoning that the two of us could make the child wholly ours by the love we gave it. You're pregnant, aren't you, Ainslie?'

'How can you possibly tell?'

'Were you congratulating yourself that nothing shows yet? You're quite right, in a way. No bulges. But there was something about the way you walked into the room. Your feet set slightly more apart than usual. And the paleness of your face. And the look in your eyes, of someone with a secret. Ten minutes ago you burst into tears. I've never seen you cry before, not in – what is it? Four years? I'm right, aren't I?'

'Yes, you're right.'

'I suppose I've no right to ask. I mean, you may be secretly married. You may want to be faithful to someone who can't marry you for some reason. I suppose you might even have chosen to bring up a child on your own. But I can't let this chance slip without throwing my hat into the ring. Will you marry me, Ainslie?'

130

For a moment she struggled with a wish to laugh and to cry at the same time. 'In order to give you instant fatherhood?'

'Of course that's not the main reason.' He came to stand behind her chair and his hands gripped her shoulders. 'I'd have asked you months ago if I'd thought there was any hope. But it was easy enough to tell then that there was someone else. You were always so – well, absorbed. It's only since this libel case came up that I've noticed a change. I thought at first that it was because you were worried about that. And then I began to wonder whether there was a baby on the way, and then I was sure, and so – I do love you, Ainslie. I want to marry you. Yes, I want your child to be my child, but most of all I want you to be mine.'

'More lies?' she said softly. 'To the child, I mean.'

'Yes. I should want your promise on that. That he'd always be allowed to believe I was his father. Or hers. Perhaps that's another reason why this seemed a good moment to speak. When you're just about to embark on a career of perjury in other areas.' He came round to stand in front of her and held out his hands, pulling her up and into his arms. 'When's the baby due?'

'November.'

'Right. We get married at once by special licence; without telling anyone. Go off on holiday as soon as the law term ends. After that, we can fudge the dates. If friends start asking too many questions, they'll simply think we jumped the gun a bit, and I shan't mind that. No one's likely to doubt that the child is mine.'

Except Gil, thought Ainslie. Gil would know that until their quarrel she had wanted no one but him. But then, by the time she had told her lies in the libel action, Gil would never want to see her again. Certainly he was not likely to come cooing over her baby and speculating on its precise age.

'But Richard,' she said hesitantly. 'This libel case. It's bound to get a lot of publicity in the newspapers. The wrong sort of publicity for someone who's hoping to become a Member of Parliament.'

'There are four answers to that point. Let's suppose that the case gets on to the list before the baby arrives. Unlikely, but

131

suppose. If you arrive at court so huge that you can hardly squeeze into the witness box and the jury discovers that you're unmarried, their bourgeois instincts will tell them immediately that you're an unreliable witness and capable of any kind of shameful behaviour. A *married* woman who is about to become a mother, on the other hand, will earn instant approval and sympathy. These things move slowly, though. It's more probable that Baby will be happily tucked up in his cradle before you have to appear.'

'You're talking about what's good for me. But I'm worried about you.'

'Well, the third answer to your anxiety is that an electorate may have different standards from the members of a property-owning jury. If I were standing as a Conservative, I agree the case might present a problem. But the sort of work you do in your Bethnal Green clinic is just what a Labour candidate needs to be married to; and if you have to pay the penalty for it as a result of the trial, I should think I'll sweep in on a sympathy vote!'

Ainslie was not so sure about that, knowing how often women voted as their husbands told them to, but she did not argue. 'You said there were four answers,' she reminded him.

'The fourth answer is that if I had to choose between being a Member of Parliament and being your husband, there'd be no contest. I want to marry you. Nothing else in the world matters.'

'Richard! Oh, darling! All the same, there's still one thing I should say. One of your guesses earlier on was right. When you thought I might be wanting a child just – well, just for the sake of having it. That was it; that I didn't want to wait much longer. I know all about the problems that older women have with babies.'

'Older women, indeed!'

'What I'm trying to make clear is, I wouldn't want you ever to think that I was looking for a husband, any husband, just because of the baby. It isn't like that at all.'

'You're saying that if you agree to marry me it's because you adore me; I'm the only man in the world for you?'

'Yes, that's right.' And suddenly a weight lifted from Ainslie's

132

mind and for the first time in nearly four months she ceased to feel sick and heavy. 'Oh Richard, you are wonderful! I do love you!'

It was true, she realized with astonishment. The strength of Gil's desire for her, and the physical passion it aroused, had swept her so completely off her feet that only an equally passionate anger could have brought the affair to an end. Her love for Richard was calmer but more exhilarating; there was laughter in it as well as reassurance. He was a good friend, a dependable companion. 'Yes, I love you,' she repeated, and from that moment the time of their happiness together began to run.

Twenty-one

Lady Ainslie finds herself unable to devote very much time to reminiscence, for soon after five o'clock she receives an unexpected visit from Daniel Carrington.

'I hope you don't mind my coming without Caro again,' he says politely.

'Of course not. Do come and sit down.' She is welcoming but at the same time suspicious. What does he want of her, she wonders, as he performs the ritual of enquiring about her health. He does not keep her waiting long to find out.

'I did mention, didn't I, Lady Ainslie, that what I *really* want to do with myself, outside the work I'm paid for, is to write biography.'

'You did, yes.'

'I've already made a start on one. Of my grandfather.'

'Gil Blakey! What's he done to deserve a biography?'

The venom in her voice startles Daniel into laughter. 'Do you think of it as a kind of accolade, then? Something that has to be earned?' He leans forward earnestly. 'It seems to me that there are two different kinds of biography which deserve publication. There are people whose lives are so important that their achievements should be recorded. And there are writers who have no aptitude for fiction, for invention, but who can make a work of art out of describing a real life.'

She listens, amused by his seriousness, as he develops this theme.

'After all, it's possible to write a biography almost as though it *were* a work of fiction, building up to the same sort of climax, using the same kind of suspense. Even presenting it as a kind of detective story in which the reader has all the clues but must find his own solution to puzzles, with no detective to assemble the characters in the drawing room for an exposition. And from that point of view it's an advantage to choose a subject who isn't world-famous. If you pick on the Duke of Wellington, everyone knows from the first page that he's going to win the battle of Waterloo. No suspense there. But if you start with one of the eleven children of a pigman, not many readers will know the plot in advance.'

'Swineherd,' says Lady Ainslie.

'I beg your pardon.'

'His father. Swineherd, not pigman.'

'My grandfather always says – Well, thank you.'

'So you see yourself as a writer for whom any old man will do as a source of inspiration, do you? I hope you haven't put that point of view to your grandfather.'

'Obviously, the perfect biography comes from a fusion of the two forms; subject and writer equally worthy of each other. But someone of my age has to get one book under his belt before other people's families are going to let him loose in their archives. It's like being a portrait painter. No one will commission you until he's seen the result of someone else's commission and approved your style.'

'Style? Do you mean accuracy?'

'I take the need for accuracy for granted in the sense of getting known facts correct,' Daniel says. 'It must always be more difficult to know what one has failed to discover. When I talk about style, I mean – well, there are so many ways to approach biography. You can just set out a chronology, and you can do that either critically or uncritically. You can do it as a kind of god's eye observer, or you can introduce yourself as a narrator. That's like writing a novel, again.'

'As a member of his family, in this particular case, you would be a personally involved narrator.'

'That's another way of tackling it. Or I could write entirely through the eyes of witnesses – another fiction-writer's method.

135

In imagination, of course. Gilbert Blakey as seen by his mother, his teachers, his mistresses, his –'

'Did he have mistresses?' Lady Ainslie realizes that the question may sound prurient. What she really hopes to discover, of course, is whether her own name is on Daniel's list. She is interested to observe that there is no glint of knowingness in his eyes. 'There was no reason, was there, why he shouldn't marry again after your grandmother died?'

'That indicates another sort of approach that a biographer can take. Trying to find the one overwhelming principle that rules a man's life. I haven't got to that yet, but I'm quite clear about a secondary one. I think I mentioned it before. He really badly wanted to have a son. I believe he had this feeling of having pulled himself up by his bootlaces, and what was the point of it all if there was no one to inherit his kingdom and his money? He never had much use for girls, and my mother's behaviour when she grew up can't have done much to improve his opinion of them. He wanted a boy, and he never had one.'

'What has that to do with mistresses?'

'Ah, well, I had a long talk with one of them – a Mrs Mainwaring – and she spilled it all out. His wife, my grandmother, died in childbirth. You probably know about that.'

Lady Ainslie nods without interrupting.

'It sounds as though he never quite got over it. He wasn't ever going to ask or expect any woman to take that risk for him again, however much he might want a baby. But he didn't intend to live like a monk either. He made it clear to Mrs Mainwaring, she told me, that it was up to her to take precautions and that he would take no responsibility if she didn't. She – she's an old lady now, of course – felt confident, all the same, that if she'd had a son he would have married her straightaway. She can't remember him saying it in so many words, but she feels quite sure. In fact he had three more daughters, after my mother, from three separate affairs. They each lasted a long time, the affairs, but came to an end when a baby appeared.'

'Sounds ruthless.'

'He was generous with money, I think. But I suppose his attitude would be that he was honest with them and so not

136

responsible for what happened. They could make their own choice and take their own risks.'

Daniel is giving Lady Ainslie a good deal to think about and she is sufficiently interested to continue the conversation.

'That's another element in choosing a style of writing, you see,' he says, returning to his main theme. 'Do you just set things down as they happened or do you go all Freudian and try to draw psychological conclusions?'

'I hadn't thought of it as being so complicated,' says Lady Ainslie truthfully. 'Well, I suppose that if you're having a trial run, so to speak, it does make it easier to start with someone who's prepared to be helpful out of affection.'

'Helpful only up to a point.' Daniel laughs ruefully. 'I mean, he knows what I'm doing, and why. He thinks it's quite a good joke. But he says, if I'm using him to practise on, I've got to practise all the difficult digging-out bits. So he won't actually volunteer any information.'

'Not even the names of the mistresses?'

'No. He let me read old letters, in the way that almost anyone would who'd agreed to be biographized. That's where I found the names.'

Lady Ainslie remembers with relief that there could have been no letters from her in any hoard. At the height of their passion she and Gil had seen each other almost every day, and it had ended with a sudden and total cutting of communication.

'So you have to discover for yourself the right questions to ask?'

'That's it. Only if I've done that will he answer them. And when it comes to the war period, the second war, he won't even go as far as that. He just says "Official Secrets Act" and clams up. Luckily, not everybody is so conscientious.'

Having no idea what Gil did in the second war, she is tempted to ask for information, but is held back by a reluctance to reveal any curiosity. Clearly she is successful in indicating indifference by her expression, because Daniel feels a need to justify his choice of subject.

'I know you don't like my grandfather, Lady Ainslie, but he has had a very interesting life. Snakes and ladders. I could almost

137

call the book that. A rags to riches story with some tremendous slithers back on the way.'

'Yes.' Lady Ainslie's voice still lacks enthusiasm. 'And I suppose it's easier – for you, I mean – to take a living subject rather than a dead one?'

'Well, him in particular. Just because I know him. There's a special advantage. I'm fond of him, you see – but of course I've never seen him as anything but an old man. By the time I was of an age to be aware of what he did, his days of buying and selling and starting magazines were pretty well over. He was still Chairman of the group, but not so much involved in all the battles. So everything comes as a discovery to me, as I hope it will to a reader, if I can get it published. A picture of a young man with fire in his belly, who couldn't ever have imagined himself as an old man leaning on a stick. Besides, talking to people is a more interesting kind of research than digging in libraries. That's why I came to see you today.'

It is a reminder that although he has politely allowed her to ask all the questions so far, he has some of his own.

'I went back to Kingsgelding, of course,' he tells her. 'It's odd, considering that he was one of eleven children, that there are no Blakeys still living there. Especially odd because when I looked back through the parish registers the name crops up regularly for more than four hundred years.'

'There are no Dangerfields there either, and *they*'d been there for far longer. The same reason in both cases, I suspect. The lure of a comfortable and manageable house somewhere else.'

'The house where Grandfather was born doesn't exist any longer. Council houses instead. He remembers a mud floor and an open cooking range.'

'I used to think how cosy that was.' Lady Ainslie is tempted into reminiscence. 'There was a most extraordinary smell. A mixture of smoke and sweat and baby urine. My mother could hardly bear to go inside. But I liked it. It was such a *hot* smell – and Kingsgelding Hall was always freezing.'

'Did you go there often, you and your mother?'

'More often than you might expect, yes. It was a very feudal sort of society, still. I'm talking now about the years before the first world war, before your grandfather joined the army and left the village. I don't suppose my father paid very good wages. But in a way he represented the social security system of his day, as far as Kingsgelding was concerned. In theory it was a bad system, because where the local squire was absent or uncaring, leaving everything to his steward, life could be bleak for anyone too sick to work. But my father was on the spot and had a sense of responsibility.'

'So you and your mother –?'

'If anyone in the village was ill, we paid the first call. My mother would send down broths from the hall for as long as that was needed, and the servants took those, but she always went herself the first time. And when anyone was going to have a baby – that was a duty I really loved, when I was a little girl. The mother was given a baby bundle before the baby arrived: a set of first clothes. My mother did the sewing herself, and my nurse used to knit the shawls. Then later, after the midwife had reported that the baby was born and looked likely to live, we took down another bundle.'

She pauses, surprising herself by her pleasure in the memories, and Daniel presses her gently.

'What was in that one?'

'A set of larger clothes: the six month size. And a gift which would depend on whether it was a first child or a twelfth. It might be a cradle, but if the family had all that sort of thing already it might only be a mug. That was all to be kept. Then there was a christening dress which was just on loan – everyone in the village used it and then returned it to be laundered ready for the next baby. Actually, I seem to remember that there were two or three of those, because often several babies arrived at the same time.'

'So my grandfather – or rather, his mother – would have had these bundles?'

'Must have done, yes.'

'This is marvellous!' exclaims Daniel. 'Just the sort of material I want. May I go on asking for your recollections of those days? My grandfather as a little boy.'

Lady Ainslie hesitates. She is not prepared to open her memory

139

as any favour to Gil. But Daniel is not Gil. Caro loves him, and that is enough to give him a claim on her help. She marshals her thoughts, arranging them in picture form.

'When I first remember him he was always dirty. Always dressed in hand-me-downs. Either too large or too small for him. You'd think there would have been one moment when they fitted. Always with scabs on his knees where he'd fallen down. And lice in his hair. He had extraordinary golden hair when it was allowed to grow.' On the verge of saying that it was hair exactly the colour of Caro's, she catches the words in time. 'But it was always being shaved off, because of the lice.'

'Marvellous!' he says again. 'May I make notes, so that I don't forget?' He is interviewing her now, as purposefully as if he were preparing one of his television programmes, but Lady Ainslie does not after all object. Later on she will ask casually about the old man's life now, and perhaps also discover more about the years between than is public knowledge.

There are, of course, questions which she will not be willing to answer, but her young inquisitor is confining himself to the village of Kingsgelding and its inhabitants in the first two decades of the century. At last, realizing that she is tiring, he puts away his notebook and pen.

'There is that other subject I'd like to discuss with you at some point, if you'll allow me, Lady Ainslie. One of the most important incidents in my grandfather's life. The Impney libel action.'

'I'm afraid I don't remember much about that. My memory –'

'Your memory is extraordinary, if I may say so. The details you've been giving me –'

'It's a well-known fact about the elderly. The events of childhood present themselves far more clearly than something which happened five minutes ago.'

She speaks crisply, intending that to be the end of the matter; but Daniel is not to be brushed aside. He leans down to pick up his briefcase from the floor where he originally set it down, and takes from it a bundle of photocopied pages.

'The transcript of the trial,' he says, laying the papers in front of her. 'It would act as a reminder.'

'I don't wish to be reminded.'

140

'Why should that be?' he asks softly. 'After all, if anybody won, it was you.' He stands, zipping up the briefcase, and smiles. It is Gil's smile. Martin has Gil's frown, but it is Daniel who has inherited the amused twitch at the corners of the mouth. 'Thank you so very much.' And then he goes, quickly, before she has time to push his pieces of paper back at him.

For a little while after his departure she remains still, and then the arrival of the supper tray provides an interruption. But after it has been removed she feels the emptiness of the evening stretching before her. And no one is watching to see her indulge her curiosity. It is not true, not true at all, that she remembers little about the trial of the libel action, but that does not necessarily mean that her memories are correct. Time distorts, and spoken words in particular rearrange themselves in the mind. 'I wish I had said this' all too quickly becomes 'This is what I said'.

She picks up the transcript and holds it on the palms of her hands for a moment, as though weighing it; unwilling to be reminded and therefore reluctant to read. But the appeal of the past is too strong. She reaches for her spectacles.

On 20 January 1939. Impney v. *Blakey. King's Bench Division of the High Court. Mr Justice Ash presiding.*

The first pages can be flicked through at speed. A record of facts accepted by both sides; sworn as correct and not disputed. Agreed: that to accuse a man of incestuously raping his thirteen-year-old daughter would expose him to hatred, ridicule or contempt and so must be considered defamatory. Agreed: that the enormity of the libel was increased when the man so accused was a public figure of hitherto unblemished reputation. Agreed: that Lord I*****, the subject of the article complained of, was identified as Lord Impney by his friends and by members of the public, and that it was intended by the writer and publisher of the article that this should be the case. Agreed: that the article was published in a magazine called *The Investigator* and that Mr Gilbert Blakey, its owner and editor, was legally responsible for all statements printed in it, whether or not he had written them himself.

A defence of justification was entered. Mr Blakey submitted that the words complained of were true; and fair comment on a matter of public interest, because of Lord Impney's standing as a public figure. Since the only matter remaining at issue was the truth of the libel, the defence applied for leave to open its case first, and this was granted.

At last Lady Ainslie's fingers, turning the pages, reach the point at which she makes her first appearance on the courtroom stage. There is no description in this transcipt; no speculation about the emotions of the actors in the drama. Only a series of questions and answers. Yet the words alone are enough to re-create the scene in her imagination. As though looking through the eyes of the reporter she sees herself at the age of thirty-four. Stepping into the courtroom. Witness for the defence.

Twenty-two

The date: 20 January 1939. The first witness for the defence answered to her name and stepped into the witness box. All signs of her recent confinement were corseted away and her slim figure was neatly, expensively dressed in navy blue and white.

Oh, what thought, what doubts had preceded the choice of that outfit! The special jury would be composed of citizens of substance, property-owners. She must impress them first of all as a competent professional woman, but at the same time must subtly make it clear that she was of the same or even a superior class to themselves. They might, as the evidence unfolded, be tempted by one lawyer or another to see her as a venal figure working on the shadowy fringes of the law. Her clothes must dispel any such impression. They were smart but not showy. The halo hat was perhaps a little young in style, but its turned-back brim showed to advantage her broad forehead and wide, honest eyes. This was a day on which she must above all appear honest.

As she took the oath, closing her ears to the words she was asked to repeat, her eyes searched the crowded room for the most important of the participants. The rows of counsel, silks and juniors in wigs and gowns, would have to be sorted out as they began to question her. Behind them sat their clerks, scribbling notes and ready to pass forward papers, but she paid no attention to these. The only familiar face amongst the lawyers was her husband's. Richard had warned her that he had no automatic right to be heard, but would have to ask the indulgence of the judge if he felt that the questioning of his client was damaging.

The judge himself appeared impassive, his eyes half closed as though he were tempted to sleep. But two other pairs of eyes were fixed on her. Lord Impney's were hostile. He still held her responsible for his being forced to bring this case to salvage his reputation. She had tried to reassure him, but he could not feel certain what she was going to say. And Gil. Gil was smiling at her as though to remind her that they were friends, lovers; that their recent quarrels were of no importance; that he trusted her to tell the truth because he knew that she always told the truth. The witness for the defence did not return his smile.

There was one other man of importance somewhere in the courtroom; sure to be. The General Medical Council would have sent along an observer to listen to the evidence and to report back to the disciplinary committee. Should she be trapped into admitting the performance of any illegal act she would have to face a second court, to show reason why she should not be struck off the register.

Gil had retained a KC to represent him: Mr Hamilton, a large, confident gentleman who settled his thumbs into the armholes of his waistcoat as he rose to question her. The implications of her very first answer would be of no significance to the barrister, but it would give the smug defendant his first shock of the day.

'You are Doctor Ainslie Anne Dangerfield?'

'That was my maiden name and since my marriage I have continued to use it in my professional life.'

'You are medically qualified?'

'Yes.'

'For the benefit of the jury, would you be kind enough to list your qualifications?'

'I hold the degrees of Bachelor of Medicine and Bachelor of Science from the University of London. I am a Member of the Royal College of Surgeons and a Licentiate of the Royal College of Physicians.'

'And what is your speciality?'

'Gynaecology.'

'In case any members of the jury are not familiar with medical terms, perhaps you would describe more simply what kind of cases you treat.'

'I specialize in the treatment of women with fertility problems. I would describe my field as that of family planning in the broadest sense.'

'You have a consulting room in Harley Street?'

'I have a consulting room in Harley Street and a clinic in Bethnal Green.'

'And do you treat the same conditions in each?'

'In both places I deal with fertility matters, but they tend to present themselves differently. Most of the women who come to see me in Harley Street are anxious to have children but have found themselves unable to do so. There are a great many different reasons for this, and as many different solutions. I do what I can to help them.'

'And in Bethnal Green?'

'My patients there are poor women – the clinic is free – and most of them already have as many children as they can cope with. They are anxious for information on how best to limit the size of their families.'

'In other words, you are prescribing contraceptives?'

'Yes. My clinic has the approval of the National Birth Control Council of which, as I'm sure you know, Lady Denman is the chairman and Sir Thomas Horder the president.'

'Not everyone, of course, approves of contraception. Can you tell the jury – very briefly – the reason why it has your support?'

'I believe that every married couple should have the freedom to choose how many children they want, and at what intervals. I believe that poorer people should have access to the methods of control which have been known to the higher class of society for many years. Four hundred women are known to have died last year from the effects of criminal abortion, and the true number is probably much greater. I believe it's better to prevent an unwanted pregnancy from ever beginning.'

'And do the contraceptives ever fail, Dr Dangerfield? Or are there perhaps women who don't learn about them in time? They come to your clinic then, I suppose, to ask that you should use a more drastic method of limiting their families.'

'I don't understand you.'

'There must be many occasions when you are asked to end an unwanted pregnancy.'

'Are you talking about abortion? My patients in Bethnal Green are very well aware that abortion is illegal.'

'But they need help. They're desperate. And you are there, with your expertise and your clinical facilities.'

'They daren't come to me, because they know that I would have to report such a request to the police. I *ought* to be allowed to help them; but I may not. So instead they continue to use the remedies which have been handed down by word of mouth for generations. Would you like me to tell the jury what these desperate women do to prevent the food being taken from the mouths of their five or six or seven children by the necessity of feeding another baby? Shall I describe the gin and the gunpowder, the boiling water and the jumping down stairs, the knitting needles and the crochet hooks and the terrible, terrible infections which result?'

Mr Justice Ash, intervening: 'I doubt if the jury wish to hear such unpleasant details, Dr Dangerfield.'

'If I'm to be asked general questions about my medical practice, my lord, I can only answer by referring to the facts.'

Mr Justice Ash: 'Then I must ask Counsel for the Defence to confine his questions to relevant matters.'

Mr Hamilton, KC: 'I sympathize with your lordship's distaste. Unfortunately, the matter which is the subject of this case is distasteful, and there is no way of avoiding it. It will become apparent, I think, that this line of questioning is both relevant and necessary.'

Mr Justice Ash: 'Very well.'

Mr Hamilton: 'You've said, Dr Dangerfield, that many lives are lost each year as the result of criminal abortion. Could these desperate women have been saved if they had been helped instead by someone like yourself?'

'In many cases, yes.'

'It's clear from your tone of voice that your feelings on this subject, and your sympathies, are very strong. There must be times when you're tempted to give the help which is needed, in order to prevent a tragedy of the kind you've described.'

146

'I'm certainly tempted, but I have to resist the temptation. Were I to break the law and perform an abortion I should go to prison. And in addition I should lose my licence to practise and with it my ability to help other women with different problems. My patients understand my situation. They don't ask what they know I must refuse.'

'So what do they do?'

'They go to the back street abortionists. The next day they're haemorrhaging or infected. If they go to hospital, the police will ask who is responsible. So the women *are* sometimes brought to me then, to save their lives. The pregnancy is already over by that time. There's nothing to prevent me from checking a haemorrhage or stitching a tear. In fact, it's my duty to do what I can.'

'Are you saying that there are no circumstances in which you would treat a pregnant woman who as a result of your treatment would no longer be pregnant?'

'You express yourself very neatly, Mr Hamilton! No, I'm not saying that. A high proportion of the women who consult me have some abnormality of the womb or genital area: that is why they come to me. Very frequently such an abnormality is only discovered when they first become pregnant. For example – my lord, if I am to answer Mr Hamilton's question accurately, I must give examples, and they may again seem distasteful.'

Mr Justice Ash: 'I think I have caught Defence Counsel's drift by now. Since I see where he is leading us, we must not allow squeamishness to obstruct the path. However, you may find it possible, Dr Dangerfield, to produce your examples without going into too much anatomical detail?'

'I will try, my lord. For example, then, there is a condition known as ectopic pregnancy. It is not possible for a live baby to be born from such a state, but if it, the pregnancy, is allowed to continue for more than a short time it presents a grave hazard to the health of the mother and would in the end prove fatal. In such a case surgical intervention is imperative and urgent. An operation is performed to save the mother's life. The effect of it is to end the pregnancy, but that is not the primary intention. Indeed, the baby may have been greatly desired. With the

147

exception of one or two members of the Roman Catholic faith, I can think of no surgeon who would hesitate to operate in these circumstances.'

Mr Hamilton: 'This condition is presumably an unusual one.'

'It's estimated that one pregnancy in every four hundred is ectopic. That's in the country as a whole. But of course amongst the pregnant women who consult me the proportion is higher, because I rarely see what might be called normal cases.'

'Let us now come a little nearer to the subject of the action under trial. The jury, I'm sure, has been left in no doubt of the sympathy you feel for any woman who finds herself expecting a baby she doesn't want. That sympathy must reach its height when the woman concerned is a victim of rape, a child, an innocent victim.'

'I try not to make moral judgements in my work, Mr Hamilton. A woman who has twelve children and is trying to limit her family by abstinence from sexual activity may be raped by her husband.'

'That is a by-way which we need not explore at the moment.'

'It's part of the answer to your question, though. I'm not allowed to help *anyone* rid herself of an unwanted baby, whether she's a raped child or a harassed mother.'

'That may not be quite true any longer, may it? I'm sure you're familiar, Dr Dangerfield, with the Bourne case.'

'Yes.'

Mr Justice Ash, intervening: 'The jury may not be so well acquainted with the details, Mr Hamilton.'

'I'm grateful for the reminder, my lord. Members of the jury, Mr Bourne is an eminent surgeon of the highest reputation. He has recently been required to face a criminal trial for abortion, after he terminated the pregnancy of a fourteen-year-old girl who had been raped by a group of Guardsmen. The operation was performed without any attempt at secrecy and, indeed, Mr Bourne reported the matter to the police himself so that a test case could be brought and defended. In the event, he was acquitted. This is well known to you, Dr Dangerfield.'

'It is now. The events which are at the heart of today's case took place, of course, before the result of that prosecution was known. It was because the position in law was not clear that Mr Bourne courageously offered to test it.'

'So now, if a thirteen-year-old girl were to be brought to you, pregnant as a result of rape, you would feel able to help her?'

'I should take legal advice. I know a great deal about the workings of women's bodies, but nothing about the law. It's certainly my impression that a precedent has been set, but I should look for reassurance from a lawyer, in case the outcome might be affected by some difference of circumstances which might be trivial in medical terms but important in the eyes of the law.'

'You show a very proper caution, Dr Dangerfield. But I think the jury may conclude, may it not, that your attitude, in today's climate of opinion, would in general be sympathetic? That you would look for reasons to help rather than reasons for turning the girl away?'

'Yes.'

'And even before the Bourne case, your sympathy would have been the same although your anxieties might have been greater?'

'That's a hypothetical question.'

'I'm only asking you to repeat that you would have looked for a way of helping rather than for a reason to refuse. And that as a result of the judgement in that very important case, you would now no longer feel that you were putting yourself at risk by admitting the fact.'

The witness was silent.

Mr Justice Ash: 'You must answer the question, Dr Dangerfield.'

Dr Dangerfield: 'It's too general. All my patients, and their circumstances, are different.'

Mr Hamilton: 'Then let us take a particular case, the case we are all here to discuss. On the morning of March 7th last year –'

'My lord, I must object. It is quite impossible for me to discuss individual patients. To mention personal details of my clients in public, and with press reporters in attendance! Anyone who comes to consult me expects me to respect her confidence, and I must do so.'

Mr Justice Ash: 'This is your own witness, Mr Hamilton.'

'I understand her scruples, my lord. I would hope that they can be removed if your lordship would give a ruling.'

Mr Justice Ash: 'I have to tell you, Dr Dangerfield, that a doctor cannot appeal to the confidence of the confessional. The interests of justice override any qualms you may feel about the betrayal of secrets. You are required to answer the question.'

Dr Dangerfield: 'What is the question?'

Mr Hamilton: 'On the morning of March 7th, 1938, you examined a thirteen-year-old girl whom we shall call M.'

'It's a little late in the day to try to protect her anonymity. If the law requires me to betray confidences, then yes, I examined a thirteen-year-old girl called Margaret.'

'Did you discover, as a result of your examination, that Margaret was pregnant?'

'No.'

'Do you mean by that that the confirmation of her condition came later, as a result of tests?'

'No. I mean that I discovered that she was not pregnant.'

'I have to remind you, Dr Dangerfield, that you are on oath. I will ask the question again. Please think very carefully before you answer. If you are trying in some way to protect your patient –'

'It's certainly true that Margaret was brought to see me in the fear that she might be pregnant: she had been suffering from abdominal pains at monthly intervals. I was able to assure her father that these fears were groundless. There was another reason for the pains.'

Mr Hamilton: 'My lord, this witness is attending court under subpoena. It was assumed that her original refusal to give evidence was on the grounds of breach of confidentiality. It appears that I must ask for her to be recognized as a hostile witness.'

Mr Justice Ash: 'I note the request and will explain it to the jury when the time comes. Dr Dangerfield, the true facts of this case are what I, and everyone else in this courtroom, are here to find out. I have no knowledge of them until they are proved. Counsel suggests that you are not stating the truth as it is known to him and as he believes it is known to you. It is my duty to point out to you that perjury is a very serious offence, punishable

150

with all the force of the law. Let us hope that some simple misunderstanding has caused confusion.'

Dr Dangerfield: 'I must again ask the jury's indulgence if I mention medical details that they might prefer not to hear. Margaret was suffering from a condition known as haematocolpos. This was caused by an imperforate hymen. To put it simply, Margaret had reached the age of puberty but there was an obstruction to the normal menstrual flow, leading to the retention of blood in the womb. With every month that passed, her discomfort – and the appearance of swelling – became greater. Her father's fears were understandable, but I was able to tell him that they were groundless. At the time of my first examination of his daughter, she was a virgin.'

Mr Justice Ash: 'The Counsel for the Defence appears to be rendered speechless! It would appear that he has failed to observe the first rule of advocacy – never to ask a question without knowing the answer in advance.'

Mr Hamilton: 'Since the witness was reluctant to appear in court, I had no opportunity to hear her evidence in advance. But I have reason to believe that what she has just said is untrue. Dr Dangerfield, you say that Margaret was a virgin when you examined her. If another doctor were to examine her now, would you expect your findings to be confirmed?'

Dr Dangerfield: 'No. Not if you define virginity in terms of an intact maidenhead. In order to cure her condition it was necessary for me to cut the hymen and stretch the cervix, and I performed this operation two weeks after first examining her.'

Mr Justice Ash: 'Do you propose to introduce the girl Margaret as a witness, Mr Hamilton?'

Mr Hamilton: 'No, my lord. Margaret now lives in Kenya with her aunt and I would think it wrong to inflict the ordeal of cross-examination on a child. In any case, it's unlikely that she understood the nature of the operation performed on her.'

Mr Justice Ash: 'So how do you propose to deal with a statement from your own witness which appears to undermine the defence of truth on which your case depends?'

Mr Hamilton: 'I shall be forced to prove that she is deliberately

151

deceiving the court, my lord. Dr Dangerfield, did you ever discuss the details of this case with anyone?'

Dr Dangerfield: 'The matron of the clinic –'

'The clinic's records appear to set down details of nursing care and costs accurately enough, but refer to your own case notes for particulars of the operation. Since you are producing a new version of the facts to the court, we must suppose that your notes have been altered to support them. But at the time, did you mention the case in private conversation?'

'Certainly not. I've tried to make clear that I regard everything said in my consulting room as private.'

'But you made a private record of the true facts, did you not? I am asking you, Dr Dangerfield, whether you kept a diary during the period under investigation?'

'If I did, it was for my own eyes only.'

'My lord, if the details which Dr Dangerfield wrote down at the time support what she has just told the court, it is difficult to see why she should object to producing them.'

'I do object most strongly, my lord. On behalf both of my patients and of myself. It's a matter of principle. The right to privacy.'

Mr Justice Ash: 'I think we have to assume, Dr Dangerfield, that your privacy has been invaded before this. You must suspect already that someone has read your diary. Whether the jury may consider that to be a shameful act is beside the point. We are concerned here to learn the truth. I instruct the witness to inform the court whether she kept a diary covering the period in question and, if so, where it is.'

Mr Hamilton: 'We are waiting.'

Dr Dangerfield: 'It is in a safe deposit box.'

Mr Justice Ash: 'How can it be recognized?'

'It's the only notebook there.'

Mr Hamilton: 'According to my instructions, my lord, the notebook in question is a child's exercise book with a dark green cover. The third entry in the book is that for Monday March 7th, of last year. It opens with a reference to a patient calling himself Mr Green and alludes to an event which took place when "Mr Green" was dressed up as Father Christmas.'

Mr Justice Ash: 'Oh, Mr Hamilton, you are throwing out a bait to the gentlemen of the press! Well, I suggest that counsels for the plaintiff and for the defendant each nominate a representative to go together and take possession of the diary. Dr Dangerfield may accompany them if she wishes. If not, she is to provide them with the key and a letter of authority. We will adjourn for lunch now and extend the adjournment for half an hour to allow the diary to be brought to the court.'

Usher: 'All rise!'

Twenty-three

So absorbed is she in the record of the libel action that Lady Ainslie, propped up by pillows in her hospital bed forty-nine years later, is almost brought to her feet as she reads the usher's words.

'All rise!' Time for the lawyers to chat good-humouredly over a more leisurely lunch than usual. Time for the judge to read a book or complete a crossword puzzle. Time in which the plaintiff and the defendant take care to avoid each other: Gil puzzled but ultimately confident, Lord Impney puzzled and uncertain. And time in which she herself, dry-mouthed with terror, must continue to act the part of a self-assured professional woman. Unable to swallow any food, she sipped alternately from glasses of wine and water while Richard, across the table, tucked into steak and kidney pie. Please God, let Gil decide to settle, let Lord Impney be run down by a bus, let the luncheon adjournment last for ever.

The luncheon adjournment ended. The witness for the defence returned to the box.

Mr Justice Ash: 'Have you secured your evidence, Mr Hamilton?'

'Not yet, my lord, but – ah, here they come now.'

'Bearing, I observe, a notebook with a dark green cover. Before offering it as evidence, you will doubtless wish to assure yourself that it contains the entry for the date in question and that the activities of Father Christmas are where you expect to find them.'

'Thank you for your consideration, my lord. Yes, the reference to Father Christmas . . . If I may crave your lordship's indulgence, I would like to consult my client briefly.'

Lady Ainslie lays the transcript down on the sheet. If looks could kill! She remembers, will never forget, the look in Gil's eyes after he had puzzled over the entry, turned to the first and last pages, stared again at the one all-important page, holding it up to the light, feeling for any trace of cutting or pasting. By the time he raised his head again he had accepted defeat in this battle. His unforgiving eyes told her that the war between them would not end on this side of the grave.

That stare of his was expected and she met it steadily, waiting as though the proceedings were no concern of hers until counsel should address the bench again.

Mr Hamilton: 'My lord, I am instructed by my client to claim that the evidence has been tampered with.'

Mr Justice Ash: 'May I see? Is this the notebook in which he expected to find a particular entry?'

'It greatly resembles it. But the entry has been altered.'

'I see no signs of alteration. There is no crossing-out or rewriting. And the entries before and after are for the appropriate dates.'

'Nevertheless, my client, who has seen the original diary, will give evidence when he takes the stand that an alteration has taken place. In the meantime, it is my submission that this witness has committed perjury and that no reliance can be placed on her evidence. I have no further questions.'

'Counsel for the Plaintiff?'

Mr Hart, KC: 'Dr Dangerfield, I remind you that you are still under oath. Do you recognize this notebook as your diary?'

'Yes.'

'In which you recorded the events of March 7th on the day they occurred?'

'On that day or the next. Sometimes I'm tired in the evenings.'

'Members of the jury, until this morning the plaintiff was not aware that this diary existed. I myself have had no opportunity to look at it. But so strong is my belief that the defamatory article written by the defendant has no basis in fact, that I propose to enter this notebook in evidence and – without pausing to approve or censor its contents – ask the witness to read aloud the entry for March 7th.'

'I must reiterate my protest most strongly, my lord, on the matter of principle.'

Mr Justice Ash: 'We can't keep being held up for this. This is a court of law, not of medical ethics. Kindly read the entry aloud to the jury.'

'Very well, my lord. This is the entry for Monday March 7th, 1938.

First 'patient' this morning was a man. So rare, this, that I found myself remembering Gil's appearance here, and smiling. The smile surprised 'Mr Green' into thinking I'd recognized him; and after a moment or two I did. His photograph was at the top of a charity appeal which came at Christmas. Homes for orphaned children. He seemed from the appeal literature to be a figurehead president of the charity as far as I remember, presumably chosen for extreme respectability – peer of the realm, chairman of a bank, lay member of the Church of England Synod.

Hadn't come to ask me for money, though. Instead, wanted assurance that everything would be confidential. Said his thirteen-year-old daughter was in the waiting room. Had abdominal pains, swelling. He believed she might be pregnant as a result of rape. Didn't want to discuss it in front of her, since she's young for her age, and innocent; no suspicions herself. Mother ill in Switzerland (sanatorium? asylum?); no female relatives in England to give advice; only one aunt, in Kenya.

Rape details – gardener's boy – sounded unlikely. Not reported to police.

Asked receptionist to bring M. up and examined her in anteroom. Extraordinarily beautiful girl; long blonde hair, rosebud complexion. Early puberty; breasts developing. Not just young, but mentally retarded. I chatted before I examined her. Where did she feel pains? Down here, as if someone had bounced on her tummy. But she wasn't supposed to talk about that part of her body.

Assured her that she could tell me because I was a doctor and that was why her father had brought her here. When did she first feel the pain? On Christmas Eve. She kept herself awake to see Father Christmas bring her stocking, and it hurt all the time she was waiting. Did she tell Father Christmas? No, because she was supposed to be asleep, and knew that Father Christmas was really Daddy dressed up.

Was she frightened of her Daddy? No, she loved him more than anyone else in the world. But she didn't want him to know she was naughty, keeping awake.

Had the pain happened again since then? Yes. It had spoilt her birthday party (26 January), and had come back again about a week ago. That was when she told her Daddy.

Examined her on couch. Straightforward case of imperforate hymen. No possibility of pregnancy.

Took blood and urine samples for testing in case mental condition has treatable cause. Sent her down to the waiting room while I talked to 'Mr Green'. Agreed to operate.

Some discussion of M.'s future; risks to beautiful girl with limited intelligence. Asked if mother's illness was mental; yes. Suggested that Mr G. should make legal guardianship arrangement with some female relative. M. will start regular menstruation after the operation; will need care. Should be protected against pregnancy. He agreed. Will ask her aunt to undertake upbringing for next seven years.'

Mr Hart, KC, Counsel for the Plaintiff: 'Thank you, Dr Dangerfield. And that is an accurate account of the consultation?'

'Yes.'

'You objected to having your diary produced in evidence on the grounds that it would infringe the privacy of your patients. Did it not occur to you that in this particular case the plaintiff would have been glad to have known that some truthful record existed? And if he *had* known, and had made the defence aware of the fact, this case would probably have been settled out of court. Your reluctance to give evidence has involved him in a great deal of anxiety and cost.'

'I can answer that in several ways. Although this court may attach little value to my belief that the privacy of medical consultations should be respected, the principle is of the greatest

157

importance to me. Most of my patients would be deeply disturbed at the thought that their personal problems might become public knowledge through a breach of confidentiality on my part. I don't see it as my duty to take sides as between the plaintiff and the defendant. My duty is to my own profession, and to my patients.'

'May I remind you that Lord Impney is one of them.'

'No. My patient was Margaret. There was nothing in the least shameful about her illness, but it distresses me very much that I have been forced to put on public record my belief that she is mentally retarded. The keeping of a personal diary is one of my pleasures, but I can only justify the inclusion of details like that if I can be quite certain that no one but myself will ever read them.'

'I might argue that your principles had a one-sided effect. You were summoned to this court as a witness for the defence and it's clear that in attempting to conceal what you knew to be the truth you were indeed aiding the defence. We must be grateful to his lordship for insisting that the facts should be revealed. I have no more questions, my lord.'

'The witness may step down.'

The photocopied pages which Daniel has brought to the hospital end at this point. They do not record the confrontation which took place a few moments later in the corridor just outside the courtroom.

'You bitch! Do you realize what you've done to me? And you've let that rat out of the trap, to mess up other children's lives. How are you going to enjoy living with that thought?'

Words tumbled and crowded through Ainslie's mind, but she was just able to control her tongue. Whatever she chose to say, whether to defend herself or accuse Gil, would be dangerous. Silence stiffened her back and banished her fear, although Gil was white and trembling with anger as he stepped forward, pressing her against the wall. Were he to hit her, knock her down, it would be a just retaliation: medicine to be taken like a man.

But she was not a man but a woman, and the swineherd's son

158

had adopted some of the habits of a gentleman. Only words attacked her, promising revenge.

'By God, Ainslie, I'll make you pay for this!'

As he turned away she felt a hand on her shoulder. It was Richard, who had been forced to make his way out of a further door. 'All right, darling?'

'No. I'm going to be sick.' She ran for the nearest cloakroom and arrived just in time.

Richard was waiting outside the door as she emerged, white-faced. 'Do you want to stay till the end?'

She shook her head. 'No. My part in it's finished.' But she knew that was true only in the most literal sense. Gil would keep his word and take his revenge one day.

Lady Ainslie lays the transcript down on the sheet. How much, she wonders, does Daniel understand about her evidence at the trial. Does he guess at the reason for it? Does he know what the consequences were? There is no doubt that his campaign to make her remember has been successful, but there is more to the affair than is recorded on these sheets of paper.

It is only when Mr Barnaby stands up at the end of visiting time that she is aware for the first time of his presence. He must have come into the room while all her concentration was on what she was reading. He hesitates before leaving, almost as though he had been hoping for conversation, and nods. It is a nod of acceptance. The hospital bed is no longer occupied by his wife, but by an elderly woman about whom he knows nothing. The door closes behind him.

The pages of the transcript slide from the bed to the floor. Lady Ainslie makes no attempt to retrieve them but lies back on the pillows, tired and troubled.

Twenty-four

That night Lady Ainslie sleeps badly – indeed, hardly sleeps at
all. Is it pain which keeps her awake or wakefulness which makes
her conscious of pain? But no, she tells herself firmly; not pain
but discomfort. Pain is something that makes you scream. This
is no more than an ache somewhere beneath the surgical incision.
Tissues which have been traumatized are perhaps once again
becoming sensitive and protesting about their rough treatment.
Or it may be that a diet of painkilling drugs has been included
amongst the tablets which she swallows without question whenever they are presented to her, and that this has now been
withdrawn.

At five o'clock she abandons the attempt to sleep, puts on her
dressing gown and bedroom slippers and goes to sit by the
window, hoping that the river will have its usual calming effect.

The tide is high, but has recently turned, allowing the water
to rush down towards the sea. Rain must have fallen somewhere
in the west, providing an extra thrust to the current and pressing
it on from its dark, silent passage through the countryside towards
the bright lights of the city. The turbulence of its haste shatters
the reflections of light from the floodlit Victoria Tower, the street
lamps on the Embankment and the green bulbs which decorate
the arches of the bridge. The effect is to increase her restlessness,
and by the time the morning cup of tea arrives she is pacing her
room as though it were a prison cell.

As the ache becomes a throbbing, movement offers the best
therapy. From time to time she walks through the ward to the
day room for the sake of exercise. It will not be too long now,

she hopes, before she is allowed home, and she must be capable at least of climbing the stairs to her own flat.

The discomfort returns whenever she is still. It is as much as she can do not to fidget uneasily during Caro's afternoon visit. At tea-time she confesses to Kathy that she is uncomfortable and half an hour later is brought two tablets to take. It is at this moment that she begins to wonder whether the operation has been successful, or whether there is something she has not been told. But a junior nurse would not know the answer to that. The question can wait until Toby makes his next surgeon's round. Early in the evening she goes back to bed again.

Lesley and Heather come into the room together to take away her supper tray and Lesley lingers after the student has pushed the trolley off towards the lift. She pulls down the blind, although Lady Ainslie would prefer to retain her window view, and tidies the room in a pernickety kind of way. It is easy to recognize that she has something to say.

'Sister told me today that you were a life peeress. I'd thought, you know, that you must be just the wife of a lord, getting the title because of who you married.'

'Is it so shameful, taking the name of the man you marry?'

'Titles are different from names. If you have the system at all, they ought to be earned.'

'Ought to be, yes, I agree. But if the system gives them to wives, it's hardly fair to blame the wives for using them. But perhaps what you really mean is that that sort of wife ought to pay for her privilege. Go into a private hospital, for example.'

It is clear that Lesley means exactly that, but her raising of the subject has been a sort of apology which must be gracefully accepted. 'Titles and money don't necessarily go together,' Lady Ainslie assures her.

'No. Sister told me you were a Socialist.'

'I'm not sure that you ought to generalize from that, either. But in my own case . . . I'm never too proud to pick up my allowance for attending the House of Lords. Why don't you sit down for a moment, if you're allowed to? We don't often have the chance of a chat.' There is something else on the young Australian's mind. Her admission of inverted snobbery about titles is perhaps only a lead into a more important subject.

'You'd be going there every day if you weren't here, would you?'

'When the House is in session, yes. I sit on a good many committees. We look at the details of the bills which are going through Parliament, so that when the debates take place – the bits you can see on television – there are always a few of us who have something useful to suggest.'

'I suppose you're dealing with this new abortion bill, then?'

So that's it! Lady Ainslie looks more closely at the nurse, whose Brontë hairstyle frames such a pugnacious face; but she continues the conversation as though it has no personal relevance to her listener.

'Not yet, no. It's still in the Commons and it may well be defeated there. If it does come up to us, we shall be expected to amend it. Even the sponsor admits that there are special cases which ought to be exempted.'

'It must be one of the things that's changed most within your lifetime, abortion. Or at least, people's attitudes to it.'

'You're right there. When I was young it was expensive, difficult to find, always illegal and usually dangerous. But in an odd way that meant that it was a very black and white affair for a woman in trouble. No grey areas. Either she wanted it or she didn't.'

'And I suppose she usually did.'

'Often. Not always. Rich women sometimes used their condition deliberately to make a good marriage which the young man in question hadn't planned on; although certainly at other times they bought their way out of the mess. Unmarried girls of the lower class – we were allowed to use phrases like that then – didn't always worry as much as you might imagine. They expected the father to marry them, and both parties might refer to themselves as getting "caught", but probably that was what they'd had in mind all along. It runs quite deep in tribal instinct, that a girl should give proof of her fertility to deserve marriage.'

'So who suffered?'

'The middle-class girl. Not allowed to learn about contraception while she was still unmarried. And if the worst happened, the only way to avoid disgrace was to abandon her education or training and accept a shotgun marriage which neither party was ready for. That's the bit that's changed.'

'What?'

'The shotgun marriage.' Lady Ainslie shifts uncomfortably in her bed. 'An unmarried girl who gets pregnant nowadays can't any longer force the father to marry her. In the old days the social pressure was really very strong. Nowadays the man can lean on her to get herself an abortion. He can also say that the whole thing is her fault, because contraception is so much more under the control of the woman than it was fifty years ago. So he has an escape route.'

'I see what you mean.'

'The girl has more choices as well, of course. The stigma of having an illegitimate child used to be so great that most unmarried mothers had their babies adopted. They still can; but now the shame has gone. A girl can have a baby without marrying and bring it up as a single parent, without even telling the father. Or she can have the pregnancy terminated without telling the father that either. So on balance, she's much more in control of her life.'

'Which do you think she ought to do?'

'How can anyone answer that question? Every woman's circumstances are special to herself. Suppose you and Heather were both standing here side by side, both pregnant, both asking yourselves the same first question: do I want to marry the father of my child and settle down to family life? For Heather the particular problem might be that she hasn't finished her training. For you the difficulty might be a quite different one – you're living in a foreign country, you probably don't intend to stay here for ever, you don't want to tie yourself down. And your moral attitudes – yours and Heather's in this hypothetical case – might be as different as your practical circumstances.'

'How do you mean, moral attitudes?'

'Your attitude to the unborn child, your views on the sanctity of life – and of when life starts. A young nurse who got herself into trouble in 1939, say, would go through a period of mental agony while she tried to free herself of an unwanted child; but it would be an agony of fear and practical problems. The need to make choices today, when there are so many more possibilities, may be just as painful. I'm sorry: I seem to be delivering a lecture.'

'I'm very interested. You've guessed, haven't you? That I'm pregnant, I mean.'

'Well, it always seems sensible to answer any questions as though the questioner has a personal interest in the answer.'

'I thought you'd tell me to start by discussing it with my boy-friend.'

'If it's going to be your own decision in the end, it must be your decision in the beginning. If what you decide is that you'll do whatever your boy-friend wants, then it would save time to ask him. But then, whichever way he jumps, you'd be lumbering him with guilt about the consequences. If you decide that you want to marry him, certainly you should talk to him. But to tell him that you're carrying his baby but that you intend to get rid of it is unnecessarily hard, don't you think?'

'Do you approve of terminations, Lady Ainslie?'

'To answer your question in clichés, I would like every baby to be a wanted one. So I approve whole-heartedly of birth control. It saddens me that there should still be a call for abortions when contraceptives are available. But I do understand what terror an unwanted pregnancy can cause. And I believe that a woman should be allowed to decide what she wants to do with something which is part of her body until it's able to live independently of her. When I was young, that was quite a radical attitude, as well as being a criminal one. Nowadays, of course, when everyone talks about the right of the baby to be born, it's hopelessly out of date.'

She is silent for a moment, tired after so much talking; but then looks sharply at the nurse.

'I would never – except for the gravest medical reasons – actually recommend anyone to have her pregnancy terminated. You mustn't think . . . It's an immensely important decision which must always be tested against individual conscience. Guilt can be a very powerful emotion. One woman can be destroyed by the same decision which brings uncomplicated relief to another.'

'It's still the woman you're thinking of, not the baby.'

164

'Yes. You must give me credit for consistency.'

'I feel myself to be the guardian of the baby, even though I never meant –'

'Then that's your answer.' Lady Ainslie smiles, pleased and sympathetic. 'Or your starting point, at least. Don't let yourself be distracted by theories which happen to be fashionable. Look deep into your own thoughts and be sure of what you really believe.'

'Before you were made a baroness, Sister said, you were a doctor. Did people ever ask you this sort of question then? Even though you weren't supposed to help?'

'Oh yes,' says Lady Ainslie. 'Quite often.'

'And what did you –' But Lesley is interrupted by the bell which rings for the end of visiting time. It is one of her duties to go round the ward, encouraging visitors to leave quickly. She smiles in a serious, grateful manner, and goes towards the door, which has been open throughout their conversation.

Mr Barnaby is standing there, leaning against the wall. It is clear to both women that he has been listening. This may not have been intentional, since perhaps he has only been waiting for Lady Ainslie to be alone, but the realization alarms Lesley into irritability.

'Visiting time's over,' she says sharply. 'You can't go in now.' She shuts the door, shuts him out.

On this occasion Lady Ainslie does not attempt to plead a case for him. She is thinking about Lesley, who may be undecided about what she should do, but will find reassurance eventually in the knowledge that whatever happens is from choice. And she is thinking also about other women, long ago, who have found it more difficult to be calm, feeling their bodies taken over by an uncontrollable force, their lives sweeping towards disaster – and carrying others, sometimes, with them.

Twenty-five

Something sinister happened in my Harley Street morning. A first appointment for D.D. Thirty-one. Smart, titled – a duchess – fashionably dressed, hat, shoes, gloves, all just so: an expensive sort of woman. No letter of referral, but often people hear about me from friends, so I thought nothing of that to start with.

She thought she might be pregnant. I examined her, and she is. Told her she didn't really need someone like me. She's fit and healthy. A little above usual age for first baby, but no reason to expect any difficulties. Gave her the name of obstetrician and maternity clinic. Said I really only dealt with problem cases. She said that was why she had come.

'You see,' said the patient. 'I do have a problem. A bad problem.'

She had dressed again by now, taking time to be sure that her appearance was as immaculate as when she first arrived. As she sat on the far side of the consulting room desk, her red-tipped fingers fidgeted nervously with the fastening of her crocodile-skin handbag. Her face, however, remained calm.

'We've been married for eleven years, Archie and I. And for all that time he's been waiting for me to produce an heir. Even before we were married I knew what he'd expect. Naturally. It's the most important thing when there's a title involved, and most of the estate as well. If I don't produce a son, everything will go to his uncle and then to some cousins he can't stand. He's worked at it, you could say, and by now he's not too pleased that I don't seem to be doing my bit.'

'It isn't always a wife's fault,' Ainslie pointed out. 'The fact that you're pregnant now –'

'Makes me wonder,' said the duchess. 'Eleven years, and suddenly it happens. Nothing inside the marriage bed has changed. But outside it . . . There is, you see, another possibility.'

Ainslie saw. She did not regard the morals of the aristocracy as any of her business and made her next comment in a neutral voice.

'Sometimes, when there's a title and a lot of money at stake, a man who suspects that he may be infertile is prepared to accept any baby born to his wife without asking too many questions.'

'That would have been the answer, I suppose, if I'd realized it earlier. To be honest, I didn't even know that men might – I mean, how can you tell? I'd assumed it must be all my fault. Archie kept saying that, and I believed him – that there was something wrong with *me*. That was why I didn't take any precautions when . . .'

Until this moment she had remained calm, almost as though they were discussing the case of someone else. But now she dropped her head to conceal the tears that were swelling in her eyes. 'I've been a fool,' she muttered. 'If this was going to happen, it should have been worked out properly.' She looked up again, weeping without restraint as she tried to justify herself.

'I'd never really enjoyed it, you see. With Archie, I mean. I always went along with it because, well, he had the right. But the idea of deliberately looking for someone else – oh, it would have been disgusting. But then I met this man. I don't know how it happened. I didn't seem to have any common sense left. Whatever he wanted, I wanted. I never knew it could be like that. Exciting. Happy. I don't expect you to understand.'

'I understand,' said Ainslie. 'I suspect it's something that only happens once. The second time, you know what to do to keep control. But the first time – especially if it happens later in life than usual . . . yes, I do understand. Do you think if you talked it over with your husband –'

'No! He'd divorce me. It would give him the chance to look for another wife to have his babies, his own. No one would ever be able to persuade him that he couldn't.'

'I'm only a doctor,' Ainslie pointed out. 'I know about bodies, but I'm not competent to advise you on your behaviour. Is it possible – from the point of view of dates, I mean – that your husband could have fathered the child?'

'Yes. But after eleven years! And you see, it may not look like him.'

'People see likenesses where they expect to see them.'

'But there are some characteristics which can't be inherited from some particular parents.'

'Are you talking about things like blue eyes or red hair? Very few people know how these matters are determined.'

The duchess dabbed at her eyes and sat up straight.

'No,' she said. 'The father, the other possible father – he's gone back to New York now – came over here for a month with a jazz band. I'm talking about black skin. Or khaki, at least.'

The two women faced each other in silence until the duchess spoke again.

'If I could be certain that the baby would be white, then I wouldn't worry. My husband would accept it, I'm sure, as you were suggesting earlier, because he wants it so much. But . . . Is there any way in which you can find out about the colour before it's born?'

'I'm afraid not.'

'Then I can't risk it. I'll have to get rid of it.'

'I'm afraid I can't help you with that.'

'Why not? You do that sort of thing.'

'No, you're mistaken if you think that.' The alarm that she felt at this direct request prompted Ainslie to be more than usually cautious. Eight weeks had passed since the end of the action in which Gil had been found guilty of libel, and the damages and costs awarded against him had forced him into bankruptcy. She had anticipated a more violent reaction than merely the few bitter words which he spat out at their last meeting. Was it possible that Gil might have sent this woman along as an *agent provocateur*, carefully prepared with a story of

168

his own invention? Did this dukedom really exist? She could hardly ask her patient to wait while she consulted Debrett, but it was odd that her face should not be familiar from the pages of *The Tatler*.

'What I can do, if you like, is to arrange for the baby to be adopted,' she said.

'A black baby? That wouldn't be easy, would it? Anyway, it's not what I want. I'm not prepared to spend the rest of my life wondering whether my child is being well looked after. I don't want it ever to be born.'

'I'm sorry,' Ainslie said firmly. 'But it's illegal, as well as dangerous, to terminate a pregnancy.'

'Not always. There was that case last year when the surgeon was acquitted.' The duchess – if she was a duchess, and not merely an actress – had passed through her tearful phase and was arguing forcefully.

'There's a good deal of difference between a married woman having an affair and a young girl suffering multiple rape. And as a consequence of that case judges are becoming stricter just because they don't want to give the impression that anyone can perform an abortion and get away with it.'

'It doesn't need to be called that. I'm only asking for a D and C.'

'I can't imagine why you should have thought that I'd be able or willing to help you,' said Ainslie. She genuinely wanted to know the explanation; but the answer came as an explosion to shatter her peace of mind.

'I read your advertisement. It seemed plain enough to me, since I know you can't say in so many words what you're offering. I called the number once before I made this appointment, and the receptionist gave me your name. Naturally, I'd heard of your reputation, Dr Dangerfield. I knew I'd be in good hands.' By now her anxious voice combined appeal and indignation, but Ainslie was no longer listening to what she said. Her attention had stopped on one word.

'Advertisement!' Hardly aware of her own movement, she stood up and leaned forward with her hands pressing down on the desk to support her. 'What advertisement?'

'In *The Lady*. I was looking for a housekeeper, actually. Your

169

notice was mixed up with domestic staff. "Qualified gynaecologist offers discreet help to women with problems."'

'I've never placed any such advertisement. You must be aware that doctors are strictly forbidden to advertise.'

If Ainslie was appalled, the duchess was angry.

'I'm hardly likely to have invented it, am I? It gave your telephone number.'

'There are about thirty doctors who work from this address. We all share the waiting room and reception facilities. I only rent this consulting room one day a week.' She had reduced her working hours since the birth of her baby.

'And it gave your initials, as well. Dr A.D. So that anyone would know who to ask for.'

'I'll have to look into it,' Ainslie said. 'This could be a very serious matter for me. In the meantime, I'm sorry that your time has been wasted. I must ask you to accept my assurance that I had nothing to do with the placing of any advertisement.'

The duchess also stood up, as alarmed as the doctor.

'I wouldn't have come here if it hadn't been for the promise of discretion. What I've told you –'

'Will remain completely confidential. You can rely on that.' She tore the notes she had made into little pieces.

'Well, the least you can do, if you won't help me yourself, is to tell me where to go instead.'

Ainslie shook her head. She was perfectly well aware of what went on in a certain country clinic which claimed to provide treatment for women suffering from stress, but her awareness of danger in this case was too strong to let her reveal the address. As soon as her patient had left, frustrated, she went down to the receptionist's office on the ground floor.

'If anyone telephones and tries to make an appointment to see me, but only knows my initials, turn them away, will you?'

'There've been three of those already this week. When I asked them for the name of their doctor, two of them rang off. This is the third one.' She turned the pages of one of the many diaries ranged in front of her and pointed. 'She sounded upset when I said you couldn't give her an appointment for five weeks, so I took her number in case there was a cancellation.'

170

'Tell her I shan't be able to see her, will you, please? Ask her to get her doctor to recommend someone else. And from now on make it clear to anyone who telephones that she *must* have a letter of referral.'

'Certainly, Doctor. Your next patient is waiting.'

'Send her up in two minutes.' It was impossible to step aside from the timetable of a busy day, or to give each patient less than full attention. Only when the last one had left did Ainslie begin to pace round the room, wondering what to do. It was tempting to telephone the editor of *The Lady*. But how many other magazines might be involved, and how could she possibly trace them?

Richard would help her. Richard, calm and sensible, would help her to control her panic. She must wait until she could talk to him.

When he returned home that evening from a late division in the House of Commons, he was pleased to find her waiting up for him, and began to tell her how the vote had gone. But within only a few seconds he recognized her anxiety and paused.

'What's wrong, darling?' He listened with a deepening frown as she told him what had happened that day.

'I could be struck off the register if it was thought I'd been advertising.' It was not really necessary to tell him that. As a lawyer, he was subject to the same sanctions as a doctor; neither of them was allowed to publicize names or services. 'Besides, if someone's doing this deliberately to hurt me, he's going to make sure that the General Medical Council gets to hear of it, isn't he? He won't just wait for them to notice it themselves.'

'Who would want to get you into that kind of trouble?'

'It has to be Gil Blakey,' said Ainslie miserably. 'He threatened me that day at the law courts. And even if he hadn't, I'd have expected him to get his own back in some way. I cost him so much money. I'm not sorry about that. He deserved it. But just as I was taking my revenge for something he did, I suppose he feels it's his turn to take revenge now. Could go on for ever, couldn't it?' She tried to laugh, but failed.

'Anyone can put an advertisement in a paper and no one can

171

prove it was you if it wasn't. Do you think your woman this morning was genuine?'

'I've looked her up. There is someone of that name, that age, no children. And I didn't offer her any treatment. But of course there may have been others before her. There was a diplomat's wife who came last week without a referral. She said she didn't have a doctor in this country and anyway their system was to go straight to a specialist.'

'Did she want an abortion as well?'

'No. She had an ovarian cyst. Painful. Quite genuine.'

'There are two separate dangers, you see,' Richard pointed out. 'Best to look them both straight in the face. The advertising could get you struck off the register. But it's worse than that. It gives the definite impression that you're offering abortions. If you have in fact performed anything that could be interpreted as *being* an abortion, you could be in real trouble. With the police, I mean. Think carefully. Are there any doubtful cases at all?'

'Not since the libel action. I've known from that moment that I must be especially careful. Before that, yes, one or two. Well covered up. The women themselves aren't likely to sneak. I did them a big favour because they were so distressed.'

Richard was silent for a little while. His advice, when it came, was definite.

'You must get in touch with the magazine at once, to make sure the advertisement doesn't appear again – and to find out, if you can, who put it in. And then I think you'll have to take the initiative in approaching the GMC. As you said, anyone who's deliberately trying to hurt you will make sure that the Council learns about it anyway, so there's no point in hoping that they never notice. There's a solicitor I know who specializes in medical affairs. I'll get him to write a letter telling the GMC what's happening and that you're taking all possible means to stop it and to discover the culprit and will then take appropriate legal action. Or whatever else he advises. So don't worry about it any more. Let's go and say goodnight to my beautiful boy.'

He put his arm round her waist as they went upstairs and stood for a moment in the nursery, smiling down at baby Leonard. Then he turned his smile towards Ainslie.

172

'Time for bed. And don't worry. We'll put it all right tomorrow.'

Ainslie smiled back trustingly, and was happy in his arms.

But the next day proved to be too late. Waiting for her on the table when she came down to breakfast was a letter from the General Medical Council.

Twenty-six

It is no longer an ache. No longer a throbbing. No longer the burning feeling which at the arrival of the drugs trolley on the previous evening has prompted Lady Ainslie to mention – without making too much of it – her discomfort. More painkillers and a sleeping pill have at least given her a night's sleep. But she awakens to the feeling that a scorpion is crawling along her gut, stinging – do scorpions sting? Or bite? – as it goes. It is as much as she can do not to cry out as her eyes open to the awareness of pain.

As soon as she has drunk her cup of tea she makes her way to the private bathroom, stooped like an old witch as though hunching over the wound will help to contain the agony. After performing her morning toilet she looks round for a mirror, but the only one on offer is fixed to the wall above the washbasin. Never mind; there is a tiny hand mirror in her handbag. She experiments with levels on which to prop it up until she is satisfied and then takes a step backwards and lifts up her nightdress.

The shape and texture of her own body has never been of great interest to Lady Ainslie. Perhaps it is her time as a medical student, dissecting anatomical specimens, which has made her think of a body, almost any body, as a mass of complicated mechanisms rather than an object of beauty. So she studies her own elderly, worn-out skin now with scientific curiosity rather than distaste or sadness at the loss of youth.

No medical training is required to tell her that all is not well. The bruising caused by the surgical clips can still be seen, although by now it has faded from purple to a marbled yellow on

174

black. Around it, like an island almost bisected by a straight but jagged range of mountains, is a circular area of smooth skin which is dark red and hot to the touch.

Lady Ainslie prods the patch cautiously, but any tenderness is deeper inside her body. On her way back to bed she stops to read the notes clipped to the end of the bed and finds them of little interest. How long is it, she asks herself, since anyone has troubled to examine her, as distinct from taking her pulse and temperature?

Far too long. Waiting in bed for breakfast she finds herself becoming angry at what appears to be neglect. Is it her own fault? She is continually asked how she is feeling, and usually replies with cheerfulness. After all, no one in hospital is in perfect health; it would be intolerable if every enquiry were to be met with a repetition of all symptoms. She remembers, too, that when Toby arrived with his train of medical students on her 'crying day' he tactfully diverted their attention by talking about general after-effects of surgery rather than her particular operation.

But the pain had not started then; not this burning feeling as of a red hot poker pressing and twisting inside her. It is not Toby's fault but the nurses' that she has been left to make a fuss about her own condition. Thinking it unfair to delay the night nurses who are hurrying to finish all their duties before handing over to those on day duty, Lady Ainslie waits until her breakfast tray is collected before asking to see the house surgeon.

Half an hour passes before Kathy, her messenger, returns.

'Mr Graham and Sister are both in a ward meeting. And at ten o'clock they'll be doing Mr Mallinson's round with him. I'll try and catch one of them in between, if you like. Or shall I ask Staff to come?'

'I'll wait for Mr Mallinson.'

Two long hours pass before he arrives. Sister, Staff and Mr Graham, ready to provide information and accept instructions, follow him into the room but stand two paces behind as he approaches the bed and smiles.

'How are you this morning?'

'Not too good.' Lady Ainslie's body is arched in an effort to

175

find a comfortable position. Her shoulders are tense, her fists clenched. She can feel that her face is flushed.

Her answer is not at all what Toby expects, since he knows her not to be a grumbler. He frowns as he pulls down the sheet, and is less meticulous than usual about arranging the bedclothes to conceal all except the area to be examined. His frown deepens as his fingertips gently rest on her skin.

'How long has it been like this?'

'I only saw it this morning. Before that, I haven't been looking.'

From his pocket he takes a fibre tip pen and draws round the outside edge of the reddened area. The touch of the pen is gentle, but cold. Lady Ainslie tries to laugh.

'Here be dragons. Like a map.'

Toby is not laughing. Without turning round he lifts a finger to call his underlings closer.

'We have an infection here. How much would you say, Sister, that it has spread in the past twenty-four hours? Mr Graham?'

They have no idea. Their silence speaks for them honestly, while Toby's own silence as he waits for an answer has a quality all of its own. His eyes are cold as he looks up. Even as his patient, Lady Ainslie has never seen him in his authoritarian surgeon's mood before, because he has always smiled at her as a friend. 'I'll be back in a moment,' he says now, pulling up the sheet and marching out of the room with his entourage at his heels.

The procession does not move far away. She can hear the angry tone of the surgeon's voice, although except for one exclamation – 'Nobody?' – it is impossible to distinguish the words he speaks. Before long he returns.

'We'll put you on a course of antibiotics. The wonder-workers. Clear you up in no time.' The coldness has disappeared from his voice. It is the business of a surgeon to be reassuring to his patients; a martinet only to his underlings.

'What caused it?'

'If we could answer that, it would be a revolution in health care. Hospitals are dangerous places, I fear. The proportion of infections to surgical operations is still far too high.'

'You don't tell the patients that before they come in.'

176

'Well, we do our level best to prevent the trouble arising. And to contain it if it does. These antibiotics really do perform miracles. You'll begin to feel the benefit in six hours. And to cover the gap, I'll make sure that you have a good painkiller.'

'I wonder about painkillers. They make you feel that you're well when you're not. Perhaps they ought to be rationed, so that pain gets a chance to speak up for itself and get noticed.'

She is doing her best to argue a case for the nurses, but it is not a very convincing one. Toby takes her hand for a moment.

'I'll come and see you again this evening. Take things easy today. Bed. Sleep if you can.'

But for the next half hour at least there is no possibility of sleep. Sister comes in person to watch the staff nurse administer the new drugs and both women make it clear without speaking that they have been hurt and angered by a reprimand. In the end Sister can hold her peace no longer.

'Why didn't you complain that you were in pain, Lady Ainslie? There's no need for anyone to suffer in silence. You ought to have told us.'

The fighting answer to that is 'Why didn't you come and look?' But Lady Ainslie is not in a belligerent mood. She feels weak and ill and longs only for her burning body to be cooled so that she can sleep. All the same, she is not disposed to take sole responsibility for her own condition.

'I asked for a painkiller last night.' To her annoyance, her voice is as weak as her body and emerges from her lips with a trace of petulance. 'Might not that have suggested in itself that I was in pain? It hardly seemed necessary to spell out the precise symptoms.'

'Some people live on painkillers for weeks after an operation. How can we be expected to know –'

'You know more than your patients do.' She manages to control the wavering of her voice and make her protest a positive one. 'We – I – come into hospital in the expectation of pain. To be sliced open and sewn up again, of *course* it's going to hurt. What good would it do to complain about that? There are ways of enduring pain. Everyone has her own preferred method. How could I be expected to know when the degree of discomfort first

177

goes off the top of the chart? When it's no longer ordinary and expected but dangerous and unusual? Most people who come into hospital have never had an operation before. We don't know what to expect. But you do.'

'You're not just any ordinary patient, though, Lady Ainslie. You're a doctor.'

The flat statement takes her by surprise and she sighs at its irrelevance even before protesting against the inaccuracy.

'I qualified as a doctor, yes. But that was sixty years ago. And I'm not a doctor now.'

Twenty-seven

Wednesday, 21 June 1939

44 Hallam Street. Such a cosy, domestic-sounding address. Inside, though, it was like living through the same nightmare for a second time. The Council Chamber was set up as a court of law. Only difference, the members of the disciplinary committee were judges and jury at the same time. And I wasn't in the witness box but the dock.

Richard was there, but left the defence to the solicitor, Mr Waring, who takes such cases regularly. A pessimistic man, who warned me in advance that the Council would have disapproved of my prominence in the libel action, even though I was forced to appear against my will. They'd have no legitimate grounds for claiming that I'd been deliberately seeking publicity for the sort of work I described myself as doing, but might start off prejudiced against me. Very cheering!

Prosecuting solicitor, Mr Berry, kicked off with a list of advertisements – including some in women's magazines which our side hadn't tracked down. Mostly using initials, but one with full name, Dr Dangerfield. Produced two doctors and a clergyman who'd seen them, assumed them to be offering abortion service, telephoned the number and were given my name.

Mr B. revealed that since November I'd reduced my Harley Street surgeries to one day a week; claimed this proved I was short of patients and needed to attract more. To my relief, no attempt to suggest that any abortions had actually been performed as a result of the advertisements. Mr Waring told me later that GMC usually leaves it to police to bring such cases, then strikes doctors off automatically after conviction in court. This case rested on the fact that the advertisements had undeniably appeared.

After such businesslike detail, Mr W. was bound to sound vague. Accepting what had been done, it was difficult to prove that I wasn't the one who'd done it. The advertisements we'd traced were all typed and paid for in cash; not unusual, proving nothing either way. First point pleaded was that any doctor would be mad to breach the rules in a way pointing straight to herself and bound to be discovered – one of the notices was in the personal column of The Times! And even madder to suggest publicly the offer of a service which would lead straight to prison. So defence (true!) was that this was a campaign deliberately designed to bring me into disrepute.

One member of Council asked whom we were accusing. Previously agreed that there was no point in naming Gil. He'd naturally deny it, and we couldn't actually prove anything. Nor would it do much for my case or reputation if I argued that he had cause to hurt me because I'd previously lied on oath, to his disadvantage. So Mr W. called me to testify that patients sometimes hoped that I'd terminate pregnancies and became upset and angry when I wouldn't. This bit went well, I thought; positive. But the suggestion that one might have tried to get her own back sounded weak.

Stronger point was that I'd cut back surgery hours deliberately after birth of baby, to have more time at home. Receptionist testified that I turned patients away instead of needing to attract them. Quite optimistic at this point.

Third hope was that enquiry might have been started by an anonymous letter to the GMC, indicating the existence of a spiteful enemy. Mr W. put this directly to the President; but to no avail. The two doctors and the clergyman had all complained.

Only thing left was for me to swear on oath that I had not placed any advertisements, nor caused anyone to place them on my behalf, nor even known that they were being placed. Since all this was true, I felt that they'd have to believe me.

End of evidence. Strangers asked to withdraw. Ten minutes of walking up and down a corridor. Only ten minutes to decide something so important! Richard and Mr Waring didn't say much. Obviously, as lawyers, used to this waiting time and saw no point in speculating

180

about what would soon be known for certain. But I felt hopeful on the whole. Worried still, but hopeful. All I needed was that the truth should be recognized.

Richard told me once, if the jury won't meet your eyes when they come back into court, you've lost. We were the ones who filed back into the chamber, but I ought to have guessed when I saw everyone at the high table shuffling papers or pretending to make notes. Back in the dock to hear the verdict. Careful consideration of the charge: serious offence, liable to bring whole medical profession into disrepute unless immediately shown by disciplinary action to be against the rules demanding high standard of professional conduct.

'Ainslie Anne Dangerfield, the Council's decision is that the Registrar be directed to erase your name.'

Arriving at Hallam Street an hour earlier, I'd tried to make myself expect this, but when it came I was stunned. Couldn't believe it. It was so unfair, when nobody had proved that I'd been responsible for breaking the rules. Richard came across quickly, fearing I might faint, but it hadn't properly sunk in. Outside, I managed to keep my chin up. Press photographers hanging around, though probably not for my case in particular. I wasn't going to let Gil open his newspaper next day and see how devastated I was.

In the taxi going home, all I could think of was my years as a medical student. All those anxieties, long hours, hard work, never enough money because my parents disapproved so much of their daughter working. All for nothing now.

I cried for two hours in the bedroom. Richard left me alone. He always knows the right thing to do.

The long case clock in the hall struck four. Ainslie pushed the damp pillow away from her face, stood up and went into the bathroom to wash her face and brush her hair. There was no need to pretend that this was not a tragedy, but no point in whining on about it. Before going downstairs she paused in the nursery, where Leonard, banging his fists with pleasure, was having rusks and milk for tea.

'Bring him downstairs earlier than usual, will you?' she asked the nurse. 'As soon as he's finished.'

181

Richard was waiting in the drawing room. Taking her in his arms he held her tightly, kissing her face and hair.

'You're marvellous and I adore you,' he said. 'How can you manage to smile? Don't answer that question, because I have to confess how relieved I am that I shall be able to hold up my head in Chambers again. I've never liked to tell you this before, but there's a pretty strong feeling in the circles I move in that a man ought to be able to support his family. I'm the only chap I know who's been sending his wife out to work. Now I can become a regular fellow again.'

'Don't be too sure. It's nice of you to prattle on like this. You're a darling, and I adore you too. But I've had time to think. This may not make too much difference.' They sat down together on a sofa, holding hands. 'I've been struck off on a technical point, you see. It doesn't mean that I'm any worse as a doctor today than I was yesterday.'

'You don't mean . . . You can't go on practising.'

'It's an interesting thing. People don't realize. If the dog breaks a leg, no one but a recognized veterinary surgeon can treat it. But if our baby breaks a leg, anyone can treat it who has our permission to try. As long as we're aware that he isn't on the register, if he isn't.'

'I don't believe it! Really? But even so, darling, you can't –'

'I shall give up the Harley Street practice,' Ainslie said. 'But I don't see why I shouldn't keep on my clinic sessions at Bethnal Green. After all, some of the people who help out in the family planning sessions have only been trained in that specific field, or as nurses. I could go down on days when there's another doctor on the premises, so that any patient would have a choice. And I could put a placard on my desk saying that I'm no longer on the register. That's the only crime, you see, pretending to be registered if you aren't. All my other qualifications are still valid. I don't think anyone can stop me calling myself Dr Dangerfield still. Women who've seen me before would want to stay with me, and I don't believe new callers would mind, either. In any argument of the Us and Them kind, they're always against Them.'

182

Richard continued to look doubtful, forcing Ainslie to press her point.

'It's such a *waste*, Richard, not to use my training. And I'm not used to living as a lady of leisure. I should get bored. And then that would make me bitter and bad-tempered.'

'Clearly we can't have that. But Leonard may need more of your time as he grows. And are you sure, darling, that other doctors would be willing to work with you? I mean, would they be *allowed* to, under the rules?'

'They would if I was only there as a helper, not as a doctor.'

'But you were saying –'

'Yes, I see what you mean. Oh, damn!' The depression which Ainslie thought she had thrown off returned as blackly as before – but Richard was still talking.

'I have an alternative suggestion,' he said. 'A favour, it is, really. About *my* sort of surgery.'

Ainslie knew what he was talking about. He had been elected to the House of Commons in a by-election five months after their marriage, and since then had spent one Saturday afternoon each month in his north-west London constituency.

'Of the people who come to see me, one or two really do need the help of their MP,' he told her now. 'Whatever they're complaining about may be most easily put right by my writing a letter to the appropriate Minister, or asking a question in the House. And then there'll be two or three more who've got in a tangle with some office of the local council and need someone to write a letter that sets the position out more clearly than they can manage for themselves. I do that as well. But for the rest, there tends to be a stream of unhappy people who have something to complain about, but aren't at all sure even what it is, much less who could help them.'

'My God!' said Ainslie. 'You're not suggesting –!'

'I can't tell you what a help it would be. You see, if I ask the agent to do any preliminary weeding out, people get resentful at not being allowed to see their MP. But if they started off by seeing their MP's wife, they'd think they were getting a double dose of attention. You've got a good surgery manner. You're used to extracting medical histories from patients. And as a matter of

183

fact, you probably know a great deal more than I do about how to solve some of the things that worry ordinary people, just from your Bethnal Green clinic.'

'So what exactly do you want?'

'D'you think you could spare one day a week?'

'In that awful office!'

'We could rent something more comfortable.'

'What would I have to do?'

'In theory, you'd be making appointments for constituents who want to see their MP, me. In practice, you'd be trying to solve as many problems as possible without me ever needing to know about them. I've realized, these past few months, what you've probably known for ages. A lot of people can't express themselves very well and don't know where to start when they need to get something done. Very often all that's needed is a form filled in or a letter written, but it doesn't seem anyone's business to help. I'm asking this as a favour to me, but really it would be a marvellous benefit to them.'

Ainslie took her time about replying. It was tempting to dismiss the suggestion as being merely a kindness on her husband's part; something to take her mind off her distress. But what he said struck a chord in her experience. Very often at the end of her clinic sessions in Bethnal Green she had called on a housing officer or a landlord to demand that a roof should be mended or a sewer cleared for the sake of a family's health – and had found that obstructions which had blocked plaintive requests for a year fell before the first blast of an authoritative demand.

Yes, she could be useful. And it might prove more satisfying to undertake a new task with full responsibility than to cling on to an unrecognized status in the medical field. She had seen her own solution as a fighting response, but perhaps after all it would be better to allow one door to close, and to step through another.

While she was considering, the baby was brought down.

'My turn!' demanded Richard. He was not as a rule at home for the regular drawing room playtime. He cuddled the little boy and jogged him on his knees, before beginning to toss him into

184

the air and catch him as he squealed with delight. Only when they were both tired of the game was Leonard put down on the carpet to kick and gurgle.

'I agree,' said Ainslie. 'I'll do it.' It seemed important that the change of direction should become part of the day which had started so disastrously.

'Darling! Have I told you recently that I love you?'

'Not for at least half an hour.' They kissed each other and Ainslie discovered that she could laugh again.

'There's just one piece of unfinished business,' Richard said. 'Gil Blakey. We're never going to prove it, but there's not much doubt, is there, that he's to blame?'

'No doubt at all.'

'Do you want me to go out and kill him quietly for you? Or challenge him to a duel? Or anything?'

Ainslie shook her head.

'I don't want to give him the pleasure of knowing he's hurt me. And I do recognize, of course, that I played him a dirty trick earlier on. Perhaps he's entitled to a revenge.' That was not quite true though, she thought, for her own lies had been in retaliation for Gil's first bad behaviour. 'If any way of getting my own back comes to hand, I shall probably take it. But I don't intend to let hatred ruin my life. I'm not deliberately planning a vendetta.'

'Good,' said Richard. 'To be honest, I faint at the sight of blood.' He bent down towards the baby, holding his finger out to be clutched. 'Leonard's never to know,' he said. 'You're never to tell him that I'm not his father.' The force of his words was unexpected, and so was the implication. He had said nothing before to suggest that he knew who the baby's father was, and Ainslie had been careful not to drop hints.

'I never shall.'

Richard looked up, smiling.

'It will have to be Mrs Johnson who takes the constituency surgery, not Dr Dangerfield,' he pointed out. 'I've been wondering whether there was ever going to be a Mrs Johnson. Will you mind? Then I shall feel myself a regular head of family at last. A man with a wife and child.'

185

She kissed him without speaking, her body flooding with a love which temporarily swept away all thoughts of the day's disaster. For a few moments they clung together. Then, sliding down to the floor, they began to tease and tickle their son.

Twenty-eight

Lady Ainslie is ill.

Instead of being borne along on the cool stream of recovery from successful surgery, she has been tipped into a thermal whirlpool. As she tosses about, seeking comfort, she finds it hard to keep her head above water. Sweat is pouring from her body and chilling her as it dries so that she is hot and cold at the same time.

Nurses come to wash her and to hold her head while she drinks. Both Sister and the house surgeon are frequent visitors. At one moment Caro is in the room, bending over to kiss her, and then is no longer to be seen. Toby returns, stern-faced because he thinks that her eyes are closed. He asks a question, but she does not hear it clearly and answers only with a grunt. If Mr Barnaby pays his usual evening call, she does not notice him.

Although she needs all her mental strength to hold on to herself, to contain all the elements of her body within its skin, her mind itself is calm. Whilst well aware that fifty years earlier this kind of infection might have proved to be a killer, she has complete confidence in the antibiotics which Toby has prescribed. She is even objective enough to recognize with amusement that she is not after all ready to die.

A second night of deep sleep brings her safely to a new day. She feels very thin, very fragile; but calm and cool. When – long before the official beginning of visiting time – the door opens to admit her grandson, wearing his police uniform and frowning anxiously, she is able to greet him with laughter.

187

'Martin, darling! Don't tell me they've dragged you off the beat for a deathbed scene! I can promise you, I'll still be here this evening.'

But Martin, although he gives her an affectionate hug, is not smiling.

'I'm here on duty, in a sense. That's to say, I asked if I could come, because it was you, although of course this isn't my patch.'

'What are you talking about, dear?'

Martin sat down beside the bed.

'It's this black chap who's been coming here. I did warn you, you know.'

'Mr Barnaby? What's happened to him?'

'Your question ought to be, what's he done?'

'All right then. What's he done?'

'He and one of his pals have beaten up one of the nurses here. She works on this ward. An Australian. Nurse Grant. Jumped her as she was going off duty last night.'

'Lesley? Oh, the poor child. Is she badly hurt?'

'I don't know the details of her injuries. But badly enough to have been admitted here as a patient, not just patched up in Casualty and sent home. One of the men kicked her hard in the stomach after she started fighting back. Her friends tell us that she goes to self-defence classes. She seems to have put up quite a good struggle.'

'But what makes you think that Mr Barnaby was involved?'

'She recognized him. She'd seen him in here on the day his wife died, and again with you since then. Both the men were black. They ran away when she screamed and collapsed. But she had time to recognize the one who kicked her in the stomach before she passed out.'

'It doesn't sound right, Martin.'

'It sounds all too right to me. He's a man with a grudge. He's been looking for a chance to take revenge. What better target than an unprotected girl, going along that river walkway in the dark. Hanging around here, he's had plenty of opportunity to find out what hours the nurses work. I know you countermanded my instructions before, Grandmother, but really now you must do what I say. The nurses will call the force in as soon as they see him, of course. But just supposing he manages to slip past without anyone noticing, you're to ring your call bell the moment he comes in here.'

There is something wrong in the picture which Martin has painted, and after a moment or two she recognizes what it is.

'If he really did plan to take revenge, Martin' – she is realistic enough to recognize that this is not impossible – 'he would have done it alone. As a personal gesture. Taking someone else along turns the whole thing into, oh, a sordid petty crime. And a stupid one, attacking someone who can recognize him. I don't believe that he's stupid.'

Martin shrugged his shoulders. 'We'll learn more about that when Nurse Grant is in a fit state to make a longer statement. In the meantime, I want you to promise –'

'I'm sure he won't hurt me, Martin.'

'Perhaps not. Probably not. But there's a warrant out for his arrest. It's your duty as a good citizen, Grandmother. Your finger hard on the call bell as soon as you see him. There'll be a couple of constables somewhere close at hand at least for an hour round about the time when he's been turning up here.'

'If he really did mug her, he won't be fool enough to come back again.'

'All your arguments presuppose that he's a rational, intelligent man. My experience of criminals is that most of them are thick as a plank. I must get back on duty now. I should have asked you, though. Caro said you were having a bad day yesterday. Are you feeling better now?'

'Yes, thank you, darling.' But although that would have been true before Martin's arrival, her mind is as feverish now as her body was on the previous day. Surely Martin's version of events cannot be true.

It has never occurred to her before that her grandson may have racist views, but his willingness to believe the worst of Mr Barnaby is clearly based on skin colour. She is clear-sighted enough to recognize that her own racial attitudes may be equally partial, although her prejudices are the opposite of Martin's. It is perhaps because Mr Barnaby is black that she is too anxious to give him the benefit of the doubt.

This is an approach which she has needed to control in the past, and on occasions like this she reminds herself of the night on which she learned the lesson. After years of battling successfully with the local councils in her constituency to give immigrants an equal share with the natives in the better grade of council housing, she was naturally unsympathetic to the complaints of some of her white constituents against their West Indian neighbours. An attempt to sleep, by invitation, in a council flat while a reggae party boomed above her head for the whole night, taught her that it was a mistake to regard anyone as perfect simply because he was the victim of discrimination.

Deliberately now she allows her memory to fill with that intolerable noise. Not in order to bring her to agreement with Martin's views, but to arrive at a state of neutrality. The situation – and Mr Barnaby's character – must be considered on its merits. Lesley will have the answer to her doubts – and Lesley also must be in need of sympathy. Lady Ainslie waits for the next nurse to arrive.

It is Tricia, the student nurse, come to give her a blanket bath.

'I was very sorry to hear about Lesley,' says Lady Ainslie as she is turned and cleaned.

'Awful, isn't it? We're always asking to have proper lights along that path. They just say that we ought to walk through the hospital and out of the main door, but it's miles further that way.'

'Is she badly hurt?'

'Her head's bruised, Sister said. They kept her in because they needed to test for internal injuries, but none of the rest of us has seen her.'

Lady Ainslie wants to ask whether the attack has brought on a miscarriage, which seems all too likely, but does not know whether Lesley has confided in anyone but herself. 'Did she lose –?' She begins the question tentatively and leaves Tricia to supply its object.

'Her purse, yes. It's crazy. Everyone knows that nurses never have any money. But she was wearing a gold chain. Sister says

190

that was what they went for first.' She goes to the door and calls for Jean, the auxiliary, to come and help her.

'Oh, I can get up,' says Lady Ainslie when she realizes that they propose to change the sheets while she is still in bed. After all, two days earlier she was able not just to sit in her chair for most of the day but to walk up and down the ward. But her head spins dizzily as soon as she sits up. Without further protest she allows herself to be rolled from one side of the bed to the other and back again.

By the time Caro arrives to visit her in the afternoon, however, she has – with assistance – made her way to the chair beside the window and is strong enough to smile.

'What *did* they do to you yesterday, poor Nanna? I was so appalled that I demanded to see the doctor. I'm not sure that Sister took kindly to that.'

'What did he say?'

'A slight setback, but everything under control.'

'Accurate enough. As you see.'

'You don't look absolutely fighting fit yet.'

'I feel old,' says Lady Ainslie. 'It's an odd thing. I mean, obviously one becomes older with every birthday, every day, and eighty-three, good heavens, that's old by any standard. But I've never felt any different from when I was sixty, say, and when I was sixty I didn't notice the difference from being forty. A little slower, a little less strong, a little less appetite, but all so gradual that it hardly registered. And then suddenly this afternoon, walking from the bed to the chair, I knew that I was old. What you said on the telephone before I came here. A helpless little old lady. It wasn't true then, but it is now.'

'Only temporary. After all, you felt a bit like that straight after the operation, didn't you?'

'Yes. That was natural, though. Whereas this –' But how can she explain to a healthy young woman how frightening it feels to lack strength, ordinary strength, and to fear that it will never return? And she must husband the little that remains to her, observing economy in both movement and speech. She waits for her granddaughter to continue the conversation.

'Now then,' Caro announces. 'I have a message for you. Your

191

loving son, my loving father, telephoned me in the middle of the night. Not last night; the night before.'

'Leonard telephoned? I didn't know they had telephones in the jungle.'

'I sometimes suspect that he's not quite as far from civilization as he likes to pretend. Obviously my letter had been carried from the airport by cleft stick or carrier pigeon to reach him in the village, but it doesn't seem to have taken him long, once he read it, to get himself to Madang. It would have been nice if he'd paused to remember that there's a ten-hour time difference, but we can't have everything. Anyway, Martin had told me that you hadn't given Dad notice of your operation, so I wrote myself. And then I wrote again after you'd had it, but that letter hasn't arrived yet. So of course he was worried.'

'Which is precisely why I didn't want to bother him. I explained that to Martin. It was naughty of you to upset him, dear.'

'There are some things that people have a right to know.'

'I disagree strongly. There are certain kinds of knowledge which impose unwanted choices. The sort of dilemma in which even if you do the sensible thing you feel guilty about what you haven't done.'

'You're a very odd mother,' says Caroline. 'A perfect grandmother, but a very odd mother. I mean, you and Dad seem to get on marvellously in the sense of being good friends and enjoying each other's company and never quarrelling when you meet; but it doesn't seem to bother you that you hardly ever *do* meet. I'd have thought you'd want him to rush back.'

'I'm afraid I was only his mother in a strictly biological sense. His aunt and I changed places, in a way, while he was growing up. Not from choice. At least, I did have to choose, but circumstances forced me into it. I remember Constance – your great-aunt Constance – telling me once that I should have to think of it as my war wound, and it was. Your father thought of me as if I were an affectionate aunt who turned up for holidays. I provided him with treats, so of course we always got on marvellously together. But if he needed to cry, it was Constance he went to. I was unhappy about it at the time, but in fact it did seem to develop a rather special sense of independence in him.'

'Is that why he found it so easy to dump Martin and me on you, do you think? Because he hadn't had a possessive mother himself, he didn't think we needed one.'

'Yes, I expect so. And I was glad. It's made me feel that I've made up for lost opportunities. Anyway, what did he say?'

'Oh, just wanted to know all the details and how you were and whether he should fly home.'

'I hope you said no.'

'I told him you were doing splendidly. That was before I saw you yesterday, of course. He's going to phone again tomorrow. In the meantime, I'm to give you all his love and best wishes and the most magnificent flowers that I can find. Which I've been arranging outside and will now produce.'

Moving with care, she carries in a flower arrangement which would have graced the high table of any banquet, and sets it down in front of the window.

For a long time after she has left Lady Ainslie stares appreciatively at the flowers and thinks about her granddaughter with affection and amusement. It is curious that Caro, whose relationship with young Daniel Carrington clearly does not fall into the old-fashioned pattern of engagement leading to marriage, should be so puzzled by a slight departure from the norm of maternal love.

But perhaps she is right to be doubtful. Leonard has grown up to be a friendly son, but there was a time when that could not have been taken for granted. Each of them was equally wounded by the war.

Twenty-nine

Tuesday, 23 May 1940

After two days in Scotland, playing with Leonard, I still can't decide what's best to do. It seemed an easy choice in September. Evacuation recommended for all London children before the start of the expected bombing, and Constance writing straight away to point out that she has a castle full of unused rooms in the safest possible area. Healthy fresh air. Plenty of staff to look after an extra child, and anyway his nurse would go with him. Her own youngest boy almost the same age, to be a playmate, and herself, a loving aunt, to be sure he was happy. Irresponsible, I thought then, to say no.

But I'm losing him. He didn't recognize me at Christmas or Easter. This time, after a shorter gap, I think he did remember, but pretended not to. Punishing me for going away. Constance is his mother. Jock and Donald and Robert are his brothers; Fiona his sister.

Ought I to stay up here with him? No, I can't. When so many other mothers are parted from their children, I haven't got the right to special treatment. And since Richard joined up and went off to France, I'm useful in London, in the constituency. Necessary, even. Women having to manage and make decisions without their husbands must have someone to talk to, someone who isn't 'official' to give advice. I feel guilty just taking this week away.

And although the bombing didn't start when it was first expected, it may now. Churchill obviously expects it. The news from France is terrible. It ought to put fear of 'losing' Leonard into perspective. Such a different kind of loss if anything were to happen to Richard. But although I know what I want for him, of course, I've no power to make any decisions. With Leonard, I can make the decisions, but don't know what's best. It makes me feel so helpless. I'm not usually a ditherer.

Thursday, 25 May 1940

Constance has taken me in hand! As though I were the younger sister; funny, really. Perhaps she's so much more decisive than me because she got married so young – and to a professional soldier, away for much of the time and leaving her to run the household. I'm good at giving advice and making decisions about other people. Not so hot, I realize now, at managing my own affairs.

So I've been given my instructions. Losing Leonard's infancy is to be regarded as my war wound. I must make whatever contribution I can to the war effort, and that means being in London. The more children Constance brings up here, the more useful she will feel. Leonard will be safe, healthy, happy. While he's so young he'll hardly be aware of my absence; when he's older it can be explained to him.

She's right that the important thing is to decide and not allow myself to regret the decision. So he stays.

Sunday, 28 May 1940

All day yesterday spent with our ears glued to the wireless. Poor reception here in the castle, surrounded by mountains; crackling and fading. The feeling that if we breathed too noisily we might miss some vital piece of news. Our men are being evacuated under bombardment. Small ships making their way to Dunkirk from all round the coast to pick them up. The number rescued rising every hour, but still thousands trapped there.

The commentators too vivid in their descriptions. Lines of men along the beach, on piers and quays, wading out to waist level in the water, with Stukas machine-gunning from the air and bombs falling. Constance was thinking of John, knowing that if his regiment was there he'd be the last officer to leave. I was thinking of Richard, an amateur soldier, out of his depth. Not hardened to death or accustomed to fear.

My own terror brought me home, even though it meant being cut off from the news for so long. An appalling train journey; long, slow, overcrowded. Impossible to read by the tiny slit of blue light. The usual camaraderie dampened by anxiety. Tried to persuade myself that every unscheduled, extended halt was to allow a troop train through, to collect more rescued men from the coast. But frightened all the time. That was why I had to get back to London, in case any news came. What I told Constance was that I must be at home when Richard turns up. We both tried to believe it would happen.

No messages, no Richard waiting. Belgium has surrendered. But news from Dunkirk encouraging. Evacuation continuing. Good weather, good order, thousands already safely away.

Friday, 2 June 1940

Constance telephoned. John is safe. I'm happy for her, but it makes it worse for me.

Perfect summer weather. A week to spend drowsing in the shade amidst the scent of roses. Driven instead by a necessary masochism to work in the constituency office. Relaxed enjoyment is impossible when so many are exhausted or suffering. In any case, after two days of listening for the telephone and the front door bell, couldn't bear to stay at home any longer. Made sure there would always be someone in the house, of course, to take messages and contact me. Then tried to concentrate on other people's problems.

Plenty of those. Even on days when 'surgery' isn't expected to be open, a stream of people needing advice. Rations, housing, health, working conditions, even some questions familiar from the old days — women who haven't seen their husbands since September but now find themselves pregnant.

I'm still listening to every possible news bulletin on the wireless. An odd, illogical atmosphere of euphoria in the words, as though there's been a great victory instead of a defeat. I can't share it, not until Richard comes home.

Monday, 5 June 1940

Evacuation reported at an end, but no news.

Wednesday, 7 June 1940

Still no news. Working daily at the 'surgery', but nothing counts as an event until I hear from Richard.

Sunday, 11 June 1940

No longer any hope that Richard was one of those who got away. But the Germans have taken thousands of prisoners, and they're civilized people. He'll be frustrated in a camp, but not wounded, please God. Bound to take a little time before the full list of names comes through. Whistling in the dark.

Tuesday, 13 June 1940

The news came today. Not a War Office telegram yet, but a letter from his CO. Richard was killed during the retreat to Dunkirk. Helping to hold the Germans back so that others could get away. Heroic rearguard action. Died instantaneously, the colonel says. How many times has he had to tell that particular story in the past few days, I wonder. Do I believe it? Yes, I must.

Gallant officer, inspiration to his men. I suppose they have to use these clichés to make it all seem worth while. But it wasn't worth while. I'm still too angry to cry. He was nearly forty. He didn't have to go. He should have wanted to stay with me. Two years we had together. Only two years.

Wednesday, 14 June 1940

Wrote that last night and then started to howl. Aware of Mrs Creevy prowling around in the hall, wondering whether to leave me alone or bring me a nice cup of tea, her remedy for all disasters. Couldn't help remembering how I cried once before – was it only a year ago? – and Richard left me to get it out of my system. Incredible to think that something like being struck off the register seemed the end of the world then!

Nothing to hold me in London now. A widow, disqualified from professional work, not useful for anything. Might as well go back to Scotland and at least act as a proper mother. But not quite yet. I can remember Richard best here.

Sunday, 18 June 1940

Went to church, but no comfort there.

I ought not to sit around like this. There must be something useful I can do. Could I appeal to the GMC for restoration to the register? There must surely be a shortage of doctors, more important than the possible breach of some stupid rule. I need Richard to advise me. I need Richard.

Monday, 19 June 1940

Richard's agent, Derek Mould, called this afternoon, wearing dark suit and black tie. We know each other well from my 'surgery' work, of course. Produced his thoughts as though working through an agenda.

Condolences first. Prepared speech about Richard's qualities, potential for future. I can't listen to this sort of thing without crying, so had to close my ears and think about the pattern of the carpet until he'd finished.

Next, a memorial service. He knew he was on thin ice in talking about the impossibility of holding a funeral, but stumbled on, claiming that constituents would want a chance to honour their Member. Told him he could go ahead and I'd come, as long as he made all the arrangements.

He wanted to emphasize how much personal respect Richard had won in the constituency in a short time. A stream of people through the office all last week, apparently. Not with problems, but to express regret.

Lastly – as I thought – formal vote of thanks to me for supporting my husband at first and later doing valuable work on my own account. I mumbled my thanks for his thanks, and offered him a cup of tea. But he hadn't finished.

He would like me to take Richard's place in Parliament. I couldn't believe it, but he was deadly earnest. Confessed that he'd originally hoped for a working-class candidate instead of Richard in 1938, but had since seen the advantage of having someone educated, articulate, able to stand up to Them. Felt I had the same qualities, and also had acquired detailed knowledge of ordinary people's difficulties. Medical background a special advantage in speaking up for better health and housing. Running the war was only part of Parliament's job, and there were enough men there to give their views on that. Important that some people should start to plan for life after war, when there might be a Labour government.

All I could say was that no one would elect a woman with no political experience. But he said that under a wartime convention the party holding the seat would not be opposed in a by-election. I'd need only to be adopted by the constituency party, and he'd guarantee that.

After thus taking my breath away, he left.

Sunday, 24 June 1940

A week of mulling over Mr Mould's offer. Scribbling down topics and then listing what I thought ought to be done, could be done. I know what the 'party line' is in most cases, of course, from talking to Richard, but tried to marshal ideas pragmatically. A good way of taking my mind off unhappiness, and I even started to become excited. Found I wanted to talk ideas through with someone. Spent an evening with an elderly Labour MP whom I know Richard respected, testing to find out whether I'd be welcome, useful, approved. Came away encouraged. As for the mechanics of Parliament – working hours, choice of committee subjects, that sort of thing – I know enough about that already. Enough to be aware that it's an impossible life for a wife with a family. But an ideal way for a widow to fill her time.

A widow. Accepting that word showed me a way ahead. Like me, hundreds of women must have become widows in the past month. There may be thousands more before all this comes to an end. They mustn't be allowed to sink into poverty like the Great War widows. I could make it my special crusade to stand up for them, and it's in Parliament that they need a mouthpiece.

Most decisive, in the end, was one simple observation. As long as

199

I was investigating, deciding, I wasn't aware of being miserable. As soon as I sat down with nothing to do, I started to cry again.

Parliament as a personal therapy. Not a very creditable attitude. But I can see things that ought to be done and I might be able to help towards them.

So Leonard, dear little Leonard, will continue to be Constance's boy. Will he forgive me for that? It must be better for him, though, to be one of five children in a rowdy household instead of being held too tightly by a weeping woman. He'll be all right. We shall have to get to know each other again later.

Thirty

Lady Ainslie sits for an hour enjoying her flowers and thinking about Leonard. Then, pushing the chair in front of her as a support, she returns to bed. She is about to turn on the radio for the news when she withdraws her hand.

How odd it is, this compulsion to be always up-to-date with what is going on in the world. She knows exactly when it began. It was during the Dunkirk evacuation in 1940 that it seemed important to listen to every possible bulletin, and the habit born in that anxiety persisted for the next five years. But that was more than forty years ago, for heaven's sake. Why should she care now what has happened in the past few hours?

Somewhere in the world, no doubt, there will have been a disaster: an earthquake, a fire, a plane crash. Give it a few hours more and the horror may be softened with stories of miraculous escapes, heroic rescues. Somewhere else in the world there will be cause for speculation. Who is going to be the next president of the United States? Will the coup d'état on some Pacific island be successful? Given time, these questions will answer themselves. She is not a financier, calculating how money rates may move; nor has she any responsibility for foreign affairs. She has no need to know and so the knowledge can wait, whatever it is.

Ah, but that's the point, that whatever it is may in fact come as a surprise, a personal shock. Disasters and presidential primaries cannot be guaranteed to fill the bulletin. She may hear of the death of a friend, the defeat of the government. Besides, the shock of reading those unfamiliar Sunday newspapers a few days earlier is still in her mind. Is she to become one of the masses who are assumed to be interested only in football results, television actors and the real or invented antics of the royal family? No. She may appear – and feel herself to be – a frail old lady, almost too weak to take charge even of anything as unimportant as her own life. But she remains one of the nation's legislators and, unless she proposes to withdraw from that responsibility, it is her duty to keep in touch with the world's affairs.

A radio news headline, however, does not wait for havering hospital patients to make up their minds. She has missed the moment. Straightening her body again from the leaning posture into which it has been frozen, she notices Mr Barnaby standing in the doorway.

He has come earlier in the evening than usual. Her instinctive reaction is to smile in welcome. Then she remembers what Martin has told her.

'Did any of the nurses see you arrive?' she asks.

He shakes his head.

'Shut the door then. Come and sit down. Here, by the bed.'

There would be time to reach for the call bell while he is making his way to the other side of the bed. But she does not move. Whatever Martin may think – and, indeed, whatever Mr Barnaby may have done – she is convinced that he has no intention of harming her. Friendship would be too strong a word to use, but there is a kind of sympathy between them. If he wants to talk, he will trust her to listen without bias.

'What happened last night, Mr Barnaby? Tell me what happened.'

He is silent, not prepared to make any unnecessary admission.

'Nurse Grant was attacked last night and you were there.'

'Who says so?'

'You were seen.' A curious form of words, when a more natural phrase would be 'Nurse Grant saw you.' Is it a vestigial memory of detective stories read in her youth which suggests that a witness named is a witness in danger? Unlike Martin, she is not taking guilt for granted, but it seems that she is not presuming innocence either. 'What were you doing there?'

'I like to sit on the wall after visiting time's over. Looking at the window. This window.'

'So you saw the nurse coming.'

He nods. 'A good bit away from where I was. But I saw this man jump her. Tug at her gold chain. The other hand over her mouth so she couldn't scream.'

'Yes?'

'She was fighting and kicking; holding him off at first. So then he, this man, started crowding her. Back against the wall. Seemed to me he was about to do her harm. So I jumped down and sprinted along. Tried to pull him off.'

'You're saying that the reason you were there was that you were trying to help her?'

'Right. That's why I went.' His voice has changed, becoming more intense, and he continues the commentary as though re-enacting the scene. 'He turned her in front of him then. Hand over her mouth still. But he had to let go of the chain to fight me off. We all went down on the ground, punching and pushing. The nurse, she's the one who saw me, I suppose. How'd she know that I wasn't ganging up with the first one? All blacks are villains. Everyone knows that.'

'So how did it finish?'

'He was taking punishment. I don't suppose he saw any future in hanging around. Grabbed her bag and ran. I ran too, the other way.'

'Why didn't you stay and help her? Call the police.'

'I did call. From the telephone box. But stay there to be picked up? No way.'

'If you'd explained –'

'What do you know about the police, lady?' His voice, his actor's voice, rises in pitch as he relieves his feelings. He is no longer now a schoolmaster who has witnessed somebody else's crime. Instead he has taken on the persona with which Martin has always credited him and is speaking as though he were an unemployed troublemaker, loafing against a lamp-post.

'Someone like you, you trip in the street, a pig'll come rushing, pick you up, brush you down, which way did he run, what colour is he? I stand still in the street and it's where you goin', where

you been, what you carryin', don't give me lip you black bastard.'
His body quivers so that she flinches away from his closeness,
the smell of his anger, and is relieved when at that moment the
door opens.

It is supper time. A nurse whom Lady Ainslie has not seen
before, presumably taking the place of the injured Lesley, carries
a tray into the room and makes sure that it is comfortably settled.
She appears not to notice Mr Barnaby's presence and makes
no comment on it, but will certainly go straight to report it to
Sister.

'Listen, Mr Barnaby.' Lady Ainslie ignores the food in front
of her. 'Now that one of the nurses has seen you, the police will
be here at any moment to ask you questions. If you were involved
in that attack, if you've been lying to me, you ought to leave
straightaway.'

'That's nice of you, to give me warning. I appreciate that.' His
voice is calm again; the voice of a Sunday School teacher. He
has never yet smiled in her presence, but is on the verge of doing
so now. 'Where should I go, though? Running off last night, that
made sense, but running for the rest of my life? I'm not a squatter,
into drugs, that sort of thing. I made a home for my wife and
children. I have an address. Anyone who wants knows where to
find me. And anyone who knows me knows I'm not a thief.
Would I be fool enough to come here tonight if I was the one
made off with that purse?'

That thought has occurred to Lady Ainslie earlier. Although,
of course, if he was clever enough to work out the advantage of
making just that point . . .

He seems to sense a doubt. 'Do they give you a Bible here,
like in hotels?'

'Yes. In the drawer of the locker.'

He finds the Bible and lays one hand flat on its cover.

'I swear by Almighty God that I never tugged at that nurse's
chain, never touched her purse.' He puts the Bible back in the
drawer. 'I wasn't waiting for her. Didn't know she was coming.
There for my own reasons. You know what the reasons were.'

'Then listen to me. You'll be arrested. Certain to be. The
nurse has identified you as being part of the struggle and until

they can sort it out they're bound to charge you. You're allowed to make a phone call to a lawyer. Have you got one?'

He shakes his head. 'I've never been in trouble. But there's a number everyone knows, written up in all the call boxes.'

'Well, if you think that's best . . . But I'll give you the name of a firm I know.' She tears a page from the diary which Caro has given her and writes down a number. Her personal lawyer specializes in such subjects as wills, trusts and leases, and is unlikely to regard a client such as Mr Barnaby with enthusiasm or to provide the right kind of help. But there is another partnership which during her years as an MP she has often recommended to constituents facing criminal charges. 'I'll telephone their Mr Brady myself in the morning, as soon as the office opens.'

Taking the paper, he nods his thanks and then walks over to the window. By the movement he is making it clear that he does not wish even to be suspected of running away from the police. It could also be, of course, that he sees the usefulness of being arrested in Lady Ainslie's presence. No one will be able to beat him up under the pretence that he is resisting arrest.

His tactics are successful. The two police constables who arrive, flustered by being late, do their best to get him out of the room in order to avoid upsetting an old lady. But his silent stubbornness defeats them and they are forced to accept her as a witness to his polite agreement when they check his identity and invite him to accompany them to the police station.

During all this excitement she has done her best to keep calm but finds herself, when at last the room empties, trembling with tension and indecision. Ought she to have offered to guarantee bail for him? Should she pass on to Lesley the version of events she has just heard? It is not clear whether Lesley is in a fit state to listen and Lady Ainslie very much doubts whether she herself is capable of making the journey to another ward. Telling herself that none of this is really her business, she looks without appetite at the cold food on her supper tray and is glad when the nurse returns to remove it.

Sister, anxious and apologetic, comes to make sure that her patient has survived all the excitement.

'I'm so sorry. I don't know how he got past. There was supposed to be someone watching. I'm going to suggest to Mr Graham that he should prescribe a tranquillizer, to give you a quiet evening's rest.'

'No, thank you.' The words emerge more abruptly than she intends, and she hastens to soften them. 'I've done a lot of work for a charity which helps widows, and some of the stories I've heard are horrifying. Stories of addiction, I mean. They all seem to start with a kind-hearted doctor who wants to help a woman through the first days of grief. A terrible mistake. Grief has to be cried out. Time is the tranquillizer. And what's happened tonight doesn't concern me personally.'

'I wasn't suggesting – well, if you're sure you don't want anything. Now then, I don't imagine there's much danger of any further visits, but we can't exactly keep you under twenty-four-hour guard. Would you like to move into the ward? With people all round, neither you nor I would feel anxious.'

'A kind thought, but no, thank you. I do very much appreciate the quietness and privacy here.'

She is left alone and sees that the diary notebook from which she has torn a page still lies to hand on the bed. Except for the notes which she destroyed as soon as they were written, she has made only one entry since entering hospital. Today it can hardly be argued that nothing worthy of recording has happened. But what would be the point of writing it down? It can never be of any interest to anyone else, because no one but herself will ever be allowed to read it. If they do, it will be by mistake and because she is dead.

The question worries her. How many hours during her lifetime has she devoted to the making of notes about mainly trivial events? Has it ever been more than a waste of time? Well, there is an answer of a kind. Until her admission to hospital, the routine of keeping a diary has been a part of her daily life, as necessary in its regularity as the taking of a bath or the cleaning of teeth. If she is to ask herself what the point is of one activity, she must ask it of them all.

So it has been a matter of choice and of values. The time she has devoted each evening to her diary might have been spent, had she been a different kind of woman, in making love or cuddling her children. Had Richard lived, everything might indeed have been different. But for most of her life she has not found it difficult to live alone. Celibacy has always come naturally to her, making any brief periods of passionate love into idylls to be savoured while they lasted rather than ideals constantly to be sought.

The writing of a diary, then, has been a hobby; a pleasure of habitude. The first choice, to devote time to it every day, has imposed other choices – of what is and is not important enough to be recorded. She has been writing, in a sense, an autobiography in serial form. Her life in words is real. These are things that have actually occurred. Whatever does not appear on the page is so much reduced in importance that it seems hardly to have happened at all.

This must be nonsense, of course. It is her body talking, using physical weakness as an excuse for not picking up the pen. Her thoughts, not so much leaping as crossing by a bridge of relevance, move back to her conversation with Daniel about the biography of his grandfather. Gil, it appears, is departing from what might have seemed his natural inclination to kiss and tell in order to encourage the young man to do his own primary research. So the name of Ainslie Dangerfield is not on the list of past mistresses. It is as though their love affair had never taken place.

For that she is profoundly grateful. But what are the implications? If the book is ever written and published, a relationship which is left unmentioned will, as far as the general reader is concerned, never have existed. There will be nothing to explain the apparent stupidity of a barrister in pressing his own witness to destroy his case, or the vindictiveness of a woman who bankrupted the man she was expected to help. Ainslie has devoted the whole of her life to keeping secrets but she is bound to acknowledge that, once a lie has gone on record, silence is a second dishonesty.

Besides, it may not be possible to remain silent. Daniel is certain to return. He has left the transcript of the trial with her specifically because he wishes to ask questions. Her choice will be the same now as it was fifty years ago: she can lie or she can

207

tell the truth. Lord Impney and his daughter Margaret have both been dead for many years, so the truth can hurt no one but herself. She had better decide what she wants to say. But not now, while she feels so washed out.

She rests without moving, except when she presses a switch to hear what Radio Three's evening concert has to offer. The music of Tchaikovsky floods the room. It is not Lady Ainslie's kind of music, for she has never been a romantic, but she allows it to sweep over her mind and stir her emotions.

Has she always been too cold? Has there been something abnormal in her acceptance of so many years of celibacy? The generation which came to maturity in the Swinging Sixties, taking for granted its right to sex on demand, would certainly say so. And even Caro's contemporaries have had a few years of guilt-free sexual activity before the appearance of AIDS as God's punishment for promiscuity.

It is hard to judge how much the ability to live happily alone is an indication of personal temperament and how much it represents the real generation gap – the gap between those who have and have not had access in their youth to the contraceptive pill. The period when guilt at sinning was so powerfully reinforced by the fear of pregnancy is past history now.

The music changes. It is Bruckner's turn, but Lady Ainslie is no longer listening. She has done her best to stay awake in order not to be roused from sleep at eleven o'clock for a sleeping pill. But the battle has been lost. Lying on her back, her mouth slightly open, she accompanies the orchestra with a faint but regular snoring. The current of time is carrying her towards recovery. Tomorrow she will be stronger; but she has had enough of today.

Thirty-one

The antibiotics are gaining the upper hand: the infection is subsiding. As her temperature falls and she becomes more at ease in her body, Lady Ainslie becomes eager to leave hospital. Toby, when asked to name a date, is not prepared to do more than murmur about 'a few days'; but he must have fed her request into the system, because within an hour someone who is no longer called a hospital almoner arrives to offer her a week in a convalescent home.

'No, thank you very much. I'd rather go straight home.'

'You may find that you're not as strong as you used to be, not for a week or two. It would be a mistake to think that you can go straight back to your normal life.'

'I shall be all right.' She has affectionate grandchildren, friendly neighbours and someone – rarely seen – who has been cleaning her flat for more than ten years and will certainly be willing to undertake any necessary errands. Even if she were to lack this support, she could not bear the prospect of sitting in front of a television set and waiting anxiously for meals in the company of a dozen other recently discharged patients. Her rejection of the offer is grateful but definite.

In the meantime, while she builds up her strength to qualify for discharge, there is a visit to be paid. Lesley, she discovers, is in a ward on the fourth floor, two storeys down. Closing her eyes to the temptation offered by the flashing numbers above a cluster of lift doors, she makes for the stairs. No one is likely to let her go home until she is capable of conquering her personal Everest in West Hampstead, where there are eight steps from the pave-

209

ment to the hall and a further twenty-one to her flat. It is time to start practising.

She takes the descent carefully, keeping one hand in contact with the banister rail although without gripping it tightly. For the first time in almost a fortnight she feels herself to be inappropriately dressed. As she wanders around her own room or the ward to which it is attached it has come to seem almost natural that she should be wearing bedroom slippers and a dressing gown whose old-fashioned shortness reveals the bottom of a warm but unglamorous nightdress. Some sartorial gesture seems necessary before she faces a wider world – but it cannot be made, because Caro has taken all her outdoor clothes home, as though she were a prisoner suspected of a wish to escape.

This small unease passes quickly, for the swing doors of Lesley's ward admit her to another world in which dressing gowns and bed-jackets are normal wear. She makes her way between the two rows of beds, glancing at each until the moment when she hesitates, unsure whether she has reached her destination.

Nurse Grant has always appeared before her patients neatly dressed, her fair hair twisted into a tidy bun beneath the frilled hospital cap, and her sturdy body trimly confined in the blue uniform dress and belt which denote her rank in the hospital.

The young woman who has begun to smile in pleased surprise at Lady Ainslie presents a different picture. One eyebrow is cut and swollen, mottling her cheek and temple with bruising. Her long hair tumbles untidily around her shoulders, almost but not quite concealing the bandage around her neck. She wears a low-cut nightdress which reveals her breasts, transforming her from a nurse into a woman.

'This is the wrong way round,' she laughs. 'You coming to see me. But it's very nice of you, Lady Ainslie. Do sit down, won't you?'

Lady Ainslie makes herself comfortable and asks the expected general questions, receiving the expected reassuring answers. Then she leans forward a little.

'I haven't liked to ask any of the other nurses,' she says. 'But I've been worried, wondering. It was a bad thing to happen to someone expecting a baby. Did you –?'

'I lost the baby, yes.' Lesley's eyes fill with tears. 'Funny how it makes one want to cry, saying that, even when . . . Something to do with one's hormones, I suppose.' She sniffs the tears away and smiles again. 'I have your black friend to thank for that. Mr Barnaby.'

'They told me you'd said so. And that made me feel guilty. I wondered – if I hadn't allowed him to keep coming back. But he came again, the night after. I was able to ask him. And he swore on the Bible that it was someone else who had attacked you. That he came to help, and had nothing to do with trying to rob you. I imagine it must all have been very sudden and confusing.'

Lesley does not comment on this immediately and, when she does at last speak, seems unsure what to say.

'You certainly oughtn't to blame yourself, Lady Ainslie. It was great of you to let him into your room. The right thing. If he'd been kept out he might have worked up much more anger, sitting on the river wall. All the same . . . I do know what happened. If he swore on the Bible, I reckon he must have picked his words carefully.'

'What did happen, then?'

'He wasn't the one who originally attacked me and tugged at my chain. He wasn't the one who stole my bag. Yes, he did come to help me and he did fight the first chap off. I was able to crawl away while that was going on, and I could see that it was a real fight. But after the first one ran away –'

Lesley pauses, upset by the memory, and makes a face before continuing. 'Mr Barnaby helped me to stand up. I was staggering a bit because I'd had a nasty bang on the head. He kind of held me steady. Leaned me back against the wall. And then.' Lesley closes her eyes for a moment. 'The expression on his face. I can't describe it. A glassiness in his eyes, as though he wasn't looking at what he was doing; but his lips were sort of snarling with hatred. I couldn't understand why he should have helped me if he hated me so much. I was more terrified then, I can tell you, than when it all began.'

'So what happened?'

'He stood back, enough to give himself room. And then he

211

kicked me in the stomach. The sort of kick that people learn in martial arts. A punch with the foot. I just doubled up and went down to the ground again. I suppose I passed out. I don't remember much more till I was on a stretcher being carried into Freddie's. There was a lot of blood. I guessed what had happened long before the doctor told me.'

'I see.' Lady Ainslie's voice is heavy with disappointment. 'Oh dear. You're right then; he chose his words carefully when he was swearing that oath. And I believed . . . I'm sorry, my dear. I really do feel some responsibility. My grandson warned me, and I didn't take any notice. How stupid of me. And how stupid of Mr Barnaby as well. He's not a hooligan – or at least I didn't think so. He's an educated man with a job and the prospect of a decent future. And now he's thrown it all away. One prison sentence and he'll probably be unemployed for the rest of his life. He must have known all that.'

'I'm not going to charge him,' says Lesley. 'I've withdrawn my complaint.'

'What?'

'When the police first started asking me questions, I was still feeling groggy. I told them what I remembered in a vague sort of way. Two blacks, one of them known to me. But I sent a message this morning, asking them to come back again so that I could amend the statement. I told them that I realize now about Mr Barnaby coming to my assistance.'

'Why should you do that, Lesley?'

'I suppose you could say that he robbed me of something, just as the first chap did. But it was something I wanted to lose. He robbed me of guilt.' She lowers her voice to make sure that her neighbours in the ward cannot hear what she says.

'That time when we talked before, Lady Ainslie. It was a great help to me. I was able to think things out. It all came clear in the end. I didn't want the baby. But I knew that I'd never be able to live with the knowledge that I'd killed it. It was exactly what you said. Some people wouldn't feel guilty at all about having an abortion; but if you *do* feel it, it's a factor to take into account. So I had decided, quite definitely, to go ahead with the pregnancy. Well, now I'm not going to have a baby any longer,

212

but it's not my fault. I don't have to feel guilty. I can just enjoy plain, unadulterated relief.'

'That doesn't alter the fact that Mr Barnaby intended to do you harm.' It must have been, she realizes, a deliberate form of harm, for she remembers that he almost certainly overheard their conversation.

'I'm giving him a thank-you present. Because I really am very happy at the way things have turned out.'

Is this the right thing to do? It means that he will be free to attack other women in the same way if he chooses. Lady Ainslie believes, as obviously Lesley does, that the violence he has shown may be a gesture necessary to get his hatred and wish for revenge out of his system, and one which is not likely to be repeated. But she has misjudged him before and may be doing so again.

Well, it is not her decision to make. She chats for a little while longer. It sounds as though Lesley's period of working her way round the world and enjoying whatever casual relationships present themselves is coming to an end. She has always been a responsible nurse. Now she is becoming a responsible woman as well.

It is time to tackle the stairs again. This time, going up, they are too much. There is no single muscle which protests against the effort, but a total failure of strength. This is how it feels to be old – weak and helpless and tempted to tears. She leans, panting, against the wall. Above and below, people will be coming and going in constant activity. But nobody has time to use the stairs, which exist mainly for emergency use. She has got herself into trouble and will have to get herself out of it. With immense effort, as though she were indeed at the top of a mountain and short of oxygen, she pulls herself up a few steps at a time.

As she pushes open the heavy fire door which admits her to the sixth floor, Sister looks up from her glass-walled cubicle and moves swiftly to help her, putting an arm under her elbow in support until she is safely settled into her chair. Lady Ainslie nods her thanks, unable to speak. She feels as though she is panting, yet her breath is emerging regularly enough. The panting is in her mind, which surges as though pumped by a piston with something near to panic.

Today's weakness has a cause. But the passing of time can only increase her feebleness. Because she so regularly reminds herself that she is old, while at the same time knowing that she is competent, she has never before visualized a time when she will be unable to look after herself. Now that picture is clear and terrifying. In an effort to control the trembling of her hands she picks up Caro's notebook.

There is plenty to be recorded today – yet even as she reaches for a pen her hand hesitates and falls back. Is it wise to set down in writing what Lesley has told her? The police may be reluctant to accept the victim's change of evidence, wishing to press charges in spite of it. They are aware of their suspect's regular visits to the hospital and may well decide to question the occupant of the room to which he has been drawn back. If they learn that any kind of written record exists . . .

'Don't be melodramatic,' says Lady Ainslie aloud. Since leaving home she has tried to keep the habit of talking to herself under control, but today finds the familiar voice reassuring. She does not in fact believe that her doubts are melodramatic, for there is a legal precedent to be recalled.

Sooner or later Daniel will come to take back the transcript of the trial. He will ask questions and hope for answers – and what will they be about? About records of conversations long ago; conversations elicited in a court of law. If experience has taught Lady Ainslie anything, it must be to put away the pen before the first word is written.

Thirty-two

Daniel Carrington arrives alone, as she has hoped. If he intends to press her to a confession of perjury, it is tactful of him not to do it in Caro's presence. He pauses in the doorway to discover whether he is welcome.

'You've come to collect your transcript, I suppose?'

Taking this as an invitation, he crosses the room to sit beside her. 'Have you had time to read it?'

'Plenty of time. Very little inclination. It's all too long ago to be of any interest.'

'To you, perhaps. But to my grandfather it was – well, the trial ruined him, you know. The damages and the costs.'

'I knew that, yes. What I never understood was what happened afterwards. How he climbed back to pick up a knighthood as well as a fortune.' She has been aware of his success, of course. Like every politician she reads each Honours List with care to discover which of her friends should be congratulated; and the amalgamation of businesses which in the nineteen-sixties made him the owner of a substantial group of magazines was headline news at the time. But she has never before bothered to enquire how he has managed it all.

Daniel hesitates. It is not Gil's later life that he wants to discuss. But perhaps he calculates that she will be more forthcoming if he trades his information for hers.

'There were two separate ladders,' he says at last. 'But it was the war which set him at the foot of each of them.'

'What did he do in the war?' In 1939, although not quite too old to fight if he wished to volunteer, Gil would have been justified in waiting to be directed to some kind of war work.

'I suppose nowadays it would be described as counter-intelligence. At the time it was called interrogation. I don't know whether you remember, before war broke out he was already writing articles about British Fascists – not just Mosley and his lot, but the social sort, the ones who invited Ribbentrop for the weekend and thought Hitler was marvellous.'

'And that Mussolini was a man who made Italian trains run on time.'

'Yes. Well, when it came to the crunch, of course, most of those proved to be patriots first and Fascists a very poor second, but it wasn't always immediately clear whether their change of heart was genuine or a cover. I imagine that it was because of the articles he'd researched earlier that Grandfather was given the job of interviewing some of these people and advising whether they should be interned.'

'He must have enjoyed that. The swineherd's son with aristocrats in his power.'

'I don't know. But he seems to have been very good at it. If he'd been born into a different class, he might have made a good barrister.'

'I can't see him arguing a case that he didn't believe.' She regrets the remark as soon as she has made it, for it suggests that her interest and knowledge are greater than she is pretending.

'Perhaps not. But he did seem to have the knack of making people admit things without realizing what they were giving away. Anyway, those first interviews led on to others. He won't talk about that part of his life, but so many other people seem to be breaching the Official Secrets Act these days that I have hopes of digging out some details.'

'I'm sure,' murmurs Lady Ainslie, but not loudly enough to interrupt.

'He was kept on after the war ended, investigating war crimes. And even after he got back to civilian life he was asked from time to time to make enquiries and prepare reports on people or organizations. Rather like his *Investigator* articles, but never published. Much later on he started getting appointed to Royal Commissions. He was chairman of one of them, as I'm sure you'll remember. Officially, that was what he got his knighthood for, but really it was for a whole string of investigations.'

'So that's the honour. What about the fortune?'

'That was helped by the war as well. I haven't had time to research that properly yet. There's a limit to the number of questions I'm allowed to ask Grandfather in any one session. After that I'm expected to go off and dig somewhere else for a bit. But what saved his bacon, he said, was *The Investigator* paper.'

'But paper was rationed during the war.'

'Yes. I may not have got it quite straight yet. Because there was a paper shortage, magazines could only print a certain number of copies, based on the amount of paper they'd used before the war. Is that right? So it was a matter of luck that after the libel action nobody wanted to buy *The Investigator*. It was put into receivership with the rest of his assets, but proved to have no cash value. I suppose possible buyers were afraid that there might be more libel actions waiting to crawl out of the woodwork. The result was that when he discharged his bankruptcy he got the title back – with the benefit of its paper ration. He met someone who had a bright idea for a new magazine but no paper, so they pooled their resources.'

'But how did he discharge the bankruptcy?'

'I think he's a bit ashamed of this. My mother's grandparents came to the rescue. Didn't like the idea of having a bankrupt son-in-law, I suppose. They'd made a settlement at the time of the marriage. After my grandmother's death it should have been held in trust for my mother, but they signed some kind of release.'

'So the bankruptcy didn't in fact ruin him.'

'It must have felt like ruin at the time. He didn't know how things were going to turn out. He had a long period of misery. And it wasn't just the money. He believed passionately in the value of what he was doing in *The Investigator*. Why did you do it, Lady Ainslie?'

She remains silent for a moment and, when she speaks, it is to ask a question in return. 'What did I do?'

'You lied on oath.'

'Did your grandfather tell you why?'

217

'To protect a patient, he said. A man who didn't deserve protection. Grandfather knew that what he'd written was true – and that you knew it too, because he'd seen it in your diary.'

'He stole the information. He had no right –'

'He's always believed that truth is more important than privacy.'

'I had the right to disagree with him.'

'But to forge a diary, a complete diary! It took him so much by surprise at the time that he couldn't challenge it on the spot. But he worked it out afterwards, that that was what must have happened. Instead of just altering the one entry you wanted to protect, you copied a complete notebook out and made it look the same. Well, it *was* the same, except for a few words. And then you played so hard to get that everyone in the courtroom took it for granted that the diary must be genuine just because you didn't want them to read it.'

'If he's worked it all out to his own satisfaction, you hardly need me to comment.'

'I was hoping that you might explain why it was you felt strongly enough to do him so much harm. And that you might perhaps allow me to read the diary.'

It is tempting to ask 'Which diary?' Daniel's understanding of the situation is accurate enough to make further concealment of the truth unnecessary – and she is acutely conscious of the fact that the two identical notebooks are only a hand's reach away. Instead, she attempts the explanation he has asked for.

'Your grandfather had – perhaps he still has – a passionate belief that nothing should ever be hidden. That everyone has a right to know everything. All journalists these days seem to work on that principle – except of course when it comes to revealing who their own sources are. *Then* they believe in the right to secrecy.'

'And you disagree. With Grandfather, I mean.'

'I disagree. It may well be that his case is better than mine from society's point of view, but I hold to my belief that people should be allowed to have private lives and preserve whatever secrets they choose. If what they choose to conceal is against the law, then of course society, through its appointed representatives, is entitled to ferret out the truth, but –'

'Lord Impney's behaviour was certainly against the law.'

'It was inexcusable,' she agrees. 'But it was not Lord Impney's privacy which was breached by your grandfather. It was mine.'

'That was a minor matter, surely, compared with the welfare of the child concerned.'

Lady Ainslie's eyebrows rise at the note of censure in the young man's voice. But she is pleased, on the whole, that Caro's friend should prove to be firm in his opinions rather than sycophantic. And she must be careful not to pursue the argument too far. A young man like Daniel, heir to twenty-five years of sexual freedom, undoubtedly sees this old lady as a member of a repressed generation, valuing virginity above passion; and such an illusion must not be shattered. It may be only because Daniel has not yet asked Gil the relevant direct question that he has not been told of the long-dead relationship which was once so close, but she certainly does not intend to hint at it herself.

'I had already taken care of the child,' is all she says. 'And the publicity aroused by the case did her far more harm than could ever have been caused by something which she never understood to be wrong. And consider something else. The accusation might not have been true.'

'The facts were taken straight from your diary. And my grandfather believed that you were a truthful person.'

'He soon found out that he was wrong then, didn't he? But even supposing I'd written what I thought was true, I could have been mistaken. Children make up stories. A doctor whose first concern is to find a physical solution to a physical problem isn't always as meticulous as she ought to be about probing for reasons. I wrote as I did on the assumption that no one but myself would ever read it. Preparing evidence for a court of law, I would have phrased it quite differently.'

'As you did.'

Lady Ainslie laughs light-heartedly. 'As I did. Your grandfather's theory is quite correct – and you're at liberty to say so as ' ng as you make it clear that I was always a hostile witness who was furious at being forced to report a confidential consultation.'

219

'Do you still have the diary concerned, Lady Ainslie?'

She hesitates only for a moment before pointing to the bedside locker. 'In that drawer.'

When he sits down again he puts the two dark green notebooks one on each knee, looking from one to the other.

'Twenty-two yards one chain, ten chains one furlong, eight furlongs one mile, three miles one league.' Lady Ainslie recites the information without taking breath.

'I beg your pardon!'

'I had to learn tables like that as a child.' She smiles at the memory. 'And these notebooks I used made sure I never forgot. Look on the back. That particular cover has Indian weights and measures as well, to indicate that in 1938 we still had an empire. But I don't recall that my governess ever bothered much about tolas and seers and maunds.'

Daniel turns the notebooks over only briefly and then continues to study the front cover, noting the identical doodles, the creases, the round coffee stains.

'You certainly took a lot of trouble with this,' he says. 'Which is the original one?'

'I can't tell from here. It's not important.'

'May I –?'

'No,' says Lady Ainslie, kindly but firmly. 'The first one was private when it was written and it's still private now. And the second one is exactly the same except for the pages which you have in the trial transcript anyhow.'

'But if I could just look at the original record –'

She shakes her head. 'I'm a stubborn old woman. Or consistent, as I would prefer to say. I haven't changed my attitude in fifty years.'

He gives in too easily. Perhaps it has occurred to him that Gil must have taken a copy of the relevant entry and may have it still. Or there is another possibility. Caro and Martin may expect to inherit their grandmother's possessions when she dies; he will wait and in due course ask Caro.

The thought agitates her. By the time her visitor leaves she has banished the indecision of the past two weeks. Tugging the pages of each of the two green notebooks away from their staples, she tears them through and tosses them into the waste paper basket.

How odd that a sudden briskness of mind should enable her to throw off the fatigue brought on by her struggle with the stairs. As though she had all the energy in the world she paces the room for a little while, knowing what she has decided but giving her subconscious mind a fair chance to produce objections if it wishes to.

The diaries will all have to go; every one of them. How can she tell what casual comment may one day prove to be an indiscretion? She has never, for example, described to her son or grandchildren how she was struck off the medical register. From the day of her election to the House of Commons her parliamentary career has occupied all her time, so there has never been any necessity to explain why she ceased to practise as a doctor. But if Caro ever learns exactly how Gilbert Blakey took his revenge on the witness who destroyed his defence, it may affect her friendship with Daniel.

No arguments come to mind to dissuade her. Checking her purse to make sure that it contains the appropriate coins, she walks through the ward towards the day room, where there is a telephone.

Thirty-three

Now she is better. Weak and wobbly still, but better. The infection has been conquered, the surgical lesion is healing. More importantly, the improvement in her bodily health has brought about a recovery in her spirits. Or is it the other way round – that the restoration of a normal frame of mind has enabled her to shrug off the feeling of being physically below par?

It is the telephone call which has cured her. She has requested the Jaffreys to burn the box which she left with them, and the relief of making at last an irrevocable decision indicates how lowering the effect of her earlier uncertainty has been. Whether her choice is right or wrong, it is definite. She is herself again.

This new-found confidence prompts her to ask Caro to bring back the suitcase containing her clothes as soon as is convenient; and when Toby Mallinson next arrives with his 'firm' of medical students to see how she is progressing she demands rather than requests her discharge.

'Oh-ho!' he exclaims, laughing, and turns to lecture the young doctors on the importance of noting the moment when the patient's attitude changes. 'Two days ago she wanted to leave because she was tired of being here. Now she's determined to leave because she's thrown off any feeling of dependency on hospital care and is sure that she no longer needs it. When someone feels as confident as that, she's probably right.'

They crowd round for what may be a last examination and two of them, a young man and a young woman, are invited to prod, probing for adhesions or tenderness. Their explorations are uncomfortable but Lady Ainslie keeps a smile on her face to prove that she is hardly aware of their touch.

'All right,' says Toby at last. 'Tomorrow then, as long as you've got someone to keep an eye on you for a few days.'

'Thank you.' She beams at the young doctors, who grin back, sharing her pleasure. When they have gone she begins to make notes of things to be done. She has always been a list-maker. Words on paper are her tool of organization; they tell her what she has to do in the future as well as recording for her own benefit what she has done.

One small piece of unfinished business catches her eye. She has not yet read through the anthology borrowed from the library trolley. This is partly because she came well supplied with books of her own, but more because during the past two weeks she has become stupid, able to listen to trivial words and background music on the radio but finding it hard to focus either her eyes or her mind on anything requiring more concentration. Now she feels guilty, as though the feelings of the library lady will be hurt by the neglect of her offering. She puts on her spectacles and begins to read.

The purple lady was right. These memoirs of the Great War are not suitable for her trolley, unless it can be argued that patients may be cheered by descriptions of horrors experienced by others. Here are letters from the Front, pages from journals, memories and histories. Lady Ainslie finds herself thinking about the old man who chose to carry such a book on his final journey to hospital; remembering, as death gently approached, a time when it threatened him violently every hour of the day and night. Somewhere inside the volume, she is sure, there will be a bookmark or pencil line to identify one incident: an experience similar to his own or a battle in which he fought. She turns the pages and finds what she expects: a Bible text keeping the place in a passage about trench warfare.

The thought of a young man living on for seventy years with such memories upsets her, and it is some time before she begins to dip into the text. The extracts which describe that most terrible of wars are poignant, tugging at her heart and memory. These are the horrors which her brother had to endure, and

223

which killed him in the end. Gil Blakey also, little more than a boy, was pitchforked into the terror of the trenches, but he was strengthened rather than destroyed by them. Anger at injustice formed his character and spurred him into a career which as a nine-year-old truant from the village school he could never have foreseen.

There is no mention in the book of the wounds of bereaved women, of brides suddenly becoming young widows, robbed of joy and love and security. Nor of the effect on girls of Ainslie's own generation who discovered as they grew into womanhood how few men of their own class and an appropriate age were still alive. Lady Ainslie, incapable of regarding any book as merely an undemanding way of passing the time, pauses to consider the effects of that shortage of husbands on the eventual acceptance of the spinster as a useful member of society and the later concept that all women should wish to work.

Her thoughts are interrupted by the opening of the door. Mr Barnaby is standing there.

'I didn't expect you to come back here again,' she says; but she nods in invitation towards the second chair.

'I came to say thank you.' He sits down, putting a hand between his knees to turn the chair in her direction. 'That lawyer, you gave me the number, he did a good job. They let me go. More than I expected.'

'It's Nurse Grant you have to thank.' Lady Ainslie's voice is cold, for she is still angry at the ease with which she allowed herself to be deceived by his earlier protestations. 'She withdrew her accusation against you.'

'The nurse? Why should she do that?'

'I can't imagine.' Only for a few seconds is she able to hold back the next question. 'She told me exactly what happened. Why did you want to hurt her, Mr Barnaby? She'd never done anything to you.'

'Hurt her? I gave her what she wanted, didn't I? If it hadn't been me, she'd have gone off to some doctor to be hurt with instruments and whatever they use. What did I do to her that she didn't want done? She didn't deserve . . . She was going to murder her own child.'

'No, she wasn't. You heard her consider it, but you didn't hear what she'd decided. You had no right to act as a judge.'

'No right? Who had the right to kill my Darleen and our baby? That nurse had no right even to think about destroying her child. A woman's body, she should think of it as a sacred temple. Who's going to protect a baby if his own mother won't? Even before he's born, he has to trust her to look after him. And even that isn't always enough.'

'But since you feel that –' and Lady Ainslie's voice is softer now, more sympathetic – 'how could you bring yourself to attack a woman in just that way?'

'What should I do? Throw a brick through a window? There had to be some way for the anger to break from my heart. I had a right to my revenge.'

'Against someone who had nothing to do with your wife's death, who'd done her best to prevent it? That wasn't revenge, just assault.'

'Then what am I supposed to do? What right do you allow me instead?'

'If we were having a theoretical discussion on ethics, I would say you had no rights at all. But since we're living in the real world –' she pauses, choosing her words carefully – 'I'd say that you have a right to rage.'

He frowns in puzzlement, trying to work it out. 'What's the difference? Between that and a wish for revenge.'

'Revenge is petty, calculated. Unless it's an instant reflex action, it comes from the mind, the darkest corner of the mind. It can be shaped and so it can be controlled; and a lack of control is an ugly thing. But to rage against the world is to curse theology, philosophy, the whole natural order of things. To feel your soul swelling uncontrollably; to recognize your own helplessness.'

'And not to do anything? You're saying I should feel all that and not *do* anything?'

'There's nothing to be done,' says Lady Ainslie. 'That's the difference between rage and revenge. You can get your own back for something small. But when someone you love is dead, there's no way in which you can bring her back to life. Nothing you can do at all.'

He shakes his head in frustration, not liking to tell her that she is talking nonsense but neither convinced nor comforted by what she is saying.

'Rage isn't something you only think. You have to express it.'

'In words, in sounds – yes, I agree. You have to scream and shout and swear. When you first talked to me, you wanted to swear, didn't you? You should have done it. I'd have known it wasn't me you were angry with, but life itself. Or God, if you believe in God.'

'I'm a Christian,' he says. 'I believe in a good God. So I can't be angry with Him. Only with the men who did it, who killed Darleen.'

'The nurse wasn't one of them.'

'I told you, I didn't do anything to her that she didn't want done. She was wishing for it. It wasn't right that she should be carrying a baby and not want it when Darleen, my Darleen –'

Burying his face in his hands he begins to sob and slides down from the chair to kneel at the bedside. His forehead touches the sheets and the metal hospital bed is shaken by the shuddering of his grief. This is the posture in which Lady Ainslie has first seen him. As she moves a hand to touch his, she notices that they have an audience. Sister is standing in the doorway. Her expression is anxious at first, but she makes no move to interfere and after a moment or two quietly moves away.

'Listen to me, Mr Barnaby,' says Lady Ainslie when at last he is calmer. 'You've had a lucky escape. What would your Darleen think if she knew you were a criminal, sent to prison for attacking a woman? You can't look for revenge against the whole world without destroying yourself. You must make a good life for yourself for her sake, to make her proud of you.'

It is hypocritical of her to talk as though she believes that his dead wife is still watching him, for she has no belief in heaven or immortality in any theological sense – although probably he has. But she is prepared to argue the case for a different kind of immortality.

'I think you ought not to come to the hospital any more,' she suggests gently. 'It's time for you to forget about Darleen as she was here and remember her from your life together. That's how

226

she can live for ever, as long as you remember her. Think of her happy, smiling, singing. Think of the good times you had together, and how no one can ever spoil the memory of them, either for you or for her. Fill your heart with good memories until there's no room for anger any more.'

The kneeling man sighs with hopelessness. As he stands up, he turns his face away from Lady Ainslie so that she shall not see his tears. He is breathing deeply in an effort to control his emotions, but the attempt is unsuccessful. When he whirls round to face her again, his eyes show no acceptance, but only a desperate fury.

'I asked you once,' he remembers. 'Hadn't you ever hated someone so much that you wanted to take revenge, I asked. And you said yes, you had. So was that a petty thing? From a dark corner of your mind?'

'Yes,' says Lady Ainslie firmly. 'But of course it didn't seem trivial at the time. It was only later, when something much worse happened, that I felt ashamed of my own spitefulness. It should have been enough, that first time, simply to hate, without trying to hurt as well.'

'So what happened later?'

She is silent, not so much refusing as unable to answer.

'I can't tell you,' she says at last. 'I've never been able to talk about it.'

She can see that her reticence annoys him. Unless she can recount a tragedy equal to his own, she has no credentials as a comforter.

'It can't be anything like –'

'Yes.' With an effort she forces the words out. 'Exactly the same. Bereavement like you. Death, and not a natural death. Murder.' She trembles as she repeats the word. 'Murder. By someone whose face I've never seen. Someone who will never be brought to justice.'

The intensity of her voice takes him aback. 'What did you do?'

'There was nothing to be done. Except to scream and shout and swear. And then remember. Rage and remember. Rage against the evil: remember the good. It's not much of a therapy.

227

But the only one I know.' She shrugs her shoulders helplessly. 'I shall be going home tomorrow. If you'd ever like to come and talk –'

Her voice fades away. What has an old woman to offer someone like him? She can only remind him of a place which he must try to forget. And yet the invitation must be extended. From Caro's diary she pulls one of the back pages, already loose because she has ripped out the front ones. She writes down her name, address and telephone number.

'Don't come here any more,' she repeats as she hands him the paper. 'Remember Darleen in the places where she was happy with you.'

It is not enough, but she has nothing more to offer. There are no goodbyes, no handshakes before he leaves. She has disappointed him; they are not likely ever to meet again.

Sister, waiting not far away, lets him pass and then comes into the room.

'So he did attack her?'

'It seems so. Not at first. I gather that he genuinely came to help her and then simply lost control.'

'He's upset you.' Sister, in a gesture so natural to the place in which they are talking that her patient hardly notices it, is checking her pulse.

'That's my fault, not his. Rage and remember, I told him. But of course, as the years pass, one does genuinely remember only the happy times. This was a reminder of the black side, that's all. I'll be all right in a minute.'

Sister is not a fusser. She nods tactfully and goes out, closing the door behind her.

Left alone, Lady Ainslie struggles to calm herself. Years of practice have schooled her in the method of bringing her feelings under control by closing her memory. She has been given a cue for the remembrance of an old rage, but is determined to ignore it.

'Oh dear!' exclaims Lady Ainslie. 'A determinist! Well, I suppose that's a possible point of view for a biographer.'

'I think so, yes. I believe that in anyone's childhood there's very often some single seminal event which influences everything that follows. And the younger the child, the more important the experience.'

'So have you managed to track down an incident of that kind in your grandfather's life?'

'I haven't got as far yet as I'd like. I thought at first that it might prove to be the death of his wife, but –'

'Has he told you about the occasion when he was part of a firing squad and had to shoot a deserter?'

'Yes. That was certainly a traumatic experience. But different young men would have reacted to that in different ways. The course of action he took – of trying to get an account of it published – was a very unusual one for a village boy. Something must have happened in his life even before that which prompted him to act as he did. This is why I'm so interested in all your memories of his childhood in Kingsgelding. And so sorry that you should have destroyed your records of the period.'

'I didn't start keeping a diary until 1917. Your grandfather had already joined up by then. Nothing that I wrote would have cast any light on his childhood.'

'But your own,' says Caro softly. 'It would have revealed something about your own.'

'Revealed it to whom? Nobody is writing *my* biography – and I don't wish that anyone should ever do so.'

She pauses only for a moment before turning back to Daniel to continue his argument.

'In any case, I don't agree with your theory. It's the final state, the established fact, that matters, not reasons or motives or influences. This is something that we're always realizing in Parliament. Draughtsmen make mistakes. A bill can be debated over a long period in both houses and in the end perhaps everyone may be agreed on what is intended and why. And then the first test case comes to court and it becomes clear that the words of the Act don't mean precisely what Parliament meant them to mean. One of the lawyers will certainly argue that the court must be aware of what Parliament *intended*. Then the judge quite rightly says that he has to interpret the law as it's been passed. The reasons behind it are none of his business.'

'That's a particular case. In most aspects of life, motive is a fact in itself.'

'In ethics, perhaps. Sin may be defined by motive. But in politics – and medicine, come to that – the final result is all that matters.'

'But even if we stick to facts.' It is Daniel who continues to argue. 'Even major events – like Acts of Parliament, or battles or treaties or deaths – they're only known about because someone has made a record. In matters of state, naturally, someone always *will* make a record. But in smaller things, that perhaps only a few people know about, we have to rely on private records.'

'Which by definition are private. Secret.'

'At the time they're written, perhaps. But as the years pass –'

'There are a good many spheres of life – in my own speciality as a doctor, for example – in which events have long-term consequences. Something which was secret fifty years ago should remain secret now.'

Out of a host of possible examples, she is remembering the duchess – who really *was* a duchess, as she claimed – who feared that her baby might be black. That baby was never born; but two years later the duchess gave birth to an heir after fourteen years of unfruitful marriage. Lady Ainslie – who has always believed that the only sensible way for titles to be inherited is through the mother rather than the father – is inclined to doubt whether the present duke has any of his father's blue blood flowing in his veins. To publicize her suspicions would no doubt serve the cause of truth; but this is a service which she does not intend to render.

'And in any case,' she adds, 'private records are not always to be trusted. As you have realized quite recently.'

By now she is enjoying herself. She cares very little whether her arguments are valid and not at all whether she can persuade Daniel to believe them. What excites her is the freedom of mind which has been restored by her bodily recovery. She turns now to smile at Caro.

232

'Daniel told you, didn't he, about my abominable behaviour in forging a complete diary? Falsifying the records.'

'Yes, he did. And I didn't understand – I mean, it's an example of something in which it seems important to know the motive.'

'And that, after all, was an unusual action,' suggests Daniel.

'You think so because you've found out about it. But how many other lies, falsifications, mistakes slip through the net, and how can you possibly recognize them? There are people –' she is thinking of politicians now – 'who write deliberately for posterity. Putting it all down on the day, perhaps, so that students of history will assume it to be a valuable source. But twisting everything just enough to boost their own reputations. Why should you believe a word they say? Or, to put it another way, how can you decide which words to believe?'

'But that wouldn't apply to you, Lady Ainslie, if you've always written your diaries with the intention that no one shall ever read them.'

'And how can I prove that intention except by making any unauthorized reading impossible? In other words, by destroying them.'

She smiles serenely at the two young people, amused to have led Daniel's argument down the one road which he is bound to find a dead end.

'You could have left instructions.' Caro, without much hope of success, is re-entering the conversation. 'To ask for things to be destroyed after your death. A lot of people do that sort of thing.'

'Let's suppose that I were to take that course,' agrees Lady Ainslie. 'And my dearly-beloved heirs respect my wishes and destroy the diaries. So what is different from the situation in which I destroy them myself? Only the niggle of doubt in my mind about whether the said dearly-beloved heirs will actually do what I've asked, or whether they'll succumb to the blandishment of their dearly-beloved biographizing friends.' She smiles at Daniel to show that she bears him no ill-will for the persuasion he would undoubtedly have exerted on Caro. 'This way the same result is achieved but in a way which allows me peace of mind while I'm still alive.'

233

'You mean that you wouldn't have trusted us to do what you asked.'

'Well, perhaps I would – just because I don't seriously think that what I've written has any value, so that the temptation to use or publish it would be comparatively small. But just think of all the people who specifically asked for their papers to be destroyed, and whose wishes weren't respected. Auden, Woolf, Eliot, Maugham. Lots of others, who knew what they wanted but had husbands or wives or lovers who weren't prepared to perform that last service. They may have had bad consciences, those people, all the same. You could say that I'm saving you from temptation.'

She laughs at Caro's expression, which shows clearly enough how much she regrets this particular salvation.

'Well, you've sniffed the smoke and seen the charred embers. My motives are no longer important. Only the fact. I gave a box of notebooks to the Jaffreys before I came into hospital, and they have burned them at my request.'

Daniel stands up, disappointed but smiling.

'You're a bonny fighter, Lady Ainslie.' He holds out a hand to indicate that he is going to leave her to chat alone with Caro.

'I'm a stubborn old woman. While I was still quite young I decided on one or two things that I thought were important, and I've never stopped since to ask myself whether I was right or wrong when I settled on them. I call it being consistent. I can understand that other people may call it bloody-mindedness.'

She clasps both her hands round his to express her liking for the young man whom Caro loves, in spite of her refusal to help him.

'It was your grandfather who's to blame for that, as a matter of fact. Not that he would remember. He told me once that girls could never keep secrets. I was so indignant that I've been keeping secrets ever since. Too old to change, I'm afraid. I'm sorry. But come to think of it –'

She has reminded herself of a conversation on a river bank many years ago. Remembering the events of that day, she wonders whether perhaps the determinist Daniel is right after all to look for some childhood event in his grandfather's life from which

234

every subsequent effect and cause may have sprung. It is not a theory in which she herself puts much faith, but she can perhaps make up for her previous unhelpfulness by making a suggestion.

'You could ask your grandfather whether he remembers the hot air balloon.'

'What happened to the hot air balloon?'

'Nothing in particular. It's what happened to Gil which might interest you. It'll be better if *he* tells you the details, not me. But it was the subject of his first ever contribution to a newspaper.'

'Thank you. Thank you very much.' He is still smiling gratefully as he leaves; but Caro shakes her head reprovingly.

'Poor Daniel! It's all very well throwing him a crumb of childhood reminiscence, but aren't you ever going to let him find out why you gave the evidence you did in that libel action?'

'No. And I'll tell you why, if you like. It's because the reason isn't to Gil Blakey's credit. Obviously Daniel has a very affectionate relationship with his grandfather. I wouldn't like to be the one to spoil it.'

'I suspect you of being a woman scorned. A mistress discarded like an old glove.'

'Old glove, indeed! Certainly not! And if you think you can tempt the story out of me by putting forward a series of outrageous possibilities you'd better think again. Better still, we'll put the subject out of bounds.'

'You can't do that. You promised me when I was twelve that I could always talk to you about anything in the world. Still, if you insist.' Caro sighed. 'It's a pity, though, when Daniel's trying so hard to write a warts-and-all biography.'

'A mistake, if I may say so. In view of the fact that he wants to use this book to earn himself commissions for other biographies.'

'Just suppose,' says Caro. 'Just suppose that Daniel and I were ever to do something really old-fashioned, like getting married. Would you come to the wedding?'

'Of course I shall come to your wedding, dearest. Wearing my Barbara-Cartland-type hat. If you feel like taking old-fashionedness to extremes and are prepared to accept a Westminster ceremony, I could even arrange for a reception on the Lords'

235

terrace. What an extraordinary question to ask. Would I come to your wedding indeed!'

'I meant, really, would you come if you knew that Sir Gilbert would be there?'

'Why not? Bride's side and groom's side never mingle much on these occasions. I wouldn't cross the room to talk to him, but if we did happen to meet you could trust me to be polite. If what you're actually trying to find out is whether I would dash up to embrace him in a grand gesture of forgiveness, that's a different matter. But –'

'Why should *you* have to forgive *him*?' asks Caro. 'Surely it's the other way round.'

'Ah!' It has not properly occurred to Lady Ainslie until now that by refraining from criticism of Gil in front of his grandson she risks giving the impression to Caro that her own behaviour was unjustified and inexcusable.

'Gilbert Blakey did me an injury,' she says. 'I had the chance to take a kind of revenge on him, and he then took revenge on me. In the dirty tricks department, he leads by two sets to one.'

'And all that is in the diaries which no one is ever going to read.'

'Exactly so. It's not fair, is it? I'm asking you to take everything I say on trust while refusing to show you the written evidence.'

'Not fair at all. So what would you feel about each other if you met?'

'Nothing. I haven't thought about that old business for years, Caro. Two people in their eighties, for heaven's sake. We've both been hurt, a very long time ago, and we've both recovered.'

This is a subject which she has discussed once already in the day, and her remark to Mr Barnaby was sincere. The betrayal of trust which sparked off her quarrel with Gil was not a small thing, but the two acts of revenge which followed from that seem now, seen in perspective, to be merely petty acts of spite. She has no intention of allowing those old events to influence her actions now.

'It's something one learns from politics,' she tells her grand-daughter. 'Wars come to an end and enemies become allies. Feuds, like friendships, can fade.'

236

She almost adds that this is one of the reasons why it is not always wise to hang on to the evidence. But instead she listens with affectionate approval to her granddaughter's hopes and plans. There has been enough talk for one day about the records of the past.

Thirty-five

On the day of her release from hospital Lady Ainslie folds away her nightdress and dressing gown and prepares to face the outside world. Even taking it slowly, dressing proves to be a tiring procedure, and the effort of slipping each stocking in turn over her toes before pulling it up is almost too much for her. It is necessary to remind herself that no amount of stretching can do any actual harm and that if she feels discomfort it is because she has not put sufficient energy into the exercises recommended by the physiotherapist.

At last the transformation is complete. She is no longer a patient but a person. Her back straightens and her eyes brighten as she contemplates a future free from the routines of temperature-taking and meals on trays. The clothes are constricting, though. She has forgotten how it feels to have the collar of a blouse tightly buttoned round her neck, or a slim skirt zipped up to a fitted waistband.

And the shoes! All her adult life she has worn heels which provide her with an extra inch or two of height and has never found the slightest difficulty in adjusting her balance to them. But after so many days spent slopping around in bedroom slippers she is insecure. Cautiously she practises walking round and round the room before making her way again to the nearest flight of stairs.

After a practice journey up and down she ceases to wobble, but instead feels her feet protesting at their confinement. Well, they will have to get used to it, just as she will have to proceed carefully for a little while. Old ladies fall down. Old ladies break their hips and are taken off to hospital. She has had enough of hospital. As she walks back from the staircase to her room her confidence increases. The return to the straight-backed posture which is Nanny Frensham's legacy makes her body feel stronger and healthier. This is the moment when she recognizes that she has made a good recovery.

The attitude of the nurses changes as decisively as her own mood. Without being able to put a finger on it – because they continue to smile and make friendly remarks – she knows that they have no further interest in her. Lunch is served, as though to a hotel guest, by an orderly who does not want to think of herself as a waitress and would rather spend time with someone in need of care. There have been new admissions; other patients are recovering from other operations. Her bed will be filled as soon as she leaves the room for the last time.

Toby Mallinson makes a farewell call – more as a friend than a surgeon, for Mr Graham, with exclamations of 'Jolly good!' has performed all the final checks. Toby nods approvingly at her neat appearance.

'You're a credit to me! Go steady for a few days, though, Ainslie. You're tireder than you know. This isn't the moment to embark on a mountaineering holiday.'

'Noted.' The question which Lady Ainslie has intended to ask in any case follows naturally from his remark. 'What's your hobby, Toby? Do you climb mountains? What do you do when you want to relax?'

'I sit on the bank of the stream at the bottom of my garden holding a fishing rod.'

'Do I detect a distinction between doing that and actually fishing?'

'You do indeed. Catching a fish is more of a distraction than a triumph. Occasionally something takes pity on my inefficiency and insists on impaling itself on the hook, but I usually throw it back again so that we can meet another day.'

'So you don't contribute much to the pot!'

'Well, once a year I accept an invitation to fish for salmon in Scotland, and that's quite a different matter. But as a regular recreation, there's nothing to beat sitting quietly by moving

239

water. Gillian plays golf. Each of us thinks that the other is merely wasting time.'

'I suppose that's what a hobby is. A pleasant way of passing the time.'

Toby knows his friend well enough to realize that there is something behind both her enquiry and her comment, and waits to hear whether she intends to explain; but all she says is 'Thank you, Toby. For the operation, I mean.'

'You've forgiven me, then, for not inserting the bare bodkin?'

'Oh, I always knew it was too much to hope for.'

He smiles in farewell.

'I'll see you next on the other side of the river. I'm due to present our case on consultants' pay to one of your committees. Naturally I shall expect to hear an impassioned speech from you saying how much we all deserve a big rise.'

They laugh together, knowing how rarely passion is expressed in the House of Lords. But the remark is enough to stir Lady Ainslie's interest in the future. As Toby leaves the room she is already clicking her tongue in disapproval of her earlier decision not to have any working papers brought to the hospital. There will be a good deal to catch up. Already she is impatient to be home.

Caro comes, as she has promised, in the afternoon, bringing with her two large and beautiful cakes for her grandmother to give to the nurses.

'We'll all get fat,' says Sue as she accepts the gifts and promises to pass one of them on to the night shift. But she is smiling, pleased; it is the right thing. Lady Ainslie looks around for the other nurses, to say her goodbyes. Everyone is busy, though; it is like the end of a holiday when new acquaintances scatter at a railway station or airport.

Outside the centrally heated hospital, the air is chilly. But the Jaffreys have made use of their key to turn on the electric fire in her flat, creating what Caro calls a good fug. Not liking to open cupboards in search of a vase, they have pushed tulips into a milk bottle which stands, inelegant but welcoming, in the middle of the table. With a sigh of satisfaction Lady Ainslie lowers herself on to the sofa and looks round her home.

240

Mrs Sumner, who lets herself in on two mornings a week to clean, has taken the opportunity of her employer's absence to shampoo the carpets and wash the walls and rub beeswax into all polishable surfaces. The flat, unnaturally neat, smells of several kinds of cleanliness. Never mind. It will soon revert to its normal state of untidiness.

Caro's first action after setting down the suitcase is to glance at the high shelf which is still well furnished with notebooks.

'You didn't have all the diaries burned, then.' There is an unusual edge to her voice. She is not sulking about the destruction of the diaries – Caro never sulks – but she has been hurt in a way which her grandmother did not expect.

'No. Only those which I remembered as describing something which could cause embarrassment if they ever became public. But these must go as well. It was a mistake to think that I could pick and choose. It's not the details which really matter, but the principle.'

Caro sighs. 'It still seems a pity –'

'All right, then.' Lady Ainslie feels an urge to tease. 'Let's see what we can do. You deserve a thank-you present for looking after me so well, and coming to the hospital every day. I wouldn't like you to think that I didn't appreciate it. So choose a diary and take it away. Or pick a date, and I'll try to find it for you. What do you think you would enjoy? My first love affair, perhaps? Or my honeymoon? My husband's death?'

Her head jerks forward as though she is trying to catch those last words with her lips and swallow them back again. Two weeks earlier that reference would have been to the unhappy diary entry on the day when the message arrived which extinguished her hopes of Richard's return. But her recent conversation with Mr Barnaby has brought back to mind the second version of that piece of news, as unbearable now as it was then. It will be disconcerting if her offer is accepted, but Caro reacts exactly as her grandmother expects. Her pale cheeks flush as she looks down at the carpet.

'I'm sorry,' she says. 'I see what you mean. It's because I only keep the appointment kind of diary that I think of everything in it as being trivial and unimportant as soon as it's happened.

241

Useful for checking facts and dates if necessary, that's all. But yes, of course. These are private things for you. I really *am* sorry.' She hugs her grandmother remorsefully.

'You were thinking about reading them after my death, I expect,' says Lady Ainslie without reproach. 'And for you, no doubt, that would make all the difference. Private life becomes history overnight. But I have to make the decision while I'm still alive.'

'I can see that does put things in a different perspective.' Caro is grinning again, her moment of regret banished.

'I *would* like to give you one, though. The very first one. A picture of a child's life. A different world. It's not quite like the others: that's why I don't mind. I wrote it for Edward, you see, my brother, not for myself.'

There are no secrets recorded in her painstaking thirteen-year-old copperplate handwriting. And Lady Ainslie has been more moved than she realized at the time by her hospital reading, the *Anthology of Armageddon*. Few of the men whose letters and diaries were quoted in it can have seen themselves as writing for publication, but the picture they have jointly painted serves to illuminate a dark corner of history. Edward, who did not survive long enough to add his own brush-stroke to this scene of terror, would have been glad, she believes now, to think that the trees and animals and peaceful pleasures of his youth might attain a kind of immortality in the mind of his great-niece.

She points up at the shelf. 'The green one on the left. Take it now.'

Even Caro, who is tall, has to pull up the library steps before she can reach. She smiles to see the miniature padlock and its tiny key, and strokes the soft leather of the binding appreciatively.

'Thank you very much indeed, Nanna. I shall treasure it. And now I must bring some stuff up from the car. Your supper, for a start, and a selection of goodies for your store cupboard, so that you won't have to go out shopping for a few days.'

'How thoughtful you are. But you must let me pay –'

'Left-overs, left-overs. Under my sort of catering plan it's only the cook who's allowed a doggy bag. Granny bag in this case. Back in a minute.'

By the time three heavy cardboard boxes have been carried upstairs, Lady Ainslie has unpacked the few possessions brought back from hospital. Caro, setting down a packet of chocolate mints before carrying a container of soup through to the kitchen, notices the brightly-patterned notebook which was her own hospital present.

'I got that wrong, didn't I?' she laughs. 'It didn't occur to me that you could ever give up diarizing.'

'Nor have I. I didn't always feel like it while I was ill. But now –'

'You surely don't intend – I mean, what's the point of keeping a diary just in order to throw it away?'

'What was *ever* the point of keeping a diary? What's the point of anything at all?'

'Oh come, Nanna, that's a bit gloomy.'

'Is it? There are some actions which are useful to other people and there are other actions which give pleasure to oneself. Keeping a diary is one of the pleasure-givers.'

'But now that you've decided to burn them all –'

'That's what puts the pleasure back into it. It's *because* I've taken the decision to destroy that I can feel quite secure as I go on writing. Only the very last book will be in danger of being read against my wishes. I did always intend to destroy them all one day, before I die. The advantage of doing it now is that I needn't continually ask myself how long I have left to live.'

'But isn't it rather a waste of time?'

'Yes. Why not? We all waste time in different ways. Except you, perhaps. Some people fish or play golf. Martin plays rugger. He can't claim that it's good for his health because he's more likely to get crocked up than fit. He does it for fun. I enjoy the act of recording my day on paper. It helps me to keep my mind orderly. But once the words are written, they're not actually of any further interest to me.'

'I have to say that there's a grave lack of logic in your position.'

'Who cares about logic? I'm an unsociable old lady passing the time in the way which gives her most satisfaction. I don't smoke or take tranquillizers. This is a harmless form of addiction – as

243

long as it's not left lying around. So I shall make good use of your thoughtful present, dear.'

It is tempting to embark on the task of bringing the diary up to date as soon as Caro leaves. There is no reason now to censor Lesley's accusation or Mr Barnaby's confession. But the timetable of her addiction is as habit-forming as the addiction itself. The hour before bed is diary-writing time.

She walks around the flat, savouring the freedom of being alone and at home, until the ringing of a bell startles her. She opens the door but no one is there. A second ring is needed before she remembers about the Entryphone and picks up its receiver. 'Yes.'

'It's Duke.'

'Duke?' As a regular attender at the House of Lords, Lady Ainslie is naturally acquainted in a general way with several dukes, but none of them is likely to call at her home or to announce himself in such a manner.

'Duke Barnaby.'

'Oh, Mr Barnaby! I didn't recognize . . . I didn't know . . .' Taking a grip on her fluster she remembers eventually to press the release.

The downstairs door opens and closes. Footsteps begin to mount the stairs. In another moment Mr Barnaby will come into sight. But why has he come? What does he want? Why has she let him in?

He has come, she reminds herself, for the very good reason that she invited him to call; or so she must presume. But so sure was she that he would never accept the invitation that as his footsteps come closer she finds herself stiffening not just with unease but with fear.

Thirty-six

How tall he is! All men are taller than Lady Ainslie, but not many of them tower over her in quite such an overpowering manner. It is because he is standing too close – but he is only so close because he has expected her to step back to admit him to the flat. She does so now, indicating the largest of her armchairs before she turns to close the door behind him.

He remains standing. The mother who taught him not to swear in front of a woman no doubt also told him that he must wait for a woman to seat herself first. His appearance has altered since their last meeting. Until now Lady Ainslie has seen him only in black casual clothes – the same clothes at every visit, taking on as each day passes a stronger scent of his body. She remembers wondering at first whether he was ignoring the dirt because it was part of his wife's duties to gather up his clothes and wash them; but deciding on a more likely explanation, that he was trying to remain as Darleen last saw him. Now that bond, like all the others, has been broken.

He is wearing a suit, although not a tie. It emphasizes the solidity of his body, which in the short-sleeved tee-shirt and jeans looked more lithe and athletic. But perhaps the difference is only in the way he is standing. In the hospital, where he was in a sense a trespasser, he invaded Lady Ainslie's room as though he had more right to it than herself. He has come here, to the flat, by invitation, but may not understand why the invitation was either extended or accepted. Common politeness prevents his hostess from asking why he has come, but they both need to know the answer.

245

'Just before you sit down,' Lady Ainslie says, 'would you do something for me? I was going to wait until my grandson came and ask him, but since you're here . . . Would you pull that electric fire a little way away from the fireplace?'

He follows the direction of her pointing finger and does as she asks.

'Can you get your arm behind it now? There's a black plastic binliner there which I'd like out. Without banging any of the contents, if you can help it.'

He eases the fire a little further before pulling out the bulky bag and setting it down on the flat-topped desk in the window bay. Lady Ainslie follows him across the room and pulls out the first of several parcels wrapped in newspaper.

'Like a lucky dip!' she says, throwing the paper on to the floor and revealing a jewel box. Opening it, she gives a quick nod of relief.

'All present and correct.' She reaches in for the next item, a felt bag containing a dozen silver forks. The silver which she and Richard bought each other to celebrate their wedding was one of the few treasures to survive the later bombing of their house. As she prepares to dip in again, Mr Barnaby puts out a hand to stop her.

'It happens almost every week with the kids in my class,' he tells her. 'The manager of the supermarket along the road comes in with names on a paper. "They've been grazing again," he says. "What are you going to do about it?" he says. And I tell him back that he's asking for trouble. Putting temptation in their way.'

'What is "grazing"?' asks Lady Ainslie.

'Taking a free lunch. Eating your way round a store before you turn up at the check-out to pay your pennies for a tube of Smarties. You know what I'm saying.'

'Quite different,' she says briskly. 'All children – well, all boys – are criminals at heart. Immature characters.' To admit in so many words that she is making a positive gesture of trust would be to spoil the effect. In any case, it is herself she is testing, not him.

'But when you saw me tonight, you were frightened. Yes?

246

Nasty things happen to old ladies these days. You can't trust anyone. Your grandson has told you, right, never to let in anyone you don't know.'

'But I do know you.' She is fishing for the next mystery object in the black bag, but pauses to look up at him. 'Although, yes, I was anxious just for a moment. Because I couldn't think of anything I could say. I meant it when I said I'd be glad to see you, but there isn't really anything I can do to help. I only wish there were.'

'I came because we never finished our last conversation,' he says. She puzzles to remember what that was. 'You were trying to persuade me that you knew what I felt because you'd felt it too, once. But you wouldn't say what happened. So how can I tell –'

While her mind freezes with alarm, her hands continue to tug away the wrapping paper, revealing a photograph in a silver frame.

'Your husband?' asks Mr Barnaby.

Lady Ainslie looks down at the laughing face. She has never wanted to display either of her two portrait photographs of Richard. The sight of his army uniform makes her angry that he should have deserted her, even in what she has always known to be a good cause; and in his barrister's wig and gown he belongs to the world of courts and justice, not to her. This is an enlargement of a snapshot taken at the end of a tennis match. His hair is tousled and the collar of his polo shirt is crumpled. He is happy, and every night the sight of him makes her happy too. But her guest is waiting for an answer.

Nodding, she sets the photograph in its place on the Victorian mantelpiece which is so much too grand for the electric fire beneath it. For a moment she is silent, considering whether she will later regret what impulse tells her to do; for she is about to break a rule. Then she looks up at the high shelf of diaries and points.

'Can you see that thick notebook, about ten from the right?' It is a notebook made black by the ruling of lines in Indian ink; horizontal and vertical and diagonal lines; hundreds of them, leaving only the smallest specks of the original redness of its cover. 'Get it down, will you?'

He hands it to her. It takes only a moment to open it at the right place before handing it back. Sitting down on the sofa, she indicates for a second time that he should take the large armchair. Then she watches his face while he reads.

Thirty-seven

Constituency surgery in the morning. The last man to turn up, a Mr Gregson, was a thirty-year-old ex-serviceman. Wanted help in getting a disability pension. Scar on his cheek showed he'd been wounded, but no immediately apparent disabilities. Said he suffered from nightmares so bad that they petrified him for hours. Literally. He couldn't move, continually lost jobs for non-attendance. I'd heard this kind of story before from men who'd been taken prisoner by the Japanese, but Mr G. fought in Europe. He told me his story.

It was in 1940, during the retreat to Dunkirk. He was in one of several groups detached to cover the retreat; staying behind to hold up the advancing Germans for as long as possible to give the rest of the regiment time to get away. Not a popular duty, obviously, with a high chance of being killed and a near-certainty of being taken prisoner. But Mr G. – he was only eighteen then – and the others did their best.

After three days of it they were exhausted from lack of sleep, hungry, running out of ammunition. Near enough to the coast to hear the bombs falling on the beach, and wishing they could run for it. About eighty of them left.

Then there was shouting from all round. One of the British officers understood German, told the men they were surrounded. Said they'd done their bit and would have to surrender. He went out by himself first of all, and then passed on all the German orders. Put down your arms, hands above your head, step forward. They were all dead tired and glad to be out of it.

The Germans lined up with machine-guns. Two SS officers with them. Mr G. realized that the officers were disagreeing about something. One was shouting orders and the other seemed to be protesting. But the shouter won. The other one clicked his heels and started giving orders. Then the British officer, the one who understood German, yelled out 'No!' And in German after that, 'Nein, nein,' and something else Mr G. didn't understand. So the shouter stepped up to him, lifted his gun and shot him through the mouth.

When Mr G. described this, his whole face changed, as though he were reliving a horror. I was concerned to notice that he was becoming rigid, having one of the nightmares he'd described to me, although still awake. I tried to persuade him to describe it from outside, as though he were an observer, but he couldn't.

All the men were marched past their dead officer, across a field and into a small barn. Shit-scared, to use his own phrase. They'd guessed what was going to happen, and it did. Grenades thrown in first. Then anyone left standing was machine-gunned. A massacre.

Mr G. was knocked down by the first blast. Saved from the machine-gunning by other men on top of him, screaming and groaning at first, then falling silent. Knew that pretending to be dead was his only hope. After several hours another survivor thought he'd waited long enough and started to work his way up through the bodies. Someone was waiting and shot him dead. After that, Mr G. didn't dare move. He reckons he spent about forty hours completely still, with the weight of dead bodies, and the smell, and knowing that they were his friends on top of him. No wonder he has nightmares.

I asked what medical and psychiatric treatment he'd had, and reckoned I could arrange for something better. Then started making notes – dates, records etc. – to pursue the pension claim. Slightly put out to discover that he's already had an MP looking into it for him, five years ago. Started to explain that I couldn't interfere with someone else's case.

Two things have changed, he said. In 1947 he couldn't get anyone to believe that the massacre had taken place. Recently, though, he'd made contact with another survivor. The episode had ended when a bulldozer started pushing the bodies into a pit. Different batch of Germans, startled to find three men still alive – sent for stretchers, not guns, and looked after them well in hospital. Mr G. was happy

250

enough to spend the rest of the war in a POW camp, but the other two made a run for it and got back to England. They only met again recently at a regimental reunion. So now he's got corroboration.

And the second thing? Well, he thought I'd be more likely to take a personal interest than the other MP. Why? I honestly didn't see the answer coming. Because the British officer who was shot was my husband.

Thirty-eight

Lady Ainslie has a photographic memory of any words which she has set down on paper herself. As Mr Barnaby turns over each page she knows what he is reading; and is perfectly well aware of the moment when he reaches the end of the entry, in spite of the fact that he continues to stare down at the diary. While he is silent, showing no sign of emotion, she begins to tremble. Her record of the interview may have ended, but memory continues it, playing the scene as though it were a film which cannot be stopped.

'What did you say?'

'It was Captain Johnson that was killed.' Mr Gregson had looked surprised that she should not know. 'They must have told you.'

What had they told her? As though her mind was groping through a fog, she tried to remember.

'I had a letter from Colonel –' She could not even remember his name.

'I can guess what he wrote. Shot through the head. Died instantaneously. That's what they always say. Well, it was true in a way. It's just that –'

'Like this, you mean?' Very very slowly and heavily, as though someone were having to crank up her arm, Ainslie Johnson raised the hand which held her pen and pointed it deliberately at Mr Gregson's mouth. 'Shot him like this? No! No!'

She shouted the words out with all the force and horror that Richard himself must have used in his last moment of life, bringing the constituency agent running from his desk in the next room. As she screamed and struggled, it took both men to hold her down.

Next morning, emerging slowly into consciousness after a night of sedation, she had asked herself why she should be so appalled by what she had heard. Richard was dead: that had not changed. Richard had been shot in the head: that had not changed either. Why should it matter so much that her mental picture of his death had been shattered?

The change was in the image of the killer. She had seen the war, while it was still in progress, as being somehow impersonal. Men in aeroplanes had dropped bombs on her, destroying her house, attempting to set fire to her place of work and twice putting her life in danger; but they had never known that she, as herself, was there. There was no emotion in it, either on their part or hers.

In a land or sea battle, too, it had seemed that guns were fired at targets rather than at people. Only later did she learn about the mass murders of the extermination camps – and, if anything, that had strengthened the impression that there was something different about the engagements of fighting men. As though even in that dark and deadly game there were rules of a kind.

That was what propaganda did, she recognized as she lay in bed, her stomach churning, on the day after Mr Gregson dropped his bombshell. It smoothed over death with a sentimental twaddle. In her case, it had deluded her into believing that her husband had been killed by a gun rather than by a man; and that his death had been in some way inevitable simply because he was in the path of a bullet. But it was not in the least inevitable. He had surrendered. He should have been taken prisoner. The rules had been broken. He had been killed by a murderer. He ought not to be dead at all. On an oppressive August day in 1952, she had staggered, sobbing, to the bathroom to be sick.

The film which has been projecting itself in her mind now splutters to an end and she realizes that she is weeping. Weeping silently, as though she is sitting in a darkened cinema and hoping for the chance to dab her eyes dry before anyone can notice.

But someone has noticed. Something extraordinary has happened. She has not been aware of her visitor moving, but he is

253

sitting beside her on the sofa, holding her tightly in his arms, pressing her head against his shoulder as he strokes and pats her back. 'I'm sorry,' he says. 'I'm sorry. I'm sorry.'

Lady Ainslie is an undemonstrative woman who rarely touches even her own son. Only with Caro does she use hugs to express and accept affection. It is very many years since she has allowed herself to be comforted in such a way. As she pulls herself together, straightening her back as Nanny Frensham once taught her, she lays her hand on his and keeps it there for a few moments before dabbing her eyes dry. Then she leans down to pick up the diary which he has dropped on to the carpet. Her hands are not strong enough to tear through its whole thickness, so she rips pages out a few at a time.

'You ought to keep that,' says Mr Barnaby. 'It might still not be too late to get those Germans punished.'

'This is only a second-hand record,' she points out. 'As my husband always used to put it, what the soldier said isn't evidence.'

'So you never did anything about it?'

'I got Mr Gregson his disability pension, and the help of a psychiatrist as well. And I reported the case as a War Crime. But only on Mr Gregson's behalf, not my own. The German officer was traced. I know his name. But at the time, in 1952, he was a prisoner in Russian hands. So the matter couldn't go any further at the time, and I chose not to press it later. I did mean what I said to you yesterday. I've never wanted to take revenge. It was too big a thing for that. I was angry; of course I was angry and upset. But I try never to think about my anger. Because I don't want to think of my husband in his moment of terror. I want to remember him like this.'

She points to the photograph on the mantelpiece and stares at the laughing face of a thirty-seven-year-old tennis player.

'In my memory, you see, he hasn't aged. But if he'd lived, he'd be eighty-six by now. Or dead. Not many men live so long.'

Her eyes begin to fill with tears again, but this time she is able to hold them in check.

'It's like having a limb amputated. Something that ought not to have happened. But once it *has* happened, it doesn't do any good to think too much about the pain suffered by the arm or the leg before it went, by Richard or Darleen. You have to learn to live as an incomplete person. That doesn't mean that you forget how it felt to be whole. But brooding on it and trying to get your own back for it doesn't help. That's why I never allow myself to think –'

She blows her nose vigorously to bring the moment of emotion to an end before turning back to face her guest.

'It's a hard thing to say, but my life has been more useful for being lonely. Domestic happiness is the enemy of altruism as well as of ambition. I've been able to help a lot of people in one way or another. I've tried, anyway. Can I get you a drink, Mr Barnaby?'

'Thanks, but I don't. And you must be tired, the first day home from hospital.' He stands up, ready to leave. There are tears in his eyes as well, but some of the despair and all of the aggression has drained away from his body.

Lady Ainslie feels that she is seeing him for the first time as he is. Not as a black man, as a distraught widower, as a threatening assailant – with shame she recognizes the stereotypes into which she has successively cast him – but as an unhappy human being: a young man struggling to come to terms with grief and searching for a way of rebuilding his life.

How will he do it? It is not for her to guide his choice. As a schoolteacher he is a useful member of society. But will a man whose ordered life has been smashed find a world of timetables and bells reassuring or intolerable? At heart, she is convinced, he is an actor; but for him to return to that insecure career will be to bid a final farewell to Darleen.

'Please come and see me again,' she says, gripping tightly the hand he holds out to be shaken. 'When you've decided what you're going to do. I'd like the chance to help, if I can.'

She has no magic wand to wave. The theatre is not her world. But if she has learned anything from her years as a politician it is the art of making things happen. As she waits at the top of the stairs to hear the downstairs door close behind her visitor, she is already planning what might be done. She is picking up the threads of her life again.

255

Thirty-nine

Like a cat reclaiming its territory after absence she wanders round the flat once more; touching, stroking, sniffing. A polite tap on the door interrupts her. The Jaffreys have called to welcome her home. Mr Jaffrey is carrying the Lowry, which he carefully restores to its place on the wall. In Mrs Jaffrey's hand is a plastic carrier bag.

'We were not sure,' she says. 'After you telephoned, we were not sure whether this bag was to be kept safely with the picture or burned with the box. It seemed best to wait and be quite certain.'

Lady Ainslie takes the bag from her with polite reassurances that it was a wise decision. Only much later, when thanks and local gossip have been exchanged and her neighbours, after agreeing to help her burn the remaining diaries next day, have had a drink and departed, does she begin to laugh at the realization that she has been offered a chance to change her mind.

Staring down at the mock-embroidered cover which she had not expected to see again, she reflects on the last of her hospital conversations with Mr Barnaby. Revenge is petty. But not every act of spite is irreversible. There is an opportunity to right a wrong now, if she chooses to take it.

'Gil leads by two sets to one in the dirty tricks department.' Lady Ainslie, who for most of her life has prided herself on not telling untruths, is shocked to remember her comment to Caro. And the reason for her lapse of memory is as shameful as the misstatement itself. It is because she has allowed a lie to endure for fifty years that she has almost ceased to recognize the truth.

Not all acts of vengeance are of equal gravity. Her false evidence in court and Gil's campaign to bring her to judgement before the General Medical Council are of no consequence now. It was possible, after the first shock, to accept her expulsion from the medical register as an atonement, a punishment well deserved. Less easy to forgive has been that first betrayal when Gil made use of her love and trust to search out and publicize her secrets. It was because of this that she concealed from Gil the fact that he is the father of her son. This has been her true revenge.

It is all past history. For most of her life she has been a practical, sensible and socially useful woman and, above all, a solitary woman. The short period in which she succumbed to desire and fury before finding love came to an end almost fifty years ago.

So is it time for her to make the truth known, whilst Gil is still alive? Never let the sun set on your anger, Nanny Frensham used to say. A good many suns have risen and set since Leonard was born, but it is not too late to amend the nursery command and forgive before dying. All his life, if Daniel is to be believed, Gil has longed for a son. Would it give him pleasure to learn now that he has had one?

No, it would not. What satisfaction could it bring him to be told the name of a stranger, a middle-aged man with an address in Papua New Guinea? To bring such an old wish back into the limelight would be unsettling for Leonard, for Caro, and even for Daniel. But most of all it would make Gil angry. The truth would bring him not the gift of an heir but the realization that he had been robbed.

She can hurt him most, in fact, by revealing her secret, allowing him for the first time to learn what he has lost. The power to take one last revenge is in her hands.

Instead of grasping it, she tears the diary into pieces. How frustrated Daniel would be if he could see her now. 'Too bad!' she says aloud. 'Girls do *not* always tell in the end.'

The memory of that long-ago accusation amuses her as she throws the scraps of paper away. Truth is the victim of time. As the years pass, what has happened becomes less important than

257

what is thought to have happened. The small girl who was Ainslie Dangerfield almost eighty years ago persuaded herself that there was a difference between telling a lie and merely concealing the truth. She was wrong; but it is too late now to make good the mistake.

A pile of letters is waiting to be opened and more, no doubt, have accumulated in her pigeonhole at the House of Lords. Tomorrow she must get back to work. But the remaining hours of this evening may be devoted to chronicling whatever has occurred since last she slept in her own bed. She puts on her spectacles and searches for a pen.

At last she can comment without fear of consequences on Lesley's pregnancy, on Mr Barnaby's assault and even, if she chooses, on her own reasons for destroying old diaries. 'Talking to myself,' she says cheerfully aloud. When no one else is listening, there can be no indiscretions. What does it matter that what she is about to record will blaze on some future bonfire in the Jaffreys' garden instead of enduring to shed a tiny light on history? She opens the notebook which Caro has given her and begins to write.